Other Gods:

Best First Novel, Bay Area Independent Publishers Association

"This mystery incorporates speech patterns, historical details of daily living, and beautiful descriptions of landscape and environment. Barbara Geisler does a highly credible job of recreating the sense of fear, despair, and loss of order that must have characterized this age, the reverse side of the faith that sustained it."

—The Midwest Book Review

"*Other Gods* brings to life an unfamiliar time and place, the scene and characters so perfectly imagined that one is immediately drawn into the lives and concerns of the abbey nuns. Readers will learn a great deal about the time and place, while being entertained by an enthralling story."

—The Living Church

Graven Images:

"An extraordinarily rich book with multiple story lines… the language and descriptions give a strong sense of the period, and the characters are fascinating. The precarious position of Jews in medieval England is vividly portrayed. The power this book held over me was such that I got up in the middle of the night to finish it—I could not fall asleep without finding out how things were resolved. I recommend it highly."

—The Historical Novels Review

"*Graven Images,* a sequel to *Other Gods* (a Ben Franklin Award finalist) brings the Middle Ages to life with authentic, nitty-gritty detailing, picturesque surroundings, and realistic characters."

—Library Journal

"A superbly written historical mystery. The title refers to religious art, but reflects the author's ability to craft visual descriptions of the medieval community. She paints realism and understanding on the canvas of her pages, clearly describing what it was like to live in these times and conditions. The book is filled with people who must rise above and beyond the routine of their lives to deal with conflicts of life, politics, and Church hierarchy, all of which Barbara Geisler skillfully weaves into the tapestry of her story. We scored this fascinating read a high five hearts."

—Heartland Reviews

In Vain:

Best Historical Fiction, Bay Area Independent Publishers Association

"In 2004, Barbara Geisler published *Other Gods,* followed by *Graven Images.* I devoured both, and highly recommend them. Geisler incorporates her historical research gracefully, and the sense of period I enjoyed earlier is evident here. The author does an excellent job of providing supporting material: a map of Shaftesbury and a plan of the abbey, information on the nuns' daily schedule, a list of characters, notes on the real characters and historical elements of the story, a bibliography, a timeline, a glossary, and even a selection of 12th-century recipes!"

—Trudi E. Jacobson, US Reviews Editor,
The Historical Novels Review

"With its strong women and historical setting, *In Vain* is reminiscent of Peter Tremayne's Sister Fidelma series. Spot-on dialogue and characterization are skillfully woven into the medieval tapestry of this novel, and its lyrical prose will draw you into the story. Historical notes and enticing period recipes nicely round out the offering."

—Ruth Hoppin, author of *Spinning the Arrow of Time*

"With plenty to enjoy for lovers of historical fiction and intrigue, *In Vain* is a top pick, very highly recommended."

—The Midwest Book Review

To Keep It Holy

Book IV of The Averillan Chronicles

Barbara Reichmuth Geisler

LOST
COAST
PRESS

Fort Bragg, California

Publisher's Cataloging-in-Publication Data
Names: Geisler, Barbara R., author. | Geisler, Barbara R. Averillan chronicles ; Book 4.
Title: To keep it holy : Book IV of the Averillan Chronicles / Barbara Reichmuth Geisler.
Description: First Edition. | Fort Bragg, CA : Lost Coast Press, [2022] | Series: The Averillan chronicles ; Book 4
Identifiers: ISBN 9781935448426 | ISBN 9781935448433 (E-book)
Subjects: LCSH: Abbeys--Fiction. | Women detectives--Fiction. | Great Britain--History--Norman period, 1066-1154--Fiction. | Murder--Investigation--Fiction. | LCGFT: Historical fiction. | Detective and mystery fiction.
Classification: LCC PS3607.E37 T65 2022 (print) | LCC PS3607.E37 (ebook) | DDC 813/.6--dc23

Library of Congress Control Number 2020934169
ISBN 978-1-935448-42-6
E-book ISBN 978-1-935448-43-3

Printed in the USA
2 4 6 8 9 7 5 3 1

First edition

Dedicated to
Mary Sutton Trafton
Frances Geisler Trafton
Elizabeth Dain Trafton

Remember thou the Sabbath day to keep it holy. Six days shalt thou labor, and do all thy work;

But the seventh day is the Sabbath of the Lord thy God; in it thou shalt not do any work, thou nor thy son, nor thy daughter, thy manservant, nor thy maidservant, nor thy cattle, nor thy stranger that is within thy gates;

For in six days the lord made heaven and earth, the sea and all that in them is, and rested the seventh day; wherefore the Lord blessed the Sabbath day and hallowed it.

Exodus 20: 8-12, KJV

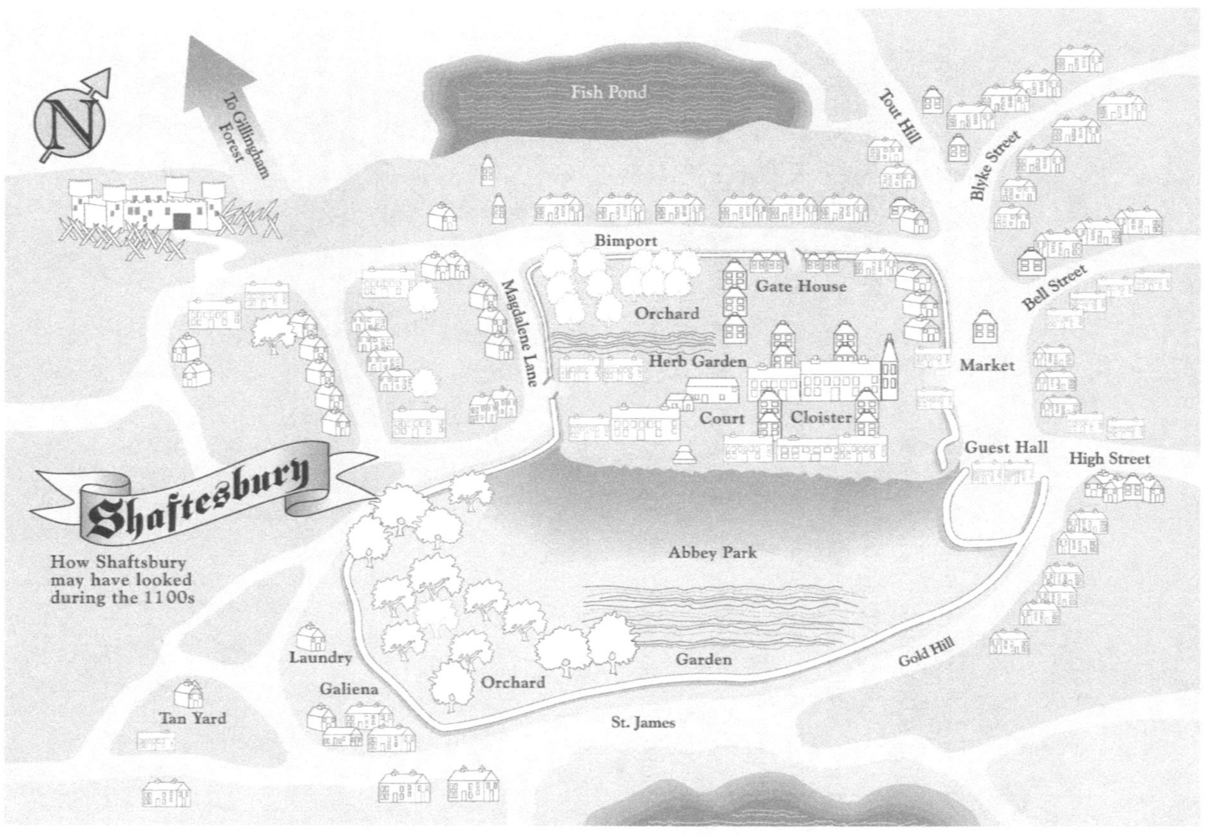

Map of the Abbey

Layout of the Abbey, Church, and Cloister

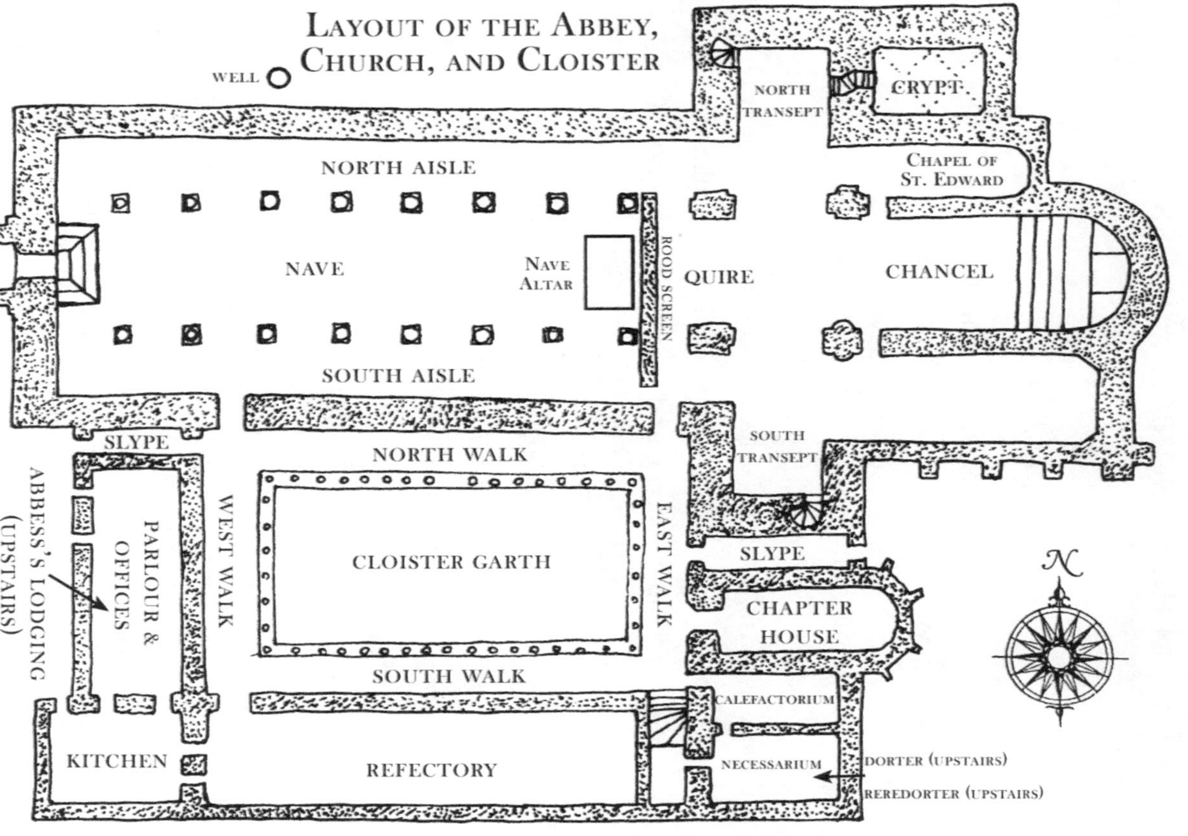

Floor plan based on and with permission from the Shaftesbury Abbey Museum and Gardens

THE CANONICAL HOURS

OPUS DEI

Matins – Midnight – in choir

Lauds* – 1 AM – in choir – Christ triumphant and glorified

Prime – 1st hour – 6 AM* or daybreak, in choir,
to ask blessings on the work of the day – morning prayer

Terce – 3rd hour – 9 AM

Chapter Mass** – 11 AM – in choir followed immediately by

Chapter – in chapter house – about twenty minutes

Sext – 6th hour – noon, in the heat of day to quench
the heat of human passions

Dinner

Midday rest

Afternoon set aside for labor, study in choir, or recreation

None – 9th hour – 3 PM – the hour of Christ's death

Vespers – evening service – sunset – in choir

Supper

Evening Collation – (short reading) in cloister

Compline – 8 PM – just before retiring – preparation for
death as well as sleep, ending the day on note of loving
submission. Mostly in choir.

---

*   Days and times varied with the seasons and hours of daylight.
At Shaftesbury, Matins and Lauds were sung together to avoid rousing the nuns twice in the night.

** On Sundays and festivals, instead of Chapter Mass, High Mass was
celebrated at 11 AM, following Chapter but before dinner.

THE CHARACTERS

Most of the characters in this book are fictious; however, Cecily (aka Cecilia) FitzHamon was an abbess. Her father, Robert FitzHamon, was a friend of William I, and her sister, Mabel, was the wife of Robert of Gloucester, the bastard son of Henry I.

Clergy and Nuns

Cecily FitzHamon – abbess

Dame Aethwulfa – prioress

Dame Averilla – assistant to infirmaress

Dame Elizabeth – infirmary and leprosarium

Dame Joan – subprioress

Dame Maud – infirmaress

Father Merowald – parish priest and nuns' confessor

Sister Ethelind – a novice in training in the infirmary

Sister Clayetta – lay sister serving as abbess's maid

Laity

Will – forester

Gervase FitzRolf – local landowner

Isabel FitzRolf – wife of Gervase

John the Mason – master mason

Madge – the town wise woman

Robert Bradshaw – bailiff

The sheriff

Wat – worker in the stables

Francine and Ellen – lepers

On November 25 in the year of our Lord 1120, Henry, King of England and Duke of Normandy and third son of William the Conqueror, set sail for England from Barfleur Normandy, confident he had accomplished on this trip all he had set out to do. He had just signed a beneficial treaty with Louis of France, had attended a church convocation, and had seen his only legitimate son, William, married to the Count of Anjou's daughter. As the sails filled and his ship pulled out into the channel, Henry saw the *Blanche Nef* cast off from Barfleur and pull away from shore. The *Blanche Nef* carried his son, William, along with his bride and their courtiers.

Henry's self-congratulation lasted until morning. Though the king's ship docked safely, the *Blanche Nef* failed to arrive. A drunken crew and a late departure caused the ship to dash itself against the nearby Catterville Rocks where it sank, drowning all the young nobles aboard, including William, Henry's heir.

Prologue

Late November 1120

Dorset, England

Pain wrenched the man from an endless fevered dark. It seemed he wasn't dead, but he wasn't sure that was a good thing. His mouth was afire with a torturous pain. He tried to swallow and… his tongue! In his mind's eye he saw the knife, its glint in the dawn light as they held him down.

He managed to unstick one eye and blinked to clear it. He knew where he was. The smell of horse, the whiffles and snorts, told him. As he struggled to open the other eye, memories slithered into his mind. Blood. There had been blood on the snow. Whose? He frowned, trying to remember. Something about a whip. Unconsciousness again claimed him.

Sometime later, an old woman plopped down beside him. *Was she here before?* He thought so. She pried open his mouth and used a straw to dribble hot broth into it. He groaned. He was so thirsty, but the broth seared what was left of his tongue. *What was left of his tongue?* Would he be able to talk? To swallow?

As the woman tottered off, he saw again the flecks of blood on the snow. Now, though, he saw Waldo, his friend, lying on the ground, back and shoulders bloody. Over him, feet splayed, whip raised, stood Alcar the reeve. Will saw himself fly down the slope and throw Alcar to the ground; saw himself kick Alcar's head, back, sides; felt again his monumental fury.

Then there had been—hadn't there?—yes, Waldo had whimpered near his left foot, grappled a weak hand onto his shin. "Stop. He's dead," Waldo had rasped.

Will's remembered rage, now in this unfamiliar barn, splintered into icy shards of fear. He had killed a man—and not just a man—the reeve, the hated overseer, an Englishman, but beholden to the Norman overlords.

But who cut out my tongue? Will couldn't remember. When next Will opened an eye, the old woman was dusting. *Dusting a barn?* He heard her mutter, and thought she said, "Here, my darlings."

Who is she talking to? he wondered, blinking through his delirium. *There is no one here.*

"I don't need much," she continued, coaxing. "Just a wee bit. Surely you don't need such a big web." Then, "Thank you, my darlings."

He could have sworn she bowed. *She's talking to the spiders? Definitely a witch.* He sank back. *This can't be happening!*

Now the woman was rolling something between her fingers. Spider webs?

She came over, bent down, and jabbed the sticky mess into his mouth. He gagged and tried to thrash his head away from her, but she held him down and massaged his throat to make him swallow until the webs were gone. Marveling at how weak he was, Will drifted back to sleep.

The next he knew, the old woman was nudging his arm. "They be coming for ye. I cain do nae mere. May our blessed Lord be with ye." She shuffled away, leaving him to his weariness.

Footsteps entered the barn. The kick was sudden, and despite himself, Will groaned.

"Well, by Lucifer's breath, after all that, 'e's still alive. Make a good serf yet."

"If we keep him shackled."

One of them made to kick him again, but the other held out a hand. "Do that and ye'll just 'ave to pick the great brute up."

They attached a rope yoke between the two horses and tied him to it. He stumbled along behind them down the hill—but where was he, and where were they taking him?

CHAPTER ONE

DECEMBER 4, 1120

SHAFTESBURY

THE ABBEY OF THE VIRGIN MARY AND EDWARD KING & MARTYR

Dame Averilla, assistant infirmaress of the abbey, sighed as she tucked in yet another coverlet, plumped yet another pillow, felt yet another forehead. Averilla's Saxon heritage was obvious not only in her unusual height but in the eager, ice-blue eyes, strong jaw, and blond eyebrows. A face that might have seemed stern was tempered by two dimples and a gap between the front teeth.

The awful storm that had savaged the last days of November had eased, but winter was nigh upon them. The abbey was a hard place when the weather turned. Doors shrank in the cold and banged in the drafts as snow sifted in beneath them. Stinging sleet and freezing slush had already brought one sprained ankle and one broken leg to the infirmary. It had been so cold that even the water in Cook's bucket of eels had frozen. *Just as well,* Averilla thought, *That we communicate mostly in sign, for the cold, added to the fasting diet of Advent, makes even the mildest-tempered testy.*

Averilla rubbed absently at the persistent pain in her back. *Simply too much to do, and no Dame Maud to tell me how it should be done!*

Two months earlier, Dame Maud, the infirmaress, had been summoned to another abbey, Romsey, to help an inexperienced infirmaress handle an outbreak of coughing sickness. Averilla had been left in charge at Shaftesbury and felt both unequal to the task and very, very tired.

It's last year's strange blindness that scares me, she now thought, remembering those three days of unrelieved dark. *And now I, who never thought to fear, dread that the blindness may return. And,* she admitted guiltily to herself, *prayer doesn't seem to help.* Burying her trembling hand in her sleeve, she forced herself to focus once again on the infirmary, where every bed was filled with victims of the flux, their vomiting and loose bowls. *I feel so vulnerable. My own malady may return, and without Maud, how can I manage?*

Averilla picked up a bowl of broth and moved slowly down the aisle, biting her lip. She hadn't yet brewed the tissanes, and she doubted that there would be time. She skirted the little piles of debris that the cripple, Mary, had swept up, knelt beside old Dame Marta, and began to spoon broth between her parched lips, trying to ignore Mary sweeping nearer and nearer. The accident was inevitable. Hearing a groan, Mary turned, and the end of her broom knocked the bowl from Averilla's hands. Mary stood, babbling in distress, humiliated. Before Averilla could stop herself, she snapped, "Well, don't just look at it, get something to mop it up with!" Mortified, Averilla bit her tongue, but it was too late. Mary had seen the pursed lips, had heard the words and the deep sigh of exasperation.

A look of panic and heaving shoulders spurred Averilla to the next bed where she grabbed the chamber pot to hold beneath the head of yet another retching nun. When it was over, Averilla wiped off the spittle with a clean cloth, picked up the filled pot, and hurried to the necessarium (toilet) with a thin-lipped grimace.

"Daughter." Old Dame Scholastica, near the hearth, held up a finger. Her eyes on Mary drew Averilla's gaze to the girl, on whose cheeks large tears glistened.

Averilla blushed. She knew she had been harsh; should apologize, should give the mortified Mary a word of encouragement—*but… I am so tired.* "In a moment, Dame."

When Averilla had emptied the slops and yanked back the necessarium door, her good intention evaporated in surprise at seeing Sister Clayetta, the abbess's English maid, waiting for her.

"*Benedicte,* Dame," said Sister Clayetta, putting a hand under her nose. "Er, the abbess's compliments." Clayetta's eyes widened at Averilla's glower of annoyance. "She, the abbess, that is," Clayetta struggled valiantly on in French, "requests your presence at the stables." The Norman French was too hard for her to manage, English as she was. Flustered, she blushed, shook her head, and gave up.

Clayetta's misery further irritated Averilla. "English will do, Sister. I too am English." Then, perplexed, "The abbess wants me at the stables? In the midst of this?" She shook her head. "Has someone been kicked?"

"N-no, Dame." Clayetta said in English. "She, the abbess, would have you and Old Turgold accompany her into the forest."

"The forest?" Averilla stared. "Now?!"

Averilla straightened her shoulders. Any request by another nun was to be obeyed without question. She rose, bowed perfunctorily to Clayetta, and said with ill grace, "Thank you, Sister. Tell the abbess I will attend her."

As Averilla thrust her dirtied apron and sleeve protectors into the laundry basket, she thought: *Of course, the abbess wants me. Someone is bound to fall on an icy patch or run into a tree, so I must neglect all my duties, as if I had no responsibility here.*

Release from the enclosure was forbidden the nuns except for "necessity." To forage for medicinal herbs, for instance, was "necessary." For that reason, Averilla and Sister Ethelind, in the care of Old Turgold, often meandered near the abbey to search out roots and herbs.

To this abbess, however, necessity had increasingly come to mean the entertaining of visiting nobility, for "If they come to love the abbey," Abbess Cecily had explained in her high, Norman voice, "they will be more inclined to donate to us benefices and tithes and great sums of money."

Cecily probably just wants to hunt, Averilla thought crossly. Court-raised, and the spoiled daughter of one of William the Conqueror's closest friends, Cecily was known to love the hunt. No nun could be unaccompanied outside the cloister, so Averilla and Turgold often attended her, as both could ride and were familiar with the environs.

Averilla explained it all to Sister Ethelind, and then shoved bread, cheese, a wineskin, medicines, and bandages into her voluminous scrip (purse). She snatched her winter cloak, which smelled dishearteningly of wet sheep, off a peg near the door and stepped outside.

A WINTER SUN, AS ROUND and red as an apple, played hide-and-seek with a low fog. Servants, ostlers, and dog handlers were everywhere. Tack clanked, dogs barked and snapped, and the horses, eager for release, stamped and snorted. The nobles stood in clusters, the fug of their breath rising. They were uniformly clad in green, their well-oiled leather boots shiny and creaking.

Benedictine abbeys offered hospitality to travelers and strangers in accordance with that portion of the Rule that bade them

"Treat every stranger as if he was Christ himself." Several nobles had taken shelter during the recent blizzard, bringing with them news of the great tragedy that had taken the life of King Henry's only son. The prince and all his court had drowned when their ship, the *Blanche Nef,* sank off the coast of Normandy. Like the rest of the kingdom, the abbey community had been weighted down by grief—many of the nuns had lost kinsmen and friends in the catastrophe.

The worst of the storm had passed two nights earlier, but the nobles lingered. It was whispered that they were eager to avoid King Henry, whose fury at the loss of his son could strike anywhere.

Averilla slipped between two horses, placed a warning hand on a shiny rump, skirted a steaming pile of manure, and barely avoided a pair of the snarling bloodhounds known as lymers.

Laughing amidst the nobles, the abbess, petite and achingly beautiful even in a habit, nodded vaguely to Averilla, who had more sense than to interrupt. Turgold, just hefting a fleece and saddle onto his mule, smiled the crinkly-eyed smile he reserved for Averilla alone, and lifted his bushy eyebrows in mute resignation. He was a tall man, his sinewy muscles knotted with the years that had grayed his hair and beard. Turgold it was who had rescued the child Averilla from a famine-induced uprising in the north and then shepherded her to the safety of Shaftesbury. His acceptance did nothing to lift Averilla's mood. The two of them would do as they were bidden. *That's the rub,* she thought. *I should be tending the sick, not chaperoning the abbess.*

Though a few plump flakes drifted down, they seemed desultory, so the nobles mounted, scarcely keeping the head-shaking horses in check, and trotted under the massive abbey gatehouse arch and onto the Bimport, the track in front of the gate, followed by yelping lymers that strained against their handlers.

Cecily, however, mounted her palfrey slowly, passed sedately under the arch, and then paced the mare between the houses on the Bimport and the High Street, smiling graciously at the numerous villagers waving and smiling and calling blessings on her. Cecily was lax in her dealings with her serfs, and they interpreted this as kindness. At the bottom of the hill, just past the town gate, Cecily reined in and frowned at the previously neat rows, torn into clumps by the headlong passage of the nobles.

Averilla pulled her donkey abreast of the abbess. "My lady, do we not follow the hunt?"

Cecily drew her brows together and glanced down at Averilla.

"I have decided not. The blizzard kept us from gathering mistletoe for the service of penance and reconciliation on the thirteenth. The sacrist needs it, and it must be the abbess who gathers it." She grimaced. "I have never quite understood the connection between mistletoe and penance, but it must be done. Luckily, I am not required to actually climb the trees."

"Turgold," Cecily asked after a moment, "know you if mistletoe appears in a nearby oak?"

"Aye, my lady." He pointed into the wood. "Farther in."

"How far?"

He looked up, judging the course of the sun. "A ways."

Watching Cecily's mare delicately pick her way through the brown leaf mold and slush, Averilla rebelled at the frivolous nature of what they were doing. *There are patients who need help now, and I am not certain how to treat this flux. When will Maud return?*

Chapter Two

Gillingham Forest

He felt he had been trudging for hours when a sudden jerk on the rope roused Will from his stupor, and he watched in awe as a huge stag sailed over the track and onto the snowy verge on its far side. Dogs, horses, and men barreled into the guards, severing the rope and knocking Will off his feet. A melee of horns, shouts, and curses roiled above and around him. Will scrambled his bound hands over his ears and head to shield himself from the onslaught. Claws dug into his back. A huge hoof landed beside his head.

His face was pressed onto the track, and dirt was in his mouth, mingling with the blood from the newly opened scab on what remained of his tongue. He didn't dare swallow. His entire world became an attempt to breathe. As the chaos ebbed, he lifted his head, wiped his lips on his shoulder, and coughed some of the mud from his mouth. His hands were still tied, but no one held his tether. His guards, preoccupied, struggled to contain their mounts. *Mary, Mother of God, thank you!*

Propelled by terror, he elbowed and shimmied his exhausted body away from the hunters, expecting a hoof in his back or a heavy hand on his shoulder. Gnarled beech roots and great clumps of desiccated bramble poked through the snow on the verge. Like an overgrown caterpillar, Will rolled and scrunched through the roots and trunks and into the thick confusion of brambles. A shout of pithy Anglo-Saxon swear words reverberated behind Will as his guards realized he had disappeared.

THE ABBESS, IN NO HURRY to find the mistletoe, was admiring a cobweb diamonded with mist when the sound of the hunt seemed suddenly nearer. Yells of fury and frustration mingled with snarls and yips. Then the uproar slowly subsided into an eerie silence.

They waited, listening. Turgold shrugged, and Averilla ventured, "That sounded somewhat amiss. Think you I should check?"

"A fall, mayhap, or a collision." the abbess said absently. "We'll know by nightfall." Dismissing the problem, Cecily pointed with her crop at the huge trees. "'Tis my hope that our oratory will look just so one day, like great beeches branching skyward."

Averilla glowered inwardly, hoping just the opposite. Cecily had caught the building bug that afflicted clergy all across England and the Continent, all of them eager to rebuild their comfortable "oratories" into massive churches. *So, the rumor is true! She really means to rebuild the whole church! Not just repair the crypt as she first intimated. Will she never stop changing things? She has no idea what such a change means to us, her "daughters."* Pretending not to have heard the abbess's comment, Averilla made a show of gazing at the swaths of snow pooled on the long arms of the beeches, and the blue shadows limning nearby rocks beneath which frozen seed vessels of cow parsnip drooped in bedraggled clumps.

The three continued up a low rise and down again into a small swale where a great rampart of holly and yew had grown together. In the bright white of the forest, the deep crimson of rosehips, holly, and hawthorn berries was breathtaking. In the midst stood a mighty oak, its bare branches swathed in mistletoe.

Cecily turned in the saddle. "The ceremonial cutting of the mistletoe allows me to—"

Before she could finish the thought, Cecily's palfrey shied violently. Cecily braced herself against the saddle's backboard, pushed her legs forward into the stirrups, and sawed on the reins. "Dear Lord," she exclaimed, "A dead man!"

Averilla peered around the palfrey and saw a huddle of bloody rags. She snatched her scrip from her saddle horn, slid from the donkey, looped her reins over a branch, and pushed aside the rump of the snorting mare. A slash of red, crude and violent, splashed across the face and clothes of a huge man who lay, crumpled, half in and half out of the brambles on the left side of the glen.

Cecily turned, aghast, to Averilla. "Blood. Is he…?"

AVERILLA KNELT IN THE SLUSH and put a hand on the man's throat. "No, not dead, but…" Her mind reeling, she pulled linen from her scrip. She had a fair idea of what had happened to this man. Cecily, however, daughter of Robert FitzHamon, sister-in-law to the Duke of Gloucester, had no notion of the cruelties Normans wielded on the subservient English.

The abbess leaned down, eyes wide. "What think you?" The whispered words caught in her throat.

"I…" Averilla temporized. "You'll…" Then, knowing only truth would do, said, "His tongue was cut out."

She wiped at the mess of dried blood near his mouth, and gently brushed the shock of grimy hair from his eyes. In answer to the unasked question, she shook her head. "I would know had I ever seen this man before." As she continued her examination, she noted in surprise that a small furrow now creased the bloody forehead. Will—for it was Will—blinked. His eyes rested on her and pleaded.

"Dumb." Turgold was matter-of-fact. He had dismounted and now held the palfrey's head. His eyes, however, probed the dell, wary. "My lady, I don't think… we must…"

When the abbess didn't respond, Turgold put a hand on her foot. Her head slewed around to him like an enraged adder, eyes firing at the liberty. "Do not ever—" she started.

"It be not safe, my lady," Turgold persisted, ignoring her rebuke. "Those as did this could be near."

"Not safe? They wouldn't dare!" Cecily's fear erupted into ire. "Hear ye," she growled, voice taking on depth and force. "This man is under the protection—the *full* protection—of the Abbess of Shaftesbury. I hereby grant him sanctuary. Any—any—who lay a further hand on this serf shall rue the day."

From some distance, as if in mockery, came the receding sound of dogs and the moan of horns as the hunt moved farther into the forest.

Then, worried, "Think you that someone actually still lingers?"

Turgold didn't respond.

"By Saint Edward, man, take your staff and check!"

Turgold gave her a level look, raised an eyebrow just enough to mitigate the twinkle in his eye. "If it please your ladyship, were there any afore in these woods, hearing you, they'd be wise eno' to 'ave gone."

Her eyes went to Averilla who had wetted a cloth with wine from her wineskin and now dabbed it onto Will's mouth. He opened his mouth as best he could, cracking the blood that caked his lips, and allowed the wine to trickle between them.

"What suppose you he did?" Cecily whispered, fascinated by the man's enormous strength and hardened muscles.

"It could have been stealing or—or anything." Averilla looked to Turgold for support.

"Since we know not, my lady—" Turgold started, but Cecily's glower silenced him.

"We will take him back."

"My lady," Turgold tried, "Ye wot not what 'e—"

"But I *do* know," Cecily snapped. "I saw his eyes."

Averilla rested her hands on her knees. Everything in her knew there would be consternation among the other nuns when they brought this man, marked as a criminal by the lack of a tongue, to the abbey. Even so, she felt gladness well inside. Someone who needed her help. Something she could do. His crime was probably not as dire as the bloody mouth would seem to indicate. She, an Englishwoman, knew that Norman justice was harsh.

Turgold nodded, knelt, and began to hack through the leather cords that bound Will's hands.

"Man!" Cecily leaned down from her horse, holding Will's eyes. "Understand you me?" She faltered on the unfamiliar English. "You will accompany us to Shaftesbury. An abbey. Perchance you will heal. We will try. You shall have sanctuary… for whatever it is that you have done." Her French accent made her words nearly incomprehensible to Will who frowned in concentration. Finally, he nodded.

Turgold firmed his lips. Despite himself, he had always liked Cecily, but she had no comprehension of anything beyond her very protected world.

Interpreting Turgold's hesitation as insolence, Cecily lifted her chin and slapped her whip against her boot. Turgold nodded, scratched the back of his neck, knelt beside Will, and propped the larger man into a sitting position.

"Let him rest a moment." Averilla held Turgold's eyes.

"Aye, Dame." Turgold then said to Will in English as he finished cutting the rope from his hands, "Ye'll 'ave to walk. There be no other way. Ye be too big for the donkey, and the mule don't like the blood."

Will nodded, head down, and rubbed his chafed wrists.

Turgold put his hands under Will's arms, and, with Averilla pushing from behind, they managed to get him to his feet.

ON THE WAY BACK TO THE abbey, Cecily kept a regal silence. Their progress was slow, as Will could barely walk. Even with a rope around his waist providing some stability, and tethered behind Turgold's mule, he staggered.

Cecily allowed Averilla to draw up beside her and confided, sorrow dimming her beauty, "William de Mortain is my cousin."

Averilla looked confused. *How does this pertain to all that has just transpired?*

Cecily continued. "William is—was—a kind and gentle man. We used to play, he and I, as children. When we were older, he would sing me his lays, poems he had himself created, accompanied with his lute. He taught me to play it as well, setting my little fingers on the strings. Some years ago, King Henry had him blinded. Blinded!" Cecily's lip trembled. "He was a poet, and now he rots in the king's dungeons for the rest of his life. All for a few words in a poem penned in jest." She paused, then said firmly, "We shall call this man Will, after my cousin. Mayhap what I do for this Will, by the grace of God, can in some way ease my cousin's pain."

BY THE TIME THE ABBESS, Dame Averilla, Turgold, and the staggering wraith of a huge man straggled up the hill after None, snow again spiraled down from dark clouds, and the horse and mule missed their footing now and again on the slippery pavement. The gateman at the bottom of the hill was appalled. They could see it in his eyes. The four made an astonishing sight as they rode along the High Street, under the gatehouse arch and into the court. The portress was stunned. Cecily, elegant and determined, as if in anticipation of battle, passed through the gate. In contrast, Averilla, on the low donkey, seemed rumpled and burdened with care. Will, bloody and bedraggled, staggered behind Turgold, astride his wild-eyed mule.

In the forecourt, Cecily dismounted. Seemingly dismissing all thought of Will, she left Averilla and Turgold to care for the wretched man.

With mixed feelings, Averilla watched the abbess glide off: *She has no idea how full the infirmary is or how much extra work she has thrust upon me.* Averilla and Turgold, supporting Will on each side, headed to the infirmary. Murmurs of alarm drifted behind them as those watching saw—really saw—the ragged hulk of the man between them.

"Not one of ours, surely."

"I have never seen a man so big."

"Then who?"

"A masterless man?"

"But look at his clothes."

"Surely that is blood."

"Look at his mouth. I think his tongue was cut out!"

"What can he have done to be so punished?"

"They should take him to the castle. Why don't they take him to the castle?"

Tentatively, Dame Mary offered, "He is hurt. She had to bring him here. They won't tend to him in the castle. He would die. We are bound to treat any stranger as if he were Christ Himself."

"But... not this kind of stranger, surely." The voice was tremulous.

THE INFIRMARY AT SHAFTESBURY ABBEY was of one story, thatched, and nestled beside the orchard and behind the herb garden in order to keep contagion well away from the cloister. With the building of a castle at the end of the Bimport by William the Conqueror, and the subsequent rebuilding and expansion of the various abbey buildings, the infirmary had been increasingly required to care for the workers' health. Accidents occurred that required more skill than the village wise women could provide. Space in the infirmary, to the right of the door, had subsequently been partitioned off by screens, and was kept for treatment of the severe ailments of abbey workers and their families.

It was into this space that Turgold and Averilla placed Will. The old man already there, suffering from aching bones, which Averilla was treating with an ointment of monkshood, looked on the invasion of his space—and at Will—with the indignant irritation of a territorial squirrel.

While Turgold removed Will's blood-soaked clothing, Averilla tiptoed to the infirmary kitchen, sliced three sides off the loaf of stale bread—blue-tinged with spots of mold—kept on a high back shelf, and poured wine into a tumbler. When she returned, Turgold bolstered up the semi-comatose Will, and Averilla again used a cloth to drip wine into his mouth. Most of it dribbled down his chin. With strips of linen, she bound the moldy bread on the gashes on Will's wrists and knees.

Turgold laid Will onto the hastily vacated pallet. Then, rubbing the back of his neck, gave Averilla a long look, "I like not his being here."

"Nor do I. Weak as a lamb now, but he will heal, I wot, and regain his strength. I saw prior healing in his mouth. I think there has been time between when his tongue was taken and whatever happened in the forest."

Turgold shook his head. "I think I best stay. We know not what he might do when he strengthens. I'd feel better—"

"As would I," piped the other occupant, who had already gathered up his bits and was preparing to leave.

Averilla made a moue of regret. "Come see me on the morrow" she told the little man. To Turgold she said, "For the nonce, get yourself some food. It has been a long, tiring day—and Turgold, thank you."

Averilla did not attend Vespers; nor did she go to the calefactorium, or warming room, following the short collation and evening meal, and thus did not hear the rumors and mutterings that bloomed among the other nuns. Keeping watch as Cecily had bidden her, she did not attend the midnight offices of Matins and Lauds either. Thunderous moans erupted from Will's soul, waking the other patients. Throughout the long night, Averilla labored to bring down his fever. She tried willow-bark tea, and when that failed, resorted to packing snow around his hot body. She had stayed beside his bed with a tenacity that surprised and exhausted her, wishing over and over that Maud had somehow returned to guide, and yes, to deal with this conundrum. Averilla's weariness threatened to overwhelm her, but she continued to moisten Will's lips with wine and sponge his head with snow-cooled water. As she labored, she found herself muttering the familiar psalms of the office of Compline, and pleading with the Almighty, "Help. Do help. Please."

As the night wended into the bleak hours of earliest morning, Will's entire system seemed to be failing. *If he dies, I will have failed to help one of Your lambs. If only I knew more.* Then, with a sudden jolt, came the thought: *If he doesn't die, what do we do with him then?*

CHAPTER THREE

DECEMBER 5, 1120

The first bell for Mass woke Averilla from a troubled sleep. She had finally taken to her bed at Prime only because Sister Ethelind, a novice training in the infirmary, had insisted that she was in no state to do Will any good. Averilla looked up now to see Ethelind, dark eyes troubled in her alert, birdlike face, standing beside her cot. "I am sorry, Dame. You have only been asleep since Prime, and I wouldn't have waked you, but the abbess sent word that you must be in church for Mass. She said that missing so many offices is 'not good for the soul.'" Ethelind repeated the phrase with a raised eyebrow. The nuns tolerated Cecily, who had been forced on them by the king. It was acknowledged among them that Cecily had no calling, but they recognized also that she was trying to understand what it meant to "give your life to Christ."

"In addition, Ethelind continued, "she wants you to attend Chapter. She said that she needs you."

"Will?" Averilla asked around the cotton in her mouth.

Ethelind just shook her head. After a moment she added, "You might like to know. Word came by messenger that though the king still grieves, he is no longer searching for anyone to blame for the death of his son." Her smile held a twist of irony.

"The treasure in the ship's hold was recovered entire from the Catterville rocks. He is somewhat mollified."

AVERILLA STAGGERED INTO THE CHURCH with a guilty sense of relief, and, as she was late, lay prone on the cold flags, the obligatory punishment for tardiness.

After Mass, with its prayers for those who had been lost at sea, the nuns processed into the chapter house for Chapter, the daily meeting of the community, which started with the reading of a chapter from the Rule of St. Benedict. Neither that nor the other readings could hold the attention of the distracted nuns. Finally came the moment when the abbess was required to ask if there were any concerns about the "affairs of the house."

The cellarer, hands in her sleeves, took the floor from her seat in the upper tier. "We… I… wonder, Lady Abbess," she looked pointedly at Averilla, "if we might be informed why there is an unknown… man… not one of our workers, in our infirmary?"

Averilla cringed and waited to see what Cecily would say.

From her armed chair on the top tier, Cecily said, blandly, "I have named him Will."

The subprioress, Dame Joan, with whom Averilla was often at odds, rose. "How can Dame Averilla place among the most vulnerable in our community this… criminal? Who knows what he will do when he heals?"

With a show of patience, Cecily responded, "His tongue was cut out. I offered him sanctuary. He accepted."

Several nuns stood.

"That is not a reason to place him where—"

"We will be murdered in our beds."

The abbess held up her hand, and when they quieted, said as if it had just occurred to her, "Old Turgold is just that, old. We needed someone to replace him as a protector when we travel.

God saw our need. Will is big. When he recovers his strength, he shall lodge with the others above the stables."

Dame Emma's soft voice could be heard when Cecily paused. "After all, Our Lord, too, was beaten."

The abbess looked to the youngest novice on the lowest tier. It was the privilege and custom of the youngest to be given voice in these meetings. Nudged by her sisters, a girl of fourteen made her way to the center of the circular room. "We know nothing about him. And he can't tell us."

The abbess considered. "King Henry once said"—Cecily had no idea if he had, but thought he ought to have—"that you can tell the nature of someone by looking into his eyes. I have looked into this man's eyes and I saw kindness."

WHILE ON THE HILL ABOVE him the nuns were in Chapter, the parish priest of St. James, Father Merowald, sat meditating in the small hut affixed like a barnacle to his parish church. He tried to ignore the cold draft that whistled through the ill-fitting shutters and lifted the rushes on the floor, flinging around the smoldering remains of last night's fire. Merowald was a thin scribble of a man, frail, fine-boned, and stooped as if his great head were too heavy to hold up. He had tufts of straw-colored floss on his scalp. His eyes were pale, he had impossibly large ears, and his ankles were twig-like. He felt restless this morning, as if something were amiss, and had prayed for guidance. The Holy Spirit had been enigmatic. The word "Will" kept repeating in Merowald's mind. *Is the Holy Spirit referring to the knotty question of free will?* he wondered. *Am I somehow abridging that greatest and most burdensome of privileges? Or is something wrong in the abbey? Mayhap if I go and look into what is transpiring there, it will become clear.*

Father Merowald crossed himself, rose, and, shaking the ash from his cassock, noticed in its shabby folds another hole. So old was the black garment that it looked green, and he had almost worn it through at the knees. And now there was yet another hole where a spark from the fire had landed. *Must have been late last night.* Merowald was never very aware as he sat "meditating" before his fire. He smiled at the term. Could he use the word "meditation," he wondered, to describe his evening's occupation? He tried—usually—to call to mind the day's gospel, tried to listen for a word or phrase that spoke to him for that day and hour. Monks and nuns had for centuries used this tool to delve into the Gospels. It had probably originated with the command of God given on the Mount of Transfiguration: "Listen to Him." *Lectio Divina*—divine listening—they called this delving into what Christ said in the Gospels, and the practice was soothing. Perhaps too soothing, if Merowald was honest with himself. The hole was evidence. Far too often his mind wandered. And he a priest. Worse, sometimes he even nodded off—ignoring the Creator of the universe—disgraceful!

Merowald's position at Shaftesbury was unusual. The bishop of Salisbury, Shaftesbury's diocesan, had the unpleasant habit of dumping ineffectual priests on the abbey, where (the bishop felt) a bumbling—or pompous—priest could do little harm. The nuns accepted the ministrations of these priests up to a point, but in matters of substance, such as confession or the care of their souls, the nuns tended to seek out Father Merowald, parish priest of the hamlet of St. James who also had the care of the abbey lay workers. Father Merowald too had been dumped—banished, actually, to St. James by the French Abbot Suger of Cluny. Merowald was a man who rarely suffered fools, and Abbot Suger, Merowald had made abundantly clear, was too fond of the things of this world and bowed too easily to the Church hierarchy. Thus Merowald found himself in a tiny parish, St. James,

where, Suger had suggested with thick irony, no worldly goods
would tempt him.

Merowald closed the flimsy door behind him and looked
around. Despite the cold, the sky was clear. The trek between St.
James at the bottom of the hill and the nave altar in the abbey
involved climbing the steep slope of Laundry Lane. *Thankfully,
the ice seems to have melted. At least I won't slip.* He began the
ascent, and, much as he hated to admit it, felt a wave of weariness wash over him. It was tiring to listen to people's confes-
sions and woes. *How does God manage it, listening to the whole
world? How does He pay attention? He is God, but…*

Merowald's mind drifted back to the problem of the hole in
his cassock. *How many holes are permissible?* He didn't like to
be profligate; yet his cassock was supposed to cover the man he
was, so that when parishioners saw him, they saw not the man
but a representative of God. Would God care about a hole in a
cassock? There were those, usually bishops and the like, such as
Suger, who seemed to think God *did* care, that He needed lavish
appointments to announce His glory. But had Christ needed
extravagance? Nothing in the Gospels indicated that Christ had
needed anything more than the attire of a carpenter.

Merowald just reached the top of Laundry Lane and was
giving his best approximation of a smile to the rapscallion
who begged at the gate, reminding himself—with this one he
felt he needed reminding—that Christ loved every soul. Then
Merowald paused, trying to remember just where he was now
headed. Remembering the hole but forgetting entirely the problem of "Will," he started off toward the church. A saw caught as
it razored a log. A man swore.

Ah, a carpenter. Merowald stopped to peer into one of the
deep holes that ringed the original apse of the old church in

preparation for rebuilding. He navigated the neat piles of rope, stacked stone, and sand where, despite the bitter cold, the men still worked. He stopped in front of a carpenter.

"Wat, God's blessing on you this fine morrow."

The wiry man straightened guiltily.

I wish they wouldn't always remember their sins when I approach, Merowald thought.

Wat scrabbled his hood off a stringy mat of hay-colored hair, wiped his hands on his leather apron, and gave a scrambling sort of bow. "Thank ye, Fader, thank ye. So…" Unless they had a problem, or a sin that they were ready to confess, the usual parishioner had no idea how to talk to a priest, much less a priest known for his learning, and, more threateningly, for his humility.

The sawing around Wat had stopped at Merowald's arrival. The masons chiseling away at hunks of greenstone, dust obscuring their features, had also stopped to listen to this unexpected entertainment. Wat ran his fingers through his hair again, making himself look like a bewildered woodpecker.

"I was wondering, Wat, what you would think of this cassock?"

The idea of putting himself in the place of the respected priest caused Wat to blush in confusion. "Well, Fader, I am… would an'—"

"What I am concerned about is this hole." Merowald poked his finger through it as a demonstration. "Do you think that if you were a priest you would leave it, or patch it, or ask for a new cassock?"

Being given choices took the pressure away, and Wat looked at the garment critically. "What I think, Fader, is 'tisn't right for a priest to be tattered. Takes away from what ye be. Makes un wonder why ye don't take better care o' yersel. Looks like ye don't respect…" He paused as another thought struck him. "See 'ere, this apron." He pointed to the leather bib covering his tunic and braes. "Keeps splinters off me, protects my clothes and body. Cain't saw through it. Same wi' ye. If ye were to approach another soul, that soul'ud wonder why ye don't take better care." His eye lit up as the thought transformed: "Didna ye say the body be the temple of the Holy Spirit?"

"Ah." Merowald held Wat's eyes for a moment, bowed his head and said, "Thank you. I am much obliged," and ambled off. Wat watched the priest walk across the court, shook his head, sighed in affection, and bent for his saw. Then he straightened and yelled, "Fader!"

Merowald turned.

"There be a man in the infirmary might need you."

"Is that so? Is his name, by chance, Will?"

Hearing a scratching from the other side of the screen that partitioned Will from the rest of the infirmary, Averilla found the kind eyes of Father Merowald resting upon her, his brow furrowed in concern.

"Oh, Father! You came! Thank you. I- I, he needs our prayer. Nothing I do seems to help!"

"I just heard something of… this man Will. Mayhap we could pray a little beside him." As he bent his knees to the floor, Merowald muttered, "Sometimes I am so blind. Even when He tells me what to do."

For a moment Averilla looked surprised, but everyone was used to Merowald's mutterings. She said, "Aren't we all, Father?"

They prayed. As they had done together many times before, they silently allowed themselves to sink into a blissful state of wordless petition for the man and soul before them, resting their hands on his body. Neither knew what it was that finally roused them, but their eyes eventually met, and they smiled. Merowald rose. It was an effort, this getting his knees to support his body. When Averilla offered a hand, he accepted it, brushed himself off, and said, by way of what—conversation?—why had the name popped onto his tongue? "Saw old Madge today. Wonderful woman, she…" He bowed and left.

Madge, Averilla thought. *Of course. Why didn't I think of her before?*

Old Madge was the village wise woman. If there was anything more that could be done for Will, Madge would know of it. Averilla shook her head at her own obtuseness, then rose and motioned Sister Ethelind and Dame Elizabeth to her. She said, "I need you to go down and ask Old Madge if she has any advice for me. About Will."

Neither protested, but both looked bewildered and reluctant, for the storm had started up again with a wild abandon, hurtling itself—and branches torn from the apple trees—against the infirmary walls. Dubiously, the two donned heavy cloaks and hats, then slipped and slid down Laundry Lane. When they reached St. James, sheltered by the bulk of Shaftesbury's mount, the snow wasn't swirling as wildly, and they could see where they were going.

Madge had lived on the outskirts of St. James for as long as anyone could remember, first with her mother, then with her husband, and more recently, for a number of years, alone. Despite the fact that she frequently talked to herself, she was respected. She was often seen praying in the little parish church of St. James, which dispelled any tendency to call her a witch, and in truth there was a certain aura of serenity about her that was healing.

SISTER ETHELIND'S EYES WERE HUGE when she and Dame Elizabeth returned to the infirmary, sooner than Averilla had expected, considering the weather. Not even pausing to remove her outer garments, Ethelind handed Averilla, tentatively, as if it might break or bite, a jar sealed with waxed parchment.

"She knew we were coming," Elizabeth said, brushing snow from her face and pulling off her cloak. Her eyes were pools of amazement as she reiterated: "We barely had to knock, and the door opened. She had the jar ready and was waiting to thrust it into our hands. Said you'd know what to do with it, nodded to us, smiled, and shut the door."

Despite herself, Averilla grinned at their youthful awe, and leaving them to tidy themselves, took the jar into the small work-kitchen, unwound the twine, and peeled the parchment from the lip. The tincture within had the consistency of cream and the odor of a pigsty.

Pot in hand, Averilla tiptoed to the screens that sheltered the momentarily quiescent Will. She had grown strangely fond of the huge man. *How can you know someone when they don't talk to you?* she wondered, yet she felt that she *did* know him, to the core. *Is it because I have watched him so closely? Oh, Lord, he isn't healing. Please help him.*

THAT NIGHT, AFTER COMPLINE, WILL thrashed into consciousness as yet another straw of Madge's noxious brew was forced through his lips, where it pooled in his mouth. He tried to push the hand away as fiery pain coursed along the stump of his tongue. His mouth was the only part of him that he knew. He clung desperately to consciousness. *I have no… tongue!* A sudden memory. A glade. A knife. Will's eyes rolled back, and he retreated into delirium, continuing to sweat and toss. He was tangled in something. Ropes? Vines? Shrouds! In his dreaming he saw a line of runaways struggling past his trussed body, their hands tied, their faces bloody. They opened their mouths as they passed him. Their tongues were gone, their mouths huge maws, black and gaping.

He replayed the last bit of the dream through his wakened mind. They'd dunked their heads into the horse trough, then tilted them back, like so many ducks, and they had swallowed! *Mayhap I too can eat. And swallow*

A cool hand touched his forehead, and he looked up into the smiling face of a young and pretty woman sitting beside his bed. *An angel?* Her features were perfect: Milk-smooth skin and eyes the color of spring bluebells. Bewilderingly, she seemed familiar, as if he'd seen her before. *Then not dead. But where be I? Who is she? What bed be this?*

When Dame Elizabeth saw Will's eyes open and then widen in confusion, she stumbled upright and, overturning her stool, gasped, "He wakes! Dame Averilla, he is awake!"

Will grabbed her tunic and groaned. "Gmnooo." The intensity and volume of his voice startled them both. He lifted his hand to his mouth and mimed drinking.

Elizabeth stuttered, "D– drink. He wants to drink."

Dame Averilla hurried over, put a reassuring hand on Elizabeth's arm, and smiled down into Will's confused eyes. Speaking slowly in English, she said, "You have been very ill. Maimed. Do you remember?"

His eyes searched the middle distance. Carefully, as if his head were glass, he gave a slight nod.

"We came upon you in the forest. We will give you drink. But slowly, slowly. Too much too soon would go ill with your body. Your tongue…"

I be with nuns, he thought, remembering the forest. *Sanctuary. But they don't know I murdered Alcar. When they find out…*

Together Averilla and Elizabeth hoisted him into a sitting position. Averilla took the wine-wet cloth from Elizabeth, squeezed out a few drops and then a few more as Will opened his mouth and tilted his head back to let the liquid run into his mouth and down his throat. The wine stung when it touched the scabbed butt of his tongue, and he groaned.

ALL THE NEXT DAY, THE sixth of December, Will was given wine with salt in it, drips at a time through a piece of straw. Later he even managed a bit of broth. By nightfall, the third night since his rescue from the forest, Will awakened to find tears rolling down his cheeks and onto the pillow. At the thought of his friend Waldo, whipped and flayed by Alcar, a lonely moan ground through his chest. Hearing it as if from someone else, someone different, he thought, *And I cain't talk. Ever again.*

As the nuns in the infirmary sang Lauds to their patients in the middle of the night, Will's mind drew up a childhood memory. Fader sitting, head in 'is hands afore the fire. Moder standing, skirts dragging at the ash. Fretting. Not about what clawed at 'er mind. Not about that. 'Twas alays some'ut else.

Chapter Four

December 7, 1120

lonely morning sun filtered through the oiled parchment of the infirmary windows as one of the lay sisters removed the shutters and woke Will. The now familiar agony in his mouth was still there. He tested his muscles. *Cain't bide here. Steward'll find me. Have to flee. But too weak.* He lay still. A misery beyond body niggled at the back of his mind. *Some'ut. What be I hiding?* Then, *Waldo!* A wave of sadness engulfed him as he saw again the lash cutting into Waldo's withered arm, saw again the fear in Alcar's eyes as he, Will, rounded on the reeve and started pummeling.

The memory ebbed. *Sure as sure, steward'll come. Or those as took my tongue. Flee!* He dug his elbows into the pallet and forced his weakened body into a sitting position. It was too much.

Averilla, heating a tincture on a small saucer atop a brazier, heard Elizabeth's cry of alarm. She glanced over and saw Will sway. "Put his head between his knees." As she turned to help, her hand—her shaking hand—brushed the saucer, and it slipped a fraction of an inch. She overreacted and, in trying to steady the saucer, jostled the brazier. The whole apparatus toppled. Live coals fell onto the dried rushes and straw that covered the floor. One or two flew onto the coverlet on Dame Scholastica's bed. A lay sister scurried to beat them out as Sister Ethelind with surprising presence of mind, calmly poured the contents of a chamber pot onto the glowing rushes.

Averilla, mortified by her clumsiness—*How could I have been so inept?*—absently reached down and picked a coal from Scholastica's coverlet and dropped it into the chamber pot.

"Dame!" Elizabeth put her hand over her mouth. "Your hand! You must have burned your hand. Let me…"

Averilla held out her hand, the thumb and forefinger only slightly reddened.

"A live coal. You picked up a coal?"

Averilla shook her head and rubbed at her eyes. "Did I? I couldn't have, could I?"

Dame Elizabeth muttered, "I am not very good with this."

Averilla raised her eyes. "Good with what, Dame?"

"With this… this continual chaos. With a giant staying among us who has had his tongue cut out and we don't know why. Who might murder us. With old women who know you are coming before you get there. With nuns who pick up live coals and are not burned. I– I thought that here, in the infirmary, I would have time to pray for the sick and be with them. That it would be serene, a place of sanctuary."

Averilla gave her a long look. "It isn't as you expected?"

"No, it isn't."

Averilla blew out a sigh, grabbed a broom, and nudged it toward the charred puddle beneath a cot. "You didn't expect—?"

"This," Elizabeth gestured around indicating the infirmary. "It's all so busy and hurried and messy. And there isn't time to pray for the sick and the injured." With a gesture of resignation, Elizabeth pushed the pile of charred rushes with her boot. "Although you did pray, didn't you? With Father Merowald and…" she looked back to Will's bed and shook her head.

As Averilla watched the younger woman dubiously head back toward Will, a wave of fatigue washed over her. *I am so weary. Elizabeth wants time to pray and meditate. I too want Sabbath. Christ went off by himself and prayed. When do I go away to rest? But...* she closed her eyes, *when does Cook? Or do any of the lay sisters? None of us has the time to spend all the Sabbath resting and listening to what God expects of us. But because we work together, we all have some time. As Benedict planned that we should.*

Averilla opened her eyes, shook her head, and moved down the aisle to Will. In English she said to him, "Your fever is gone. But you are still very weak. You will be for some days. At the end of that time, we won't force you to stay with us. The abbess would have you stay and will give you sanctuary for as long as you want. But if you want to, you will be free to go, though I don't think you are yet ready."

Will looked at Averilla and frowned. *How does she know what I be thinking?* He shook his head, rolled to his knees, put one foot underneath his body, and, putting out a hand for support, rose. Elizabeth steadied him.

Reverting to French for Elizabeth, Averilla said, "In any case, Will needs to be up and moving around. Walk him as far as the stables. Get him a sheepskin and shoes from the stores there. Show him the abbey. As much exercise as he can take. When he tires, sit him down and have someone fetch bread dipped in broth. And some ale. Whatever you do, don't leave him."

AFTER MASS, BUT ABSTAINING FROM Chapter, Averilla returned to the infirmary, plunked her cloak onto a peg near the door, and noted with relief and anxiety that Will and Elizabeth were still gone. *She is alone with him, and we don't know what...* She couldn't worry about it. She moved down the center aisle, checking on her patients. At the last cot, one called out. Averilla turned too quickly, and her left foot caught the leg of Dame

Scholastica's bed. Averilla fell, sprawling atop the frail old woman. They looked at one another for a long moment.

"Thinkest thou indeed" Scholastica quipped with a raised eyebrow, "that this is the most comfortable cot in the infirmary?" The wry wit challenged Averilla's worried embarrassment, and her surprised giggle quickly turned into hiccoughing laughter. And then tears. Scholastica let Averilla cry and then, her voice soft, said, "Dame, I suppose it is a heresy, or perhaps superstition, but…" She trailed off.

The words were calculated to catch Averilla's attention. She wriggled into a sitting position and sniffed. "Heresy?"

"I watch you. There is little for me to do here but watch and pray. And prayer is of course a luxury beyond imagining." Scholastica's thin lips turned up at the edges, splaying a cobweb of wrinkles across her face. "Yet even when I am resting in God's palm" her eyes twinkled, "sleeping might be a better term, or when He and I are discussing, well, even then, I hate to admit this, but maybe that is why it happened."

Seeing that the old woman had begun to wander, Averilla prodded, "What happened?"

"Did I say 'happened'? I meant to say, sometimes my eyes see things happening here and my brain saves them to mull over, or they are linked one with another. Yes, that is it." She stopped, bewildered, but her self-pity had vanished.

"You were saying that you saw things and remembered them."

"Oh, yes. Yes, indeed. It appears to me that… you seem not yourself. Have not done so for several months."

To Averilla's chagrin, tears again brimmed. *Finally, someone has noticed.*

"So, it seems to me that you may not know" Scholastica cleared her throat, "of the fairy well."

"The fairy well?" Averilla's incredulity was barely contained. Heresy indeed!

"I lie here day after day," the gentle voice, scratchy with age, pattered like a soft rain, "and I see and hear things. Several from the village have had diseases such as your clumsy tremors. Diseases that bear no easy resolution. Such ailments I think have neither the blood-bearing of an open wound nor the peculiar angle of a limb destroyed.

"I get bored sometimes," she continued slowly. "I shouldn't, I know, I should pray as I lie here, but I find myself fascinated by watching others. It whiles away the time. Whilst you have been attending to—as you should, Dame, as you should—nuns or others from the village, I have heard more than one of them speak of the woman called Madge."

Scholastica held up her hand to forestall Averilla. "Yes, I know her salve just cured Will, but do pay attention, for what I have heard is important. To you. I couldn't ask any of them, of course, what they were piecing together for one another, but finally one of the villagers had to stay—something only you could solve—and when the one waiting beside her spoke at length it became clear. The woman, she who was ill, had as you do, a palsy or some such. 'Spend the pennies you have hoarded,' said the other, 'to see Madge. She knows of a fairy well.'"

Averilla huffed.

"Wait. Don't say me nay. The woman speaking was wary, looking to see if any heard. 'Tis hallowed to Thor.' Then she added that Madge might refuse to tell the route without the pennies."

"If it heals," Averilla interrupted, "others know of this place—"

Again, Scholastica raised a hand. "My question as well. The very same words the woman waiting used. It seems Madge uses many paths one can travel, and there are briars and brambles—"

"But I too know the forests."

"Mayhap, but have you come upon a fairy well?"

The question left Averilla silent, for she rarely strayed from well-trodden ways. The deer paths and bylanes near the abbey were many, and the nests of brambles daunting. She had always stayed near the abbey, wary of masterless men and wild boar.

Scholastica continued: "'Tis said that the way to the fairy well must be walked at night and during a full moon. Madge lights the path by magic. Some, having gone there once, have tried to retrace their steps, knowing where they started, but on the next attempt, full moon or no, the path had vanished."

"Gone?" Averilla was skeptical.

"Dame, I, as you, know nothing of these matters, but the ending of this story needs to be told. Apparently, those who have hoarded their pennies and trodden the lighted path have indeed met with a slow healing; not a miracle, but continued relief—at least according to the stories I have heard again and again—for a malady such as ails you." Her eyebrows rose.

"So, you would have me trot down the hill to Madge's," Averilla heard the sarcasm in her own voice, "having first lied to the abbess about where I was going, and then pay Madge with what? I have no money, but say I stole alms, then I should go off into the woods at a midnight hour, missing Lauds and Matins, in search of a fairy well that appears and disappears, and then come home again, miraculously cured?"

"You gave to this Will, this maimed serf, one of Madge's… preparations? So, it might be well to ask her. I know but what I have heard. Not a miracle mayhap, but some relief. Just because we don't understand how God works doesn't mean He doesn't." Scholastica shut her eyes, effectively ending the whispered conversation.

Averilla slowly rose, shook out her habit, and, musing on what Scholastica had said, walked back to the kitchen, straightening pillows on her way, her spirit… tempted. *So, this is temptation. To do something you know to be wrong. Or is it wrong? Both St. Paul and the Old Testament forbid sorcery? Is what*

Madge does a black art? Our Lord said it was right to heal on the Sabbath. Doesn't Paul say that anything done in the name of Christ...? What I need to do, she concluded firmly, *is talk with Father Merowald. He it was who recommended Madge. Called her a wonderful woman.*

Dame Elizabeth returned after None, eyes alight. "He walked. He did. Think ye it is Madge's tinctures?"

"He ate?"

Elizabeth nodded. "I gave him broth. He tilted his head back and swallowed."

"And he walked?"

"Aye. I showed him the gates and the church and the graveyard."

"Went you into the church?"

"No." She brought her brows together. "He wouldn't. Shook his head and grunted. I certainly couldn't force him."

"No. I wonder why he—"

"I left him in the stables near the brazier. I showed him the privies. Should he bide in the stables from now on? Recuperate there."

"Yes," Averilla said dubiously. "The men can look after him. We can see to him here each day, but as he heals, what can we expect? Is the abbess right about him, about his kind eyes? Or..."

Chapter Five

December 9, 1120

A flurry of nuns, most with hacking coughs, minor colds, and runny noses, and one with a cut finger, kept Averilla busy in the infirmary for the next few days. On Saturday, she was able to haul her aching body down Laundry Lane to the church of St. James where she knew she would find Father Merowald. *Worse and worse,* she thought as she picked her way along, *I am starting to believe in the powers of a witch.*

The sky held patches of blue as clouds had drifted farther apart, but a sort of ground mist blurred her vision of the path, a running together of colors, like a dyer's overturned vat, with a fuzziness to the outlines. The familiar panic seized her. "Lord, please, not my eyes again!" She blinked. A year ago, her sight had deserted her one day in the middle of Prime. It had come like a bolt of lightning. Dame Maud, frantic, had led Averilla to the infirmary where she had lain unseeing for three days, a strange gray cloud obscuring her sight. Then, miraculously—for what else could it have been—her vision, totally and without warning, had returned. They had had a Mass of thanksgiving, and Averilla was grateful, truly grateful, but the lurking fear that the blindness might again strike would sometimes, as now, shake her like a cat with a mouse.

At the bottom of the hill, Averilla stumbled to her left, and pushed open the door to the cozy church where Merowald was preparing for the next day's Mass. He smiled at her, then cocked his head like a robin listening for a worm.

Averilla said, "Thank you for your prayer for Will. He is well enough now to bide in the stable."

"Is he? Well, then, we thank you, Lord, for—"

Before he could kneel or prolong the prayer, she blurted. "Knew you that there is a fairy well in the forest that Madge uses to– to cure ailments?"

"Aye, I am aware of it." His eyes twinkled.

Averilla started. "You *know* of it?"

"Your interest in this fairy well is because?"

"Because," a tear trundled down Averilla's cheek, "I am so very tired."

"Ah."

"I have been told," Averilla's blush deepened, "that this well can cure maladies that defy my skill. Maladies such as fatigue." She dipped her chin, then raised her eyes beseechingly. "A fairy well seems– seems not of God."

"How can you be so sure? Since the well heals, mayhap it should rightly be called a holy well, think you not? Perhaps the ancients who named it didn't understand God's ways and thus called it a fairy well. I presume you would seek it yourself to cure this fatigue." He raised his eyes. "I imagine the abbess might allow you to seek a holy well—not a fairy well, mind, but a holy well. Of course, I am not sure it is a holy, but can anything that God gives us to use be wrong? Be that as it may, many sat around the pool of Siloam, did they not, in our Lord's time. It, too, healed. Our Lord said not why.

"You could thank Old Madge for the preparation for Will, and then…"

As Averilla turned to go, the priest said, "But keep in mind, child, that what you might need more than this well is a Sabbath rest."

Chapter Six

December 10, 1120

Feast of Elfgiva of Shaftesbury

Lady Isabel FitzRolf, wife of Gervase FitzRolf, opened her eyes slowly. Her head ached ferociously, and her leg, when she tried to shift it, forbade her with a lancing shard of pain. She blinked, trying to make sense of her surroundings. "Where am I?" The words were querulous, but since she could hear them, she decided she was not dreaming.

Isabel roused herself, whispering the words a few more times before some consciousness entered the question. She grew aware of her own voice, not just petulant now, but fearful. She examined her surroundings more closely. Wherever she was, it was dim, almost as dark as the unconsciousness that had been hiding her. Is that a gleam? A crack in the wall? She squinted. No, not a window, a crack, and not a wall at all. Her brow puckered into a frown as she tried to make sense of what she saw. Cobwebs? Surely the maids needed to do something about them. And the walls seemed to be tilting. It must be a dream, Isabel decided, and closed her eyes.

AFTER PRIME, WITH A SENSE of guilt for pursuing her own desires on the Sabbath, Averilla mounted the stairs to the abbess's lodgings. Sister Clayetta was not there to let her in, but from inside came the sounds of a lute strummed by a competent hand. It was neither plain chant nor hymn, but one of the lays sung at the court. It was rumored that the abbess amused herself thus, but Averilla had never heard it. She listened entranced. Finally, she knocked. At the expected "Deo Gratis," she peered around the door and entered.

The abbess looked up from the lute. "Dame Averilla," she said, setting the instrument on the table and motioning to a chair. "What brings you up my stairs during this time of rest?"

Averilla perched. Aware of the probing of the abbess's eyes, she opened her mouth to answer, then shut it, swallowed, and said, "Lady, when we—you and I—went to gather mistletoe for the office of penance, we didn't have a chance to gather any… because we found Will."

"I remember."

"Since that day, the weather has been uncertain, and I have been taken up with—"

"With Will. For me."

"Today looks to be a day of relative fairness. But it is a Sunday."

"Ah. The Sabbath." Cecily's chin rose a fraction. "Were you to gather mistletoe, it would be for the Lord, but I am required to…" she frowned. "I saw them, so I suppose it matters not that I gather them myself. You could take Will. I saw him walking. He looked quite recovered—apart from the tongue—and the trip would acquaint him with the environs." The abbess picked up her lute, ending the interview.

After the Sunday Mass and the midday meal, with its extra pittances and meat in honor of the abbey's patron saint, Averilla donned her cloak. Traces of Will's blood stiffened it here and there. She stepped outside. At her heels, Sister Ethelind wrestled with a huge basket for the mistletoe. She had already managed to skew her veil while putting on the huge straw hat she insisted on wearing. Averilla, as she stood waiting for Ethelind to sort herself, examined the sky to test her sight. A wind had blown the clouds away.

Ethelind straightened her veil. "Do we take Turgold?" she asked.

"Turgold?" Averilla shook her head like a cat pretending unconcern when it has knocked something over. "No. The abbess said Will. He has not seen the abbey lands. Mayhap this would be a good time to take him. If he decides to go or stay, he needs to have walked to get his strength back."

Ethelind looked at her superior in disbelief. "But Dame, Will? We know not what he…" Then, "How can we offer sanctuary if he is in the woods? He must be in the church or the abbey enclosure, surely."

Averilla, testy, said, "Sister, these are our woods and our lands. There are foresters. Surely no harm can come to him or us."

Ethelind looked rebellious, the first time Averilla had ever seen her so. "I think we shouldn't take him. Not yet. After all, it was in these woods that you found him." She stopped, flustered.

During this interchange, Father Merowald had sauntered toward them, then stood off at a discrete distance until, the conversation with Ethelind at an impasse, Averilla turned toward him, a smile lighting her eyes.

"God be with you, Father Merowald."

"Deo gratis, Dame. Sister. Head you into the forest? Need you someone to accompany you?"

Averilla, assuming Merowald himself was offering to accompany them, and certain that he would be more hindrance than help, hesitated.

An apologetic smile lifted one side of his mouth. "No, indeed, Dame. I offer not my own services. I would be of no great help to you, but I met a carpenter—well, I did know him from before, of course—who might be of use. His name is Wat. I will fetch him. Where shall I tell him to catch you up?"

"Near Old Madge's cot."

He cocked his head like a puppy, raised an eyebrow, and then nodded.

Averilla beckoned to Will, who was seated on the bench outside the infirmary, his great hands busy whittling. The three of them took the shortcut from behind the infirmary. A ground mist dampened their footfalls, and an abbey pigeon swept close enough for them to hear the wind ruffle its feathers.

WHEN ISABEL AGAIN ROUSED, IT was the next day. Her head still throbbed, and she was nauseated. *Not just a headache.* Shakily, she felt her temple, and her hand came away sticky. The grinding ache in her leg had not eased. Just moving her hips sent a fiery brand down the leg and up into her spine. She gently fingered the place on her shin whence the hurt radiated. Swollen but no protruding bone. The slight movement deepened the throbbing, and she straightened. *Broken. Must be broken. But how?* An intense effort brought no answer. The memory was there but wouldn't be bidden. She took a deep breath and consciously relaxed her shoulders, and after a moment, somewhere between oblivion and waking, a partial memory surfaced. She saw herself riding at night, held before someone. *Who? Peter. Yes, Peter.* Her hands had been bound. She now lifted her right hand and looked at it. No longer bound but—and this was frightening—her wrist was chafed, red and sore. *So, it wasn't a dream. I was really bound.* She drifted off.

MADGE'S COTTAGE NESTLED AT THE bottom of Laundry Lane. So covered was its stone with tufts of frost-seared moss and fern that it looked like an old grizzled bush. Patches of thaw mingled with the snow on the ground.

Angular signs—runes—squiggled up the door jamb and along the windowsills. Averilla clenched her teeth, ruing what she was allowing herself to do.

At their knock, the door opened and Old Madge, looking like a *grand-mère* from a children's tale, smiled in welcome. Her face was well lined, and her hands and shoulders were bent inward and cramped from rheumatics. Despite the effort it must entail, her coif was meticulously clean.

"Dame Averilla."

"Old Madge."

They bowed to one another, low, in affirmation of mutual respect. Then Madge turned, flapping her hand. "Come in, come in. The heat will get out." Madge's eyes flicked to Will and she gave him a twinkling smile. "Better ye be, I see. I'd hoped 'twould do the trick, but oft…" Averilla made a sign to Will to stay, but Madge said, "No, let him come in. I have no wish to foil the good effects of the tincture by leaving him out in the cold."

Averilla couldn't stop herself: "You knew about Will even before I sent Sister Ethelind to you?"

The eyes sparked with mischief. "'Tis naught, just gossip. I bide by the laundry. They wot all in the laundry. Mothers oft leave their babes to crawl on my floor, while others, with sores on their souls, troubling, but not of such merit to bother good Father Merowald, talk to me. While I listen, I spin. It soothes them, and the twirling thread of my spindle draws out more of their woes than they might intend to share." She turned back into the warm cottage. Averilla ducked under the lintel to follow, noting with surprise the tidy cleanliness of the cot.

The cottage was neither hut nor hovel, though made in the old style: withies intertwined between uprights of bent trees, the whole neatly plastered with clunk. The plastering caught Averilla's eye, for it meant that the hut was snug in winter and would hold its heat against the wind. Like the infirmary, the roof was thatched, and there was a proper vent flap, now propped open, to allow smoke from the hearth to escape. The two windows had well-made shutters. Averilla allowed her eyes to wander among the neatly aligned hanging herbs, examining and cataloging them in her mind. Amulets with strange symbols hung here and there from the rafters among the dried herbs. *From whom exactly, am I asking help? Surely Madge is not of God. Not with amulets and runes.* She felt Ethelind stiffen.

A pot, like a spider with three legs, stood in the bed of coals on the hearth. Nor did Madge lack for wood. How she came to be so well supplied was a mystery. *Surely, Madge can't carry a faggot, much less the logs needed for a winter's warmth.* Madge put her foot into the still-glowing coals on the hearth and nudged the pot away from the flame.

"There," she said, wiping her hands on her apron and shooting Averilla a knowing look. "Aye, I do have plenty. Folk rely on me for… my wortcunnings and such as I gave you." She looked at Will. "Will… do I wist that they call you Will?"

He nodded, cocking his head.

"Well then, Dame, now we can discuss what you have come to learn of me."

Madge plumped down onto the stool. Her skirts whooshed an outrush of air, which spread a gust of ash. Averilla perched on a long bench, the only other piece of furniture. Madge was stooped with advancing years but well enough fed. Her tunic was simple and of the usual dun color, but clean, and her coif was spotless. The time and care that such personal grooming must take at her age was impressive. The old eyes smiled as Averilla caught them.

Madge answered the unasked question: "They all help me, the nearby folk. I need time to prepare my cures, so" she gestured to the room around them "they see to it that I want naught. There always is a young maid to do my running and fetching, or a young man to pull down the dried plants I canna reach. "So, Dame Averilla," Madge asked, suddenly serious, "why come you now to me?"

"I am tired."

Madge's eyes narrowed, her whole being suddenly focused on Averilla "Your many tasks tire you?"

"Yes. Increasingly, as the day wends into night, sometimes the slightest task seems too hard."

"And?"

"I– I overturn things or stumble."

"Well, Dame, so do I," said Ethelind, eager to erase the implied stigma. "I am so clumsy."

Madge smiled at Ethelind. "I think, Sister, your problem is an eagerness to please. And youth. For you, Dame Averilla," she turned, serious now, to the infirmaress, "there be more?" An ember sparked.

"Last year, around Michaelmas, I could not see for… some days."

"Ah. I did hear about that." There was a pause as Madge thought for a moment, then said, "Know you of the fairy well? Some few call it St. Mary's well?"

"St. Mary?" A shiver ran up and down Averilla's spine. Surely this trek must be of God, for how else would it happen that this woman, this "witch." would speak of the Virgin on St. Elfgiva's day?

"Aye. The Virgin has appeared to some few who made the trek."

Averilla opened her eyes wide. "Surely such a miracle would cause many to seek."

"She does not always appear. Besides, anything too easily won is not valued, so I hide the way. Those who might profit from it, I send by night in a full moon."

"How find they it at night?"

Madge pointed over their heads to a mass of gray-green lichen that hung from the eaves in the corner. "That moss. I found it when I was but a maid. I liked the soft color. I thought to dye the wool I was to take to my lad after our handfast. It was at night when I first noticed its power. We were wedded by then, my lad and I, awake in the night as is the wont of youth, but had the shutters open for the light of a full moon. Hanging from the ceiling that lichen caught the moonlight, held it, and shone it back as if to honor that brilliant orb. 'Tis not magic, but yet those as see it think it is. I had my lad drape it for me from the oaks in the forest so there came to be a path that catches the light of the moon, or of a torch, and leads those I send to the fairy well. 'Tis the quest that they need, you see, and it is the quest that draws them nigh."

"I see."

"But for you," her eyes on Averilla were soft with compassion, "there be no need of a nighttime quest. The well is a marvel, and with or without the Virgin, I know not why, but oft it heals that which I, of my own wisdom, cannot. Seemingly, in order to draw out the dis-ease, the seeker must walk with bare feet in the mud around the well. Three times."

"Three times around the well?"

"Barefoot. Although I am not sure that now would be the best time for you to go. Snow will linger in the shade. I have never sent anyone in midwinter. Verily this well heals. Sounds daft, which is why I go to the trouble of the lichen. Folk are more apt to believe if the light from the 'magic moss' has softened their hearts."

Again, the fire popped. "I have naught to pay you."

Madge's eyes twinkled. "We help one another, do we not?"

On the ashes in the hearth, Madge drew a map for Averilla, and made her repeat the incantation to use as she slogged around the well.

"You tell me your secrets? Why?"

"I am old. I had thought at one time to train the maid Galiena, but she is now wedded and bides in the north, and… and something dark entered her. I would not give her my arts even came she back. There is none other to come after me. I hope you will protect this knowledge."

And," her eyes twinkled, "mayhap it does belong to the Virgin."

CHAPTER SEVEN

DECEMBER 10, 1120

When Isabel waked, her mind could comprehend but not make sense of what she now saw. *I am inside a stump!* Her eyes traversed the interior of a tree cut down in the distant past and hollowed out by ages of rot and decay. Dawn light now peeped in from a hole on one side, illuminating the webs that hung from huge splinters of wood reddened by beetles.

The memory still crouched in a dark crevice of her mind, but seemed determined to stay hidden. She forced her mind to probe it. *I was riding through the forest in the middle of the night in front of someone. Peter? Why was I tied in front of him?* She tossed her head in frustration. Even that small movement sent a tremor of pain down her leg.

No one can find me hidden in a stump in the middle of a forest. I have to get up. But how? I can't even move, much less walk. I must make noise. Mayhap someone, a charcoal burner, a forester, even a masterless man, will hear?

"Help!" Her voice even to her own ears was weak. *No one can hear that. Something louder. I could bang on the stump's wall.*

She was close to the wall, and the stump would reverberate like a drum. Carefully, moving only her arm, she pawed at the duff, recoiling from the feel of scat and drifts of small bones. Finally, her left hand closed around something. A stick. She swung it against the wall. It made a satisfying thump. Exhausted, she laid it back down. Her mind told her that the stick wasn't rotted and that that was somehow important. So, how did it get there? Suddenly, she saw in her mind's eye Peter swinging a large stick toward her. *He hit me! Peter deliberately hit my leg. And then my head. Bafflement mingled with horror. Did he mean to kill me? But why leave the stick within reach of my left hand? Why take off the gag and unbind my hands?* She had known Peter from his earliest days. *So… he didn't want my death on his conscience? And that must mean?* It hurt to think. *That means, no one can hear if I scream. But why? Because I am so far away from any help that…* She thumped again, hard, in frustration.

A woodpecker hammered nearby.

I need to make it rhythmic if I am to attract attention. As if a person is doing it, not a laughingale.

ETHELIND, AVERILLA, AND WILL EMERGED from Madge's cottage to find a cheerful Merowald and a very uncomfortable Wat standing in the wind. Wat awkwardly bowed to Dame Averilla and Sister Ethelind, but it was beyond his station to speak to those so high above him in rank and—he thought—sanctity. With a special smile for Merowald, Madge shut her door.

Merowald said, "Wat was uneasy at the idea of coming with you. I told him that Turgold needed a rest. It will be well, I think, for Will to better know some of the men." Merowald raised an assessing eye at the two men standing together silent. "Mayhap not through speech, but…" Merowald bowed and left.

Next to Will, Wat seemed puny. Angling an inquiring eyebrow at Averilla, he handed an ax to Will. Averilla nodded dubiously, recalling Turgold's warning, but was reassured by Wat's lack of concern. *Probably came to an understanding during the night, all sleeping together in the stables. Somehow Wat senses that Will is trustworthy. It is a sense Turgold, Ethelind, and I don't have, but the abbess does. Strange.*

Wat had an axe as well, slotted in a loop of his belt, and had an eating knife of impressive length with a wicked curved blade. Noting Averilla's surprise, he muttered, "A Saracen's, this. My granda' had it off one at Antioch. The steel is…" he shook his head at a loss for words and handed it to Will for the latter to examine. It was a vicious-looking thing, but Wat's acceptance of Will eased Averilla's worry.

The way between the last house in St. James and the forest wound among shaggy winter grasses, where frost melting in the ditches glittered and the bare branches dripped. When they reached the rock at the entrance of what Madge had referred to as their path, Averilla paused, unsure. She had never taken this path, knew not where it went. She pushed a bramble aside. Overhanging branches forced them to walk in single file. Behind Averilla, Wat and Will seemed to be in a kind of conversation. Wat, who had been almost wordless when confronted by Merowald and the nuns, found his voice while walking with Will. He asked and then answered his own questions. Averilla wondered at it, but didn't look back, fearing to ruin a burgeoning friendship. The words "oak," "hornbeam," and "beech," drifted forward. Wat became so enthusiastic that Averilla wondered if perhaps Will too had worked with wood. *A forester? Of course. A man his size could well perform such work. They both seem to know wood! How could Father Merowald have known?*

THE COLD WAS DEEPER UNDER THE leafless trees. The group struggled up and over three small berms, leaving behind the wild crabapples and hawthorns, and descending into the forest proper with its huge oaks and beeches. Hollies grew to a great height, and the ground was covered with the nuts and desiccated leaves of autumn. Lichens, protected from frost, gleamed here and there from under the beech mast. Eventually, where a strange purplish light clung to the winter branches, the four found themselves following a stream.

Wat's words dwindled and then ceased.

Will trudged on, immersed in thought. *Murder. And I can't confess it. Can't speak to confess it.*

It was the first time Will had been able to enter that dark room in his mind. He saw himself clearly loping away from his bruised and bloody friend. *Left Waldo and ran into the forest with Alcar dead over my shoulder.* Will had run up into the denuded forest, eventually reaching the clearing where the charcoal burner had built a mound of billets, pieces of wood the length of a man's forearm and as wide as a hand and covered with a layer of turf or sod. Will and the burner were friends, both otherwise alone in the forest for long stretches of time. Tightly constructed, the mound had a tunnel left in its middle so at the last the burner could light a fire and the billets would not burn to ash because of the covering turf. Instead, the fire would smolder, turning the wood into the charcoal needed for village braziers.

Then I stood at the edge of the clearing to see if 'e was gone. Lucky for me the mound was near completed. I dragged and stuffed Alcar's body into the tunnel, didn't I? Mayhap when 'e came back 'e saw what I 'ad done and lit the pile afore the dogs come. If not… Will shuddered at the thought.

THE FOUR CONTINUED STEADILY UPHILL until Averilla, exhausted, allowed herself to slump against a boulder. Despite the cold she was sweating and fingered her handkerchief from her sleeve to wipe her forehead. Every bone and joint ached. She closed her eyes. No one spoke. The wind sighed high in the denuded branches.

Will I, she wondered, *be granted sight of the Virgin?* Hope gave her a spurt of energy. She rose, wobbled momentarily, and then steadied into a walk, slower this time. Beyond the boulder, the path turned and for a while ran alongside one bank of a stream before crossing to the other.

"I suppose it is necessary to keep to this sodden path?" Ethelind asked.

Averilla nodded grimly, pushed away yet another trailing bramble, and trudged on. They had hiked for more than two hours when she rounded a bend and gasped in surprise, for encircled by shrubs was a wide pool overhung by a canopy of thick branches. The spring. All around in the muddied slush on its edges were the footprints of everything from squirrels to people. *So,* Averilla thought, *despite Madge's precautions, others do know of this well or find it on their own. Strange the ground is not harder.*

"'Tis beautiful."

Averilla smiled distractedly, and then really looked. The pool was quite large, larger than she would have thought possible, the water clear and deep and coming from… nowhere. "Living water."

"Where can it possibly come from?" Ethelind asked, then added, grumpily, "I don't really understand anything about this: I don't understand taking tinctures from a witch who uses amulets and wortcunnings; I don't understand taking an injured serf from sanctuary to danger; I know not why we are here or whether it is of God."

A weed drifted lazily on the bottom of the pool, and a swift water rat that ought to have been hibernating swam among the weeds, bubbles of air caught in the forked teeth of his fur. Averilla responded, measuring her words, "I am unsure as well, of both my motivation and of whether I am listening to God or to my own needs." She rubbed absently at her neck. "I have felt increasingly ill, have not had the energy to do all that needs doing in the infirmary." She looked down, her voice lowering as she confessed that which she so hated to admit even to herself. "I have tried to give this disease up to God, but I don't see any way He can help, and…" her voice lower still… "apparently I don't trust Him to get it right, so I went to Madge."

Ethelind chewed on her lips and shook her head.

Will and Wat stood silent.

Averilla gave a curt nod, raised her chin, and looked for the place where Madge had instructed her to start. "The place near a green rock" turned out to be a muddy patch on the far side, now limned with ice. Madge had been clear. Averilla was to remove hose and shoes before thrice circling the spring. Feeling foolish, Averilla sat on a boulder, untied first one and then the other of the thongs that fastened her stout shoes. She reached under her tunic and released the cords above her knees that gartered her hose.

Embarrassed by exposing her bare feet, and mortified by what her neediness was forcing her to do, yet at the same time desperate to find relief for her body and her anxiety, Averilla squelched her feet one by one into the freezing mud, revolted by the feel of it, squishy and unbearably cold between her toes. As she walked, she whispered the words Madge had made her memorize.

> Light of sun
> Water fierce
> Ease the toil

Of my body
Cleanse each part
Through your power
Empty my heart.

The first time Averilla squelched around the spring, she felt surprise at the cold. Halfway around the second time, her left foot sank deep. Will started forward, ready to lend his arm, but she waved him off. She avoided the sinking place on her third circuit, deciding that despite any meaning the chant might hold for Madge, to her, Averilla, the meaning of the water *must* be Christ. Living Water.

She squished her way back and probed within herself. She felt nothing. What had she been expecting? Light? A puff of smoke? Relief? Joy? A vision? Something. Madge hadn't said what to expect. Disheartened and depressed that there had been no sign of the Virgin, Averilla took one last glance around, rubbed off the mud with her hose, and retied the thongs on her wet shoes.

The group splashed back down the same path by which they had come. Despite her determination to not believe in magic, Averilla was afraid to turn aside or stray in any way from the trail, not knowing which actions were important, which deviations might break the spell. Ethelind's disapproval bored into her back. Averilla wondered idly what Wat and Will thought about the exercise. She had so hoped that the holy well, or the walking in the mud, or something would heal her, but indeed she felt no better, only more tired and definitely foolish and frightened at her mind's turmoil.

Was Madge a witch? William the Conqueror had used witches when he was warring in the fens. It was said that the Crusaders had used them in Jerusalem. No, no. Was it not the Saracen who used them? She wasn't sure. Most wise women used herbs to good effect. True, some of them were a bit fey, probably from poverty and loneliness. What if the blindness came again? Was it really hazy today? She couldn't see very well. *If I lose my sight, how will I know one plant from its kin, the one poisonous the other not? And this weakness…*

WHEN THEY FINALLY REENTERED THE glen where the mistletoe hung, Averilla took a shaky breath. "Mistletoe." Her voice to her own ears sounded exhausted. She eased onto a boulder, fatigue sapping not just her limbs but her entire being. Will plopped beside her. He was gray. His shoulders drooped. *Here I am again,* Averilla thought, *letting my need demand too much of another.* Wat, unfazed, settled down on a stump, and with bored efficiency pulled a packet of bread and cheese from his jerkin and began to munch.

"We are to gather mistletoe?" Ethelind seemed to still have some energy.

Averilla glanced around. "I think there might be mistletoe." She raised her hand to point, and saw it tremble like a leaf in the fall—*so Madge's spring didn't help.* She lowered her arm to control the trembling.

Pointing, Ethelind said, "There?"

"Not there," Averilla snapped. "'Tis always found on oaks, and that is not an oak." Her voice sounded impatient and… dismissive? "On the oaks. You see…" Averilla broke off. There was no point.

"That's not an oak?"

"No. Over there. High. "A fuzzy green."

"Oh. Verily I cannot climb so high. Mayhap Wat?"

Averilla shook her head. "It has to be a nun."

"I have not been very supportive today, have I?" Ethelind said.

No, by St. Matilda, Averilla thought, *you haven't. Questioning me every step of the way.*

Ethelind waited, expecting Averilla to catch herself, look up, and say, "You came. You tried to understand. You gave me considered counsel. I know it is confusing."

When Averilla didn't reply, Ethelind asked, "Do you think I can still have a vocation in the infirmary if I can't tell one tree from another? I might well poison the patients."

When no answer came, Ethelind said sturdily, "I'll just look for another tree with mistletoe lower down. And I think I see one farther up that berm."

Averilla sighed and closed her eyes. *Why do I find it too hard to call out words of encouragement?*

Chapter Eight

Will listened to the nuns' interchange because it was so unusual to hear them talk. During the days of his convalescence, the silence of his nun-nurses had given him an insight: *I will now have to be as they are, live as they do, without words. Strange it 'appened so. Dame Averilla uses words with those in pain, to find where the pain lies. Others use a few words. With most, though, 'tis the eyes as talk. Or they gesture. That I won't ever be able to talk shouldna worriet me so. I was alays quiet, wasn't I, before?* His face dissolved into sadness. *Liked the quiet and didna want to speak. Now I cain't.*

Even so, words don't alays help. Some of the nuns speak English, while others babble on in French. His eyes opened in surprise as his mind finally found a tendril of memory. *That's it, isn't it—the men who took my tongue spoke French. They were Normans. 'Tis why I didna understand 'em.* He tried to remember what they had said. *Roi, I know, means king, and Atheling means crown prince. Were there any others?* He frowned, concentrating. *Yes! They kept repeating one phrase, Blanche Nef,* but he didn't know what it meant.

Will found himself reliving those moments. *The men were talking. Then I must have gasped or moved. On me in a second. Trussed me like a dressed pheasant and then...* Even now he could see the knife glinting against the dawn sky. *They took my tongue.* He rubbed his eyes. *They thought I understood what they were saying about the king and the prince. But what were they saying?*

Will shook his head and looked around. Averilla was asleep. He could no longer hear Ethelind bumbling through the woods. Will liked Ethelind. From what he had seen, everyone did. Averilla might think the woods were safe; he had reason to know otherwise. He got up and, reasserting his woodsman's stealth, strode past the edge of the clearing to where he'd seen the young nun ease into the shrubbery. His eyes probed the crevices of light and shade. Nothing moved. *Should I go after her? How do I tell Averilla that the nun be gone?*

IN HER ROUNDED PRISON OF wood Isabel dreamt of her husband, beloved Bernard who from the very first had made her restless in her maiden bed and giddy for she knew not what. Bernard, who had caused her to wander her maiden chamber and won-der… about men. She then began to pay attention to the furtive glances between the maids and ostlers; their shallow gropings and stolen kisses had aroused in her a longing to feel Bernard's arms around her. To wed. Then, finally, when her aunts had clothed her in her mother's bridal finery and the marriage vows had been repeated, she and Bernard had stayed in the house of her maidenhood, the great estate entailed on her at her father's death, and wrapped themselves in one another.

They had had two babes, eventually, she and Bernard, two beloved sons.

So why hasn't Bernard found me? How did he let this happen? He seems so distant. More distant than the dream of Peter, which seems so real. The confusion was terrifying. She roused herself. *Must keep hitting.* Thump. *Rhythmic.* Thump. *Not like a woodpecker.*

She inched her hip sideways in order to lever her hands closer to the wood. Even that slight movement caused fire to career up and down her left leg. The amount of hurt was mesmerizing and slammed another memory into her mind. *I was in the solar, wasn't I, embroidering....*

ETHELIND MEANDERED ALONG A PATH bordered thickly by brambles, the canes brittle, dried-up black nubs dangling on dirt-colored skeleton leaves. As a cold mist wound around her knees, she thought she heard a faint knocking. *Not the rat-tat-tat of a woodpecker,* she thought, *but a repetitive, rhythmic knocking. A buck? No, too late to be making his stand.* The hairs on her arms and neck rose.

ON THE BOULDER, AVERILLA SLOWLY awoke into the stillness around her. Wat alone stood near, immobile like some woodland gnome turned to stone. "Will?" She looked around. Where had he gone? Did he decide to flee? A feeling of betrayal shadowed her eyes. *No, not Will! Or did whoever cut out his tongue come after him? They could have. He had been a valuable serf to someone. Was that someone here in the forest? Had they snared Will and hauled him off while I was busy worrying about my shaking hands?* "Will," she called. "Will."

"Over there, Dame," said Wat.

And suddenly there he was, silent, on the edge of the brambles. He gave the grimace she knew for his smile and pointed up the berm.

THE STRANGE THUMPING SEEMED LOUDER now. Ethelind pressed on, determined to follow the odd sound, but half her mind worried about Dame Averilla. Using a witch and going to a fairy well? What about prayer and… and God? Ethelind had finally elbowed her way to the top of the berm and looked down past a line of trees. Before her lay a mossy path that wound down the other side into some sort of bowl. An old keep?

Thump!

Of course. A lamb or a ewe. Yes, surely sheep. She hurried down the bank. "How am I supposed to get through to help you?" she said aloud, frustrated as only sheep could make her. "Oh, Lord, why do you always compare us to sheep?"

The nuns owned many flocks, and as a young novice, Ethelind had been out with the lambs one spring. It hadn't been a success. Newborn lambs do die, or their dams are not strong enough for birth, or the ewes reject them. The obedientiaries had agreed that "mayhap," and then "probably," and finally "surely," Ethelind's calling was not with lambs but with the sick in the infirmary where her motherly empathy could flower. Ethelind had found lambs and sheep depressing. "They can't go to heaven as we can," she told the novice mistress.

The increasingly frenzied thumping brought Ethelind fully back to what she was doing. *Poor lamb,* she thought, then frowned. *Why doesn't it bleat?*

When she reached the bottom of the berm, she found no frantic ewe or lamb, but an empty clearing enclosed by the encircling wall-like slope down which she had scurried. On the other side of the clearing loomed a huge stump, *as high as the top of the workmen's lodgings,* she estimated. The roots of its base had twined and stretched themselves among nearby stones. Lichen peeped between them. A stool? *It should be called a stool, shouldn't it? No- no, 'tis a stump, for it died long ago and has probably rotted inside. Probably hollow.*

Thump!

The sound is certainly coming from inside. Ethelind paused then tiptoed across the frost scarred grass. *Why am I tiptoeing?* she wondered as she stood below the gnarled remains. *Is that breathing?* Ethelind took a step up to the base of the stump.

Thump, thump, thump!

The sudden noise startled her, and Ethelind jumped, tangled her foot in her skirt, and teetered, arms flailing. She regained her balance, suddenly aware of her solitude. The air seemed hostile.

"Hallo? Is someone there?"

The sound that answered her was neither a bleat nor a thump, but a long murmur.

Not a sheep, a person. The hair on her neck rose.

Straightening her shoulders and muttering a prayer for guidance and courage, she slowly circled to seek an entrance. She came to the place where the disintegrating bark had been crudely arranged against the stump. Like a kitten having caught its first bird, she plucked and then, hearing a louder muttering from within, *a woman's voice,* pulled more vigorously at the final slab apparently placed to disguise the entrance. She took a deep breath, stooped, and peered inside, and as her sight gradually adjusted to the dim interior, her mind registered the luster of silk and fine linen. A woman. The woman had gray hair, and though intertwined with twigs and dead leaves, it was still partially bound by a silken coif.

Isabel and Ethelind gaped at one another.

"Mother of God, help me!" Ethelind muttered, crossed herself, dropped to her knees, and half-crawled, half-crouched through the opening toward Isabel. The idea of a trap or the presence of a threat flickered on the wall of her innocence.

Isabel lay on her right side. Her left leg draped at an odd angle on top of her right.

"Oh, *pauvre petite!*" Ethelind clucked as Isabel's eyes held a depth of pain. "*Quoi...* who?"

Ethelind fumbled in her scrip to reach her wineskin, lifted Isabel's head, and held it to the chapped lips. Isabel sipped, and then gasped, "*Merci.*"

Her arm under Isabel's right shoulder, Ethelind tried to raise her to a sitting position. A groan erupted from Isabel's lips.

"Where? What? How have I hurt you?"

"My leg."

That silk-encased left leg looks broken, Ethelind decided. Wishing she had listened harder to Dame Averilla, she asked, "Can you rise?"

"I'll try." Isabel tried to lever herself up by pressing against the ground with her right elbow, but her whole arm was numb from lack of circulation and she collapsed onto her back. "I- I'll try again. But we must be quiet. And hurry, he may be..." She strained, groaning through clenched teeth. The effort was too much. Her eyes rolled back, and she fainted.

I don't know what to do, Ethelind thought. *I can't lift her by myself.* She looked around for a tool, a splint, but there were no pieces of straight wood in the bat droppings and duff. She compressed her lips. *I'm not even sure how to splint a leg. And I certainly can't carry her.*

Chapter Nine

The Forest

Hoping her own need to escape was not driving her, Ethelind eased her arm from under Isabel's shoulder, scrunched back to the opening, turned, and peered into the glade. What had before seemed peaceful now seemed ominous. It was quiet. Too quiet. *Who is "he"? Where is he? She said to hurry.* Ethelind stood, re-kilted her habit and, leading with her left leg, sprinted for the woods on the other side.

She saw no more than a glimmer of movement to her left.

It was too late.

Something—someone—moved in the shrubbery behind the stump. Like a small dog that has never before met a large one intent on a fight, Ethelind felt terror. Malice and evil did exist. Instinctively, she veered. It was the wrong move. It gave the arrow the wide expanse of her back. The piercing iron thumped below her shoulder blades. "Averrrillaaa!" The force of the blow toppled her and sent her skidding onto her nose. She felt the grinding ache of bones shattered, the screeching vibrato of severed nerves, the lessening control over her legs. It all took but an instant. "My God, my God," she whimpered.

ISABEL SWAM AGAIN INTO CONSCIOUSNESS. She looked around her prison. Empty. The nun had gone. "No! Come back!" she cried, the hoarse sound little more than a whisper. She sagged back. *I will not cry! Not at my age. Did she abandon me? No, I saw her eyes.*

Isabel heard the swift hiss of the arrow and the hollow thunk as it sank into human flesh. *No! No! No!*

Ethelind's agonized scream destroyed Isabel's burgeoning hope. Tears streamed from her eyes even before her mind could contend with the enormity of what had happened. "Peter? No! No, Peter. Not a nun," she groaned.

THOUGH MUFFLED BY DISTANCE, THE young nun's shriek, her drawn-out "Averrrillaaa," scraped through the shrubbery and knifed up Averilla's spine. Will turned. Wat vaulted to his feet.

Ethelind's entire consciousness centered on a depth and breadth of a pain she hadn't imagined could exist. *What had…? Why…?* Something inside insisted that she continue to flee, but… *I am… comfortable here.* Sensing it might help, she tried with the last of her strength to draw her arm under her body. *Something is very wrong with my legs. And my arms.* She ordered them to crawl. They wouldn't.

She was roused by the sound of pounding feet and a slashing in the underbrush. Someone dropped down beside her. She dimly heard the words "Oh, God! No!"

Averilla?

"Ethelind! Oh, Ethelind. Answer me."

Ethelind tried to move her head.

Averilla lifted a hand to caress her fallen friend. "Oh, Ethelind!" Averilla's hand shook, hovering over the arrow. "No! No! My God, please!"

"Try…" Ethelind's voice was faint, barely audible. Averilla craned her head close to Ethelind's mouth, the better to hear. "To help…" Ethelind coughed… "her."

"We will. We will." Then, "Her?" Averilla put her hand to Ethelind's suddenly limp shoulder, willing life. "Who, Ethelind?" she said. "Who?"

Lethargy, warm and strongly comforting, crept up from Ethelind's legs. She frowned. "Forgive me, Father.…"

WILL PUT AN IMPATIENT HAND on Averilla's shoulder. She looked at the hand dully. Wat said, "'E's right, Dame. Be not safe. Some'un be here."

Averilla's voice was that of a little girl. "Who would…? She was a nun, and someone shot her! In the back!" Bewilderment rounded her eyes. "A nun! Who could?"

Will scanned the berm farthest from them and then headed back toward the scrim of denuded foliage through which they had just come.

"Where are you going?" What are you—?"

Wat said, "'E probably figures the only way to get you to leave is to take 'er back with us. Going for poles, I wist."

As if she were two people, one part of Averilla nodded, eased the scrip from her shoulder, and upended it. The other part keened inside her, *Oh, Ethelind, don't be dead.* She stared woodenly at the items from her scrip lying on the ground as if she had never seen them before.

Will stumbled down, hauling two sapling poles. With Wat's ax he denuded them of branches as Averilla tugged at the thongs that had held her scrip together. Will cocked his head and raised a questioning eyebrow at Wat. The latter shrugged.

"We need lacings," Averilla said, in explanation. Unsteadily, she rose, unkilted her tunic, pulled out her arms, and handed the garment to Will, who passed the poles through the armholes and laid the improvised stretcher beside Ethelind's body.

ISABEL HEARD THE BLUNDERING CRASHES as the three of them came down the berm, heard Averilla's cry of anguish.

The nun? What happened? If I hadn't... if Peter hadn't... She heard the low rumble of a man's voice. *I can hit again. Where is the stick?* She scrabbled in the duff trying to find it. She struck once, twice, three measured thumps on the inner surface. *They'll hear me, surely.* Denying the pain, in a spurt of anger, she hit so hard the stick shattered.

AVERILLA HEARD THE MUFFLED THUMPING that came from across the glade. She felt the hair on her arms and neck rise.

"Hear that? From the stump, I wist," said Wat.

"Ethelind said 'she.'" Averilla took a hesitant step toward the stump. Wat put a hand on her arm. "Dame, we mun leave. Get the bailiff. Whoever did this may be by."

Jaw jutting, a line of pain slashing his closed mouth, Will put one huge hand on the arrow shaft protruding from the dead nun's back. He paused, glancing at Averilla, who nodded, eyes huge. Placing his right palm flat on the back of the body, fingers on either side of the shaft, Will snapped the arrow off and handed the remainder to Wat who broke it again and slotted the fletched end into his belt. Together the two men shifted Ethelind onto the crude litter. Averilla held out the thongs. Wat lashed

Ethelind's shoulders onto the poles, then hefted the front pole ends; Will, the taller man, those at the back. They broke into a half trot up the path, Averilla stumbling ahead.

The three moved with fear-induced speed. A fog of grief enshrouded Averilla's mind. *Never to hear Ethelind's voice again,* something inside kept insisting. Something else staunchly denied it, flashing memories of Ethelind into her mind's eye. *Oh, the pain.* Her heart actually hurt. *Never to watch her joy, her gentle kindness. Never, never, never. And today Ethelind just wanted a word from me, a word of praise and encouragement. And I withheld it. Just one kind word!*

Chapter Ten

Shaftesbury Abbey

By the time they reached the abbey gate, Averilla was numb with shock and sadness.

Word had passed from the townsfolk and into the abbey. The sorry little group straggled down the High Street, then passed under the wide eaves of the gatehouse and continued into the court between a line of bewildered nuns. A beloved member of the community—as Paul would say, a hand or a foot—had been severed from the body whole. As the news of Ethelind's death spread, others ran to stand and watch, their gasps and moans of dismay creating a low hum.

Hearing the turmoil, the abbess rushed downstairs from her lodgings, hand over her mouth.

"It's Ethelind!" said someone.

Cecily's eyes widened.

"Oh, Lady, she's dead!" said a third.

Cecily's eyes drooped into grief, then slitted in glittering anger.

Prioress Aethwulfa held out her arms; Averilla fled into them and was enfolded. As she sobbed, Dame Agnes, Dame Elizabeth, Dame Joan, and Sister Blythe motioned for Wat and Will to

65

maneuver the litter into the dark of the Lady Parlour where Agnes and Blythe shifted two benches into a makeshift bier.

Averilla pulled back from the embrace of the prioress, hiccoughed, scrabbled at the tears, and turned to the abbess with an awkward bow. The face that met hers was implacable in its steely ire, the blue-gray eyes sparking with rage.

"Who dared attack my nun?"

"My lady, I- I know not." Averilla stuttered. "The arrow was shot true and—"

"The temerity! To attack a nun! What miscreant…?" Then, "Summon the bailiff!"

Wat and Will backed out the door and into the courtyard. Will, stumbling with fatigue, made for the stables where he collapsed onto the hay and immediately fell into a sound sleep.

Dame Elizabeth followed the men out, intending to fetch perfumed water for the cleansing. Aethwulfa laid a hand on her arm. She said, voice calm and low, "Dame Elizabeth, please send someone to fetch the bailiff."

"Think they that we are but a mealy-mouthed passel of meekness," muttered Cecily darkly. "They will find to their—"

"My lady. There… this…" Averilla's voice rasped.

Cecily ignored her and turned to Wat. "Have you the arrowhead?"

He pulled from his belt loop the fletched end of the shaft. Cecily examined the feathers.

Averilla's voice was louder now, trying to get the abbess's attention. "Ethelind bade us find… 'her.'"

The abbess finally heard Averilla's words. "You think a woman shot her?"

Averilla shook her head and turned to Wat. "Can you find the place again? Lead the bailiff to it?" Wat nodded.

Cecily frowned. "You would have Wat return? To save her? Who?!"

"I know not, but Ethelind…" Averilla gagged on the name. With an enormous heft of will, a raft of tears sliding down both cheeks and mingling with the drops from her nose, Averilla said again, "told us to save her."

"Mayhap she meant herself."

"No. There was noise. A thumping. From a stump. I think 'her' is a woman trapped in a stump."

Though confused, Cecily addressed Wat. "Are you willing to go back?"

Wat clenched his jaw but nodded. Before he had taken two steps, Averilla said, her voice flat, "You will need to wait for the bailiff. And Wat? In the officina?" She pointed. "Get another wineskin from the peg by the door. She may be wounded. The bailiff should be here by the time you get back. You can lead him."

Wat raised an eyebrow as he waited, expectant, for her to remember more, then loped off toward the officina. Nuns surrounded the abbess and Averilla, attempting solace.

An interminable time elapsed before a clatter of hooves announced the arrival of the bailiff, Robert Bradshaw, from the castle at the end of the Bimport. He leapt from his horse, bowed, and looked from Cecily to Averilla.

"Sister Ethelind was shot in the back with an arrow. Apparently in the old deer pen," the abbess said when it became obvious that Averilla could not speak. "At least that is where Averilla thinks it is," she added looking round for Wat. "Oh, here you are, Wat." To the bailiff she continued, "Wat can lead you there." She held out the fletched end of the arrow.

Bailiff Bradshaw glanced at it. A frown carved twin furrows across his brow. "A FitzRolf arrow." He handed back the shaft.

"FitzRolf?" asked Cecily. "Surely not.

"Could 'ave been found or stolen," Bradshaw said, but dubiously. "You want me to find the archer and… he's probably long away."

"No, not the archer," croaked Averilla. "Before Ethelind died, she bade me 'save her.' We heard something from a nearby stump. I think someone, a woman, is in there."

The bailiff raised an eyebrow.

"Please go and see if someone is there." Averilla's eyes were pleading. "I promised Ethelind."

AFTER WATCHING THE MEN HEAD for the gate, the abbess paused at the door of the Lady Parlour. Then, "Dame Joan!" Her voice was peremptory.

The subprioress appeared from inside the Lady Parlour, wiping her hands on her habit. At Cecily's nod, she followed the abbess into her own office next door.

Dame Joan, as subprioress, was the abbey bursar, and with the help and advice of the steward—one Master Chapman—was in charge of the abbey's money and business affairs. Her office was simple yet spacious, part of the newly rebuilt two-story "lodgings" that made up one side of the cloister. Rushes covered the floor tiles. Lavender and rosemary still gave off a faint scent from the autumn strewing. An iron-bound coffer with three hanging locks crouched in one corner. Account rolls littered a table in the middle of which stood a slanted writing desk. Holes across the top of the board held an inkhorn, sharpened quills, a lead plummet for ruling lines, and a stylus for pricking the parchment in preparation for ruling. Cecily paced back and forth with the jagged energy of a caged wolf.

Joan couldn't sit if the abbess stood, and there was but the one chair. The abbess stopped and, in an irritated voice, said, "Sit. Oh, do sit. You will take a letter. To the king."

There was a fresh piece of vellum affixed to the board, already ruled. Joan chose a quill, dipped it in the inkhorn, and waited. Cecily began:

To the noble prince, lord, and our very dear
friend the Lord Henry, by the grace of God,
King of England, Lord of Ireland, and Duke of
Normandy, his devoted Cecily FitzHamon, by
his grace, abbess of the Abbey of the Virgin Mary
and Edward King and Martyr at Shaftesbury,
sends greeting and both devoted and due obedience and reverence in all things....

As she dictated, Cecily wriggled the huge abbatial ring from
her forefinger and then stood, absently caressing the intaglio
stone incised with an image of an abbess. Joan would seal the
completed letter with ribbon and a disc of wax. Cecily laid the
ring on the table and said, "Tell him about Ethelind. You will
phrase it," meaning the body of the letter. "Send to the bishop
of Salisbury and the sheriff, as well." The question was whether
either would come in time to help them.

Chapter Eleven

The Forest

Knowing not whence came the strength, Wat, followed by the horses, loped down the hill. Bradshaw made a sign, one of the men held out a hand, and Wat, running alongside, leapt up and struggled onto the saddle, his body between the man and his saddle board, legs dangling.

When they came to the boulder where Averilla had rested, Wat pointed to the path leading through the copses of hornbeam, beech, and ash. The party rode quickly up the berm, horses unhindered by the brambles and holly. On the other side, toward the bottom of the berm, the bailiff pulled back on his reins and held up a hand. Wat dismounted. When the jangling of the tack had quieted, they all listened. At first, they heard nothing but the rumble from one of the horse's insides. Then, very faint, they heard something that sounded like a voice. Senses alert, the bailiff probed the verges of the clearing with his eyes. Wat pointed silently to where he thought the arrow had been loosed. Two men dismounted and, at a sign from the bailiff, fanned out, keeping within the undergrowth and stopping every few feet to listen and observe through the leafless twigs. Eventually they found trampled snow and horse droppings where the archer must have stood. One man came out into the open and whistled to signal that all was clear.

The murmurings from the stump had ceased.

Wat and the bailiff walked to where Ethelind had fallen. Footprints through the sere grass led to and from the huge stump. "Must be in there, only place someone could still be. We better check."

Wat and the bailiff eased around the clearing, staying well within the scrim of denuded branches, and circled the stump. The pile of bark Ethelind had torn off told them where to enter. The bailiff peered in. In the filtered light lay a woman, her eyes round with terror. She looked to be a noblewoman in a tumble of fine silk, coif displaced, white hair tangled, lips blue from the cold, and despite the fur-lined cloak, she shivered.

The stump smelled of ancient wood, must, dead insects, and piled debris. Robert doffed his hat and, as best he could, folded his body into his most courteous bow.

"My lady, I am Robert Bradshaw, castellan and bailiff at Shaftesbury."

Bradshaw had always had a way with animals—familiarity? Empathy? Or just kindness? Knowing this, he smiled. It was a sweet smile. His handsome stern face became something else altogether when he smiled.

The panic in Isabel's eyes receded.

Deliberately slow, he shrugged off the wineskin Wat had handed him, unstopped it, and knelt. Seeing her wariness ease, he shuffled on his knees toward her, the wineskin held out. She took it, gasping with the pain of effort, and put it to her lips.

When she had drunk a deep draught, she patted delicately at her lips with a forefinger as if the finest linen draped from her hand. "*Merci.*" Vapor from the cold surrounded her words.

She pointed to her leg and switched to English. "Broken."

Bradshaw nodded and looked around for a splint. He said, "I am bid by the abbess to take you back."

The word "back" rewound her terror. "No!"

Sensing a misunderstanding, he elaborated. "Nuns. To the nuns. At the abbey. They will care for you."

She bit her lips, grasping at reason. After all, she had never seen the man before, so he couldn't be coming from FitzRolf.

Her mature voice, though shaking, held the crisp notes of good sense and long experience. "Master Bradshaw," she said, "forgive me. I do not know you or understand what has transpired here. I feared further violence. You said 'abbey,' and I believe a nun did come, so I am in your hands." Then, "I am Isabel, daughter of Robert de Geroi and wife of- of Bernard FitzRolf, and he needs to know that I am here." She frowned then, looking suddenly both vulnerable and bewildered.

Her eyes held Bradshaw's as she visibly gathered her sliver of remaining strength. "My gratitude and that of my sons will always be at your service." Then vulnerable again. "My- my leg is broken. There was a branch here—thank the Good Lord—but I shattered it trying to…" She frowned as a sudden thought hit her. "A young nun came to me. There was a young nun and then…"

"Madam, she was shot in the back with an arrow and died."

It was as if Isabel had known Ethelind for years, so great was the pain that darkened her eyes. She shut them and breathed deep. "May the Good Lord have mercy on her soul and mine. She died because of me."

Robert said, "My lady, your lips are blue. There is downed wood outside. We'll fashion a litter and lift you out of here." His eyes appraised the interior of the stump. Over his shoulder, to Wat he said, "Think you could make that opening a bit wider? At Wat's nod he said to Isabel, "I'd drink that wine were I you, my lady. You are cold and this will hurt."

Bradshaw hunched his way back through the opening and gave the necessary instructions.

WHEN THE ABBESS AND DAME Joan had gone, Aethwulfa led Averilla by the hand into the Lady Parlour where Averilla sank to her knees beside the bier and, curling into herself, sobbed in great gulping gasps that heaved from deep within. Although there would be no administration of the viaticum to the dying, and no confession, even so the sacrist placed a scaffold of ritual over the horror of murder. Death was death, and there were prescribed ways of handling it and dealing with grief, rites that had been honed and polished over the centuries to give the bereaved words, concepts, and movements to cling to. The murder of a nun was a horror, but still, the body needed to be cleansed. Averilla neither heard the wet sounds of cloths being dipped and wrung out nor the gentle whispers of the others. She did hear the words of the sacrist as she reiterated "I am the resurrection and the life" from the Gospel of John. The words seeped deep inside Averilla, bringing a modicum of peace.

"Murder." The word snaked itself around the courts and into the cloister, gathering to itself huddles of whispering nuns.

THE SHADOWS HAD LENGTHENED INTO a drear winter afternoon by the time the cleansed body had been sewn into its shroud. The coffin, smelling of new wood, was brought and the body reverently placed within. They would wait for the Vespers bell to take Ethelind to the church for the first of the liturgical hours that comprised the Office of the Dead.

Finally, Averilla lifted her head, rose, and walked stiffly outside. Father Merowald was waiting. He had heard Bradshaw's men canter through St. James, and fearing—something—had hurried up Laundry Lane, where he had been informed of

Ethelind's death in solemn whispers. Hearing of Averilla's part in it, he had gone to the Lady Parlour, where he still sat on a large chunk of greenstone and waited for Averilla to emerge.

"Child."

"Father." She bowed to him, the respect ingrained. Gesturing vaguely toward the infirmary, she added, her voice flat and dull, "I... there is much to do. Ethelind is..." She paused for a moment as if she had forgotten what she had intended to say. "Did you know that?" She saw the sadness behind his eyes as he nodded. "Someone told you. Wat and the bailiff went to find 'her.' Ethelind said, 'her.' Averilla looked around absently as if Wat might be standing nearby, having found "her." "Where is Will?" She broke off, bewildered by the cascade of conflicting disasters and duties, too many to comprehend.

"Your loss, my child," he started but saw that her mind was still on Will.

"He is still not recovered," she bleated, rubbing her hands together. "And I left him in the forest. He didn't know his way back. He doesn't know anything. I was showing him—"

"No, child. I was told he is in the stable."

"Oh."

THE NUNS WAITED.

As is the case in any village where the ordinary sounds patter against the brain like soft rain and are intuitively identified and fitted into their niches without remark—yes, the blacksmith is whetting the scythes, or the shepherd is taking the sheep out, or the wagon with wood for the kitchen is right on time—the nuns half heard those ordinary sounds as they readied for the Office of the Dead, but at the same time listened for the grinding sound of the gate that would signal the arrival of they knew not whom.

The main gate ground open, and the litter carrying Lady Isabel, more efficiently constructed than that on which Will and Wat had carried Ethelind, rocked inside, carried by four of Bradshaw's men.

The nuns formed a black-and-white pattern against the gray slush of the cobbles.

Beside Merowald, Averilla watched the men maneuver the litter through the gate. A woman. Ethelind's "her." And on a litter, so… injured. Averilla straightened her shoulders, took in a long breath—*oh, Lord, give me strength*—and pushed herself forward through the mass of nuns to the litter. The woman was conscious. Averilla noted the silken clothes, hair, more white than gold, the thinning skin webbed with lines of age, and the leg cocked at a strange angle. "May God be with you, my lady. You will be made welcome by a superior, but now it would be best if we took you to the infirmary."

Isabel gave a wan attempt at a smile. Every step the men had taken out from the deer pen, over the berm, down onto the lower fields, and again up the steep hill to the abbey had jolted her leg into renewed agony. "My husband, Bernard, must be sent for." Her teeth were clenched. Averilla frowned. *Bernard FitzRolf is long dead,* she thought, *and the arrow that killed Ethelind has FitzRolf feathers. This is odd indeed.*

Averilla stumbled through the herbarium to the infirmary. "Sister, I need a bed. In the north aisle." Averilla's "please" was a tattered, whispered word. She grasped a sheet, folded it, and placed it lengthwise atop the bed. Dame Elizabeth hovered behind her, clueless. "Please God 'tis but a simple fracture." Averilla muttered in Norman French, and, to the men just arriving at the door, added more loudly and in English, "Ye'll have to pick her up and carry her from there."

Wat grappled Isabel from the litter into his arms, and Dame Elizabeth placed her hands under the injured leg to support it. Then the two sidestepped down the aisle to the waiting bed.

Safely thereon, Isabel dragged herself back into awareness. Her eyes found Wat's face. She used halting English. "You understand me?" He nodded again. "Peter, the man who hit me… was he… did he—?"

Wat shook his head. "Nay. He rode off. Bailiff's men saw the horse droppings. The snow showed us where he 'ad been."

Isabel laid her head back on the pillow and shut her eyes. The mishandling in the forest had taken its toll. The old face was slack. Together Averilla and Elizabeth turned Isabel onto her side, gentling the injured leg onto pillows, and Averilla muttered to Elizabeth, "She will need poppy."

WILL, LYING IN THE STABLES, was wakened by the sounds of the horses and men in the court. His mind skittered around and then settled on the memory of the run he had taken from the charcoal burners to the glade. Being in the woods again had brought it back, and he took it out and examined it like some newfound pebble.

I was running. He squinted, his eyes seeing the winter trees, leafless, slashing his face. Sloshing down a stream—even now he could feel the cold air searing his lungs—*to keep my scent from the dogs. No, not at first.* The image of an old boar shuffled into his memory. *I stumbled into a boar run. I bent double,* he now saw, *to duck under a branch. Aye. That was it.* But the branches made a roof strangely open underneath. He could still feel the horror of the scent of boar. *Turned, then, didn't I, and saw 'im. Great savage brute, tusks like lances. Could he really have been that big? And I was trapped. Crouched and vaulted upward, didn't I? Trying to shove through the branches. It was then the boar stopped and looked.*

He saw himself backing until his left foot struck a tree. *I- I backed farther and fell, rolled over a cliff, and bounced down into a swale.* He remembered the bruising. *But the boar didna take my tongue. Worst he did was give me ticks.* Even now the feeling of the ticks that had dropped on him in the boar run made his entire body itch.

And then what? Started to run again, didn't I, sloshed through another stream 'til I could go nae more. He felt anew his sweat falling in great drops, twilight making clawing fingers of the bare branches overhead. *I curled up under a hazel, burrowed down into the leaves and duff, and slept.*

THE ABBESS APPEARED IN THE infirmary just before Vespers. It was expected of her. To Isabel, she said in Norman French, "My lady, may God be with you in your distress. You are in the infirmary of the Abbey of the Virgin Mary and Edward King and Martyr at Shaftsbury. I am Cecily FitzHamon, the abbess." Cecily held out her hand.

"Ah." Isabel put a hand under one hip to shift her weight in order to kiss the abbatial ring, gasped in pain, and made a fluttered gesture of apology.

She took a deep breath and coughed. "I- I am Isabel de Geroi, married to Bernard FitzRolf. We have met a number of times, Lady Abbess." Averilla placed a bolster behind Isabel's head. "But I assume I look now not as I usually do."

Cecily tilted her head in surprise. "Forgive my lack of recognition."

Averilla frowned. There it is again, *The Honour of FitzRolf is close, no more than eight miles away; and Bernard FitzRolf died more than fifteen years ago.* Cecily met Averilla's eyes across Isabel.

Isabel's comment caught Cecily's attention. Tentatively, she said, "I did meet a Gaston FitzRolf at court...."

"My lady," Averilla interrupted, holding a tumbler to Isabel but including Cecily with her glance. "The setting of the limb needs to be done now, and it will be most painful. This is poppy and wine. It will ease the hurt."

Isabel took the cup with a shaking hand and gulped, grimacing at the bitterness of the poppy. She wiped her lip and took the proffered piece of honeycomb, knowing to suck on it to take away the bitterness.

Confused, Cecily again responded to Isabel's long-ago recollection: "I did meet a Gaston FitzRolf at court."

My eldest son." Isabel leaned back on the pillow and looked at the ceiling, brow furrowed in confusion. A moment passed. "I have two sons by Bernard, but..." she broke off, eyes taking on a glazed look. Cecily gently finger-combed Isabel's hair back from her forehead.

As she took the wide strips of dripping leather from Sister Susanna, Averilla said, "Forgive me, Lady Abbess, Lady Isabel, but the leg. I need to... Sister Susanna and Dame Elizabeth, if you would..." She looked at the latter uncertainly. Neither she nor Susanna had any confidence that Elizabeth had any idea as to what would be required, but Elizabeth nodded gamely.

"My lady," Averilla said to Cecily. "If you would allow Lady Isabel to grasp your hands. To Elizabeth, she continued, "What I am trying to do is to straighten this leg. Susanna will pull on the upper half of the leg, you grasp the foot. I will try to give a shove to get the bone back into place." Everyone looked anxious.

Averilla put her hands on either side of the leg and prayed: *Oh, Lord, help me do this right. Maud would know, but I... without Ethelind...* She then pushed one way and pulled the other.

Isabel screamed. Her nails pierced the skin on Cecily's hand, and she slipped—gratefully—into a numbing unconsciousness.

Averilla examined the straightened leg, nodded, and wound the dripping leather strips around it, then bound them in place with wet leather thongs. "The leather will draw tight as it dries. Now the arm."

Cecily whispered, "There is a gash on her temple." Averilla nodded. Isabel's left arm had several other nasty gouges already reddening. "The salve from Madge." Averilla stuck three fingers into the smelly black goo Blythe held out to her and slathered it on the wounds. Quickly, she put linen on the sores and bound them as well, tearing the ends into tails with her teeth and tying them together.

The abbess, having seen more than she had bargained for, breathed deep and glided to the door. "I will visit again on the morrow." She turned. "You need to be at Vespers." It wasn't a question. Averilla looked around vaguely. Her extreme tiredness drew lines down her face and hollowed her eyes. She nodded, wiped her hands on her apron, untied it, handed it to another lay sister, and followed the abbess toward the door.

THE NUNS ALIGNED THEMSELVES BEHIND Cecily and the coffin, and then entered the church to begin the Office of the Dead. When Cecily reached the chancel, the men shifted the coffin onto the abbey bier under the hearse, an ornate post-and-lintel assemblage with candles arranged atop the lintel. The sacrist brought out the pall, an embroidered covering, white for Ethelind's virginity, and fussed over the heavy folds, making sure that the cross was straight atop the tent-like piece. At the sacrist's nod, Cecily intoned the first words of the antiphon. "O gracious light, Lord Jesus Christ…"

When Vespers ended, most of the community remained in the church to keep the Great Vigil—ceaseless prayer—that would continue on through the night.

The familiar words from Matins: *Dirge, Deus Meus in conspectus tuo vitam meam,* rose into the gloaming, followed by the *De profundis* of Lauds. "Out of the depths have I cried unto thee, O Lord." Texts from Job on the alienation of the sinner from God, and the parable of Dives and Lazarus, followed by the numerous psalms would keep them awake through the night.

Chapter Twelve

December 11, 1211

The Infirmary

ernard! Where have you been? Isabel's lips smiled in sleep. *I have missed you sorely.*

Where had Bernard been? She couldn't remember. She just knew that she hadn't seen him in ever so long. It didn't matter now. They could go riding. They loved to ride. He liked to see her hair loose and flowing in the wind, just as he liked it when she danced for him in the firelight, barefooted on the bear rug, toes nestling into the fur. She was so lucky to cherish her husband; lucky that they had been espoused when they were young and in love.

When the Mass of the Dead ended the following morning, the nuns lined the way to the crypt. They sang the penitential psalms as eight men muscled the awkward coffin down the narrow curving stairs into the charnel house between two pillars in the crypt. Here were stored the bones of the previously departed, dug up from the graveyard.

In the spring, when the ground could be dug, the coffin would be moved to the graveyard where the priest would etch a cross in the dust, the ground would be broken, the coffin opened, and the corpse asperged with water and incense and checked for decay. The shroud would then be resewn, covered in incense and laurel, and the body placed, without the coffin, in the ground.

WHEN THE ABBESS REENTERED THE infirmary, Averilla put a finger to her lips. Isabel was dreaming. Her eyelids fluttered, and a soft smile had erased the lines. *There is no help for it,* Averilla thought. "My lady," she said. Isabel's eyes opened and the lines returned, scoring her aged face once more.

The abbess said, "I am Cecily FitzHamon, the abbess of the abbey."

"You were here before."

"Aye. You husband must be told of this. I shall send a messenger."

Isabel frowned. An elusive memory slid forward tentatively, like a cat's paw. Then she smiled, a softening beam that took years off her face. "Oh, do. Send to Bernard and tell him. He is just back, you know."

Cecily frowned. "But my lady…"

A lay sister plumped a hummock of pillows so Isabel could sit up. Sleep had done much for the woman. Even so, the color around her eyes was still the purple of a bruise, and the abrasion on her temple oozed. Averilla handed Isabel another draught. A lay sister scuttled over with a chair for the abbess.

Isabel said, "I was found in an old stump, wasn't I?"

Cecily nodded. "So I have been told."

Isabel's eyes were bewildered. "I think it was Peter who put me there. Why would Peter hit me with a stick on my leg, and on my head as well?" She put her hand to her temple.

"Who is Peter?"

"One of our men. I have known him since childhood, watched him grow. But why would he have put me in a stump in the forest?"

"Are you sure?"

"I am." Her eyes took on a bewildered look. "Though I don't know why. I can't remember...." She trailed off, then held up her hand and examined the still-raw chafing. "My hands were tied. Oh- oh, I remember. He took a stick and hit me below the knee with such strength that I felt inside me the sound of the break. It was a screaming red pain. Then the branch came at my face." Isabel let the silence lengthen. "When I awoke, I was in that... that stump. Peter was always my man. I don't understand. And then he unbound my hands, but why would he?"

"So he left you?"

"Aye. Am I muddling this up?" Her eyes were uncertain.

"A nun came, sometime." Then eagerly, "Have you sent for Bernard?"

Cecily looked blank.

"My husband, Bernard FitzRolf. He must be told."

"Er, not just yet," Cecily hedged. "Dame Averilla thinks it is not yet safe for you to travel."

"But he needs to know. He will be distraught."

"My lady, it shall be done."

"Surely you can send for him and he shall be here within the day. Just to see me. 'Tis not far." Even to Isabel's own ears, something gave distance to the words, like a hollow memory.

"I shall see to it."

"I remember a stump. I think I was in a stump in the forest."

"You were, my lady."

"I remember a nun coming to me in the stool. Is it possible?"

"Yes. Sister Ethelind found you there."

Isabel closed her eyes for a moment. "Then she left, didn't she?" Isabel's voice became tinny, like that of a child. "I was so frightened. I didn't understand why she would leave me. Then I heard a scream. An awful, horrible scream. Did she, did she…?"

"Aye. She died. An arrow."

"But… why?"

"We know not why nor who did it, but you are here and safe, and Ethelind is with our Lord." Cecily crossed herself.

Tears trickled down Isabel's face. Lady abbess, I- I—"

Cecily patted Isabel's shoulder. "Sleep now. You need to sleep."

Cecily motioned to Dame Averilla as she made her way out the door. Outside, the abbess shivered. Averilla carefully closed the door behind her. "My lady."

The abbess gazed off into the misty white distance. "There is something gravely amiss here."

"Indeed."

"Not the obvious hurt to Lady Isabel's body. Bernard FitzRolf died many years ago."

Averilla nodded grimly. "The wound to the back of her head could make her forget the present for a happier past.

"So, Lady Isabel is forgetting, and has no memory at all, not only of what happened to her but of a whole swath of her life."

"It can happen with a fall. Jack, the hodman, fell from the tower last year—"

Cecily blurted, "Bernard FitzRolf was killed in Cranborne Chase," she shook her head, "mayhap fifteen years since."

"And Isabel was wed to his brother?! Against church law and all… all nicety"

"If I remember aright, Gervase FitzRolf received a dispensation to wed the lady, and she had no living kin to object."

"And now, after a blow to the head, fifteen years are gone, and she remembers only her first husband?"

"Indeed. I think we shall not send word to Gervase until we know more. The arrow."

Averilla nodded. "The arrow was fletched with FitzRolf feathers, but why would FitzRolf hurt his lady or kill a nun? It must have been someone else."

Chapter Thirteen

December 13–14, 1120

The Abbey

The quiet of Advent, tinged with deep grief for Ethelind, descended like a pall on the abbey. The thaw continued. Will was gaining in strength. He slept in the stables, but during the day sat in front of the infirmary in his filthy sheepskin, often whittling. He seemed to like the closeness of the infirmary and the quiet of the nearby orchard. Dame Averilla went about her duties, although without alacrity or enthusiasm. Ethelind, with her endearing bumbling, was truly gone. Averilla felt not only grief but the burden of guilt. Her hands still shook.

Father Merowald had just finished saying the Mass of penance for the lay servants of the abbey and was leaving the church when Dame Elizabeth touched his arm. "Father." She bowed.

Like a robin hearing a worm, Merowald cocked his head. "My child." He glanced around vaguely, and then said, "I'm feeling tired, child. Sit with me and tell me what ails you."

"Is it that obvious?"

"You have a certain… translucence. 'Tis a blessing that you are so open." He continued leading her to the Lady Parlour. "I do so hate to probe." Leaving the door ajar, he waited for her to speak.

"The abbey is not... not right for me" The words issued forth in one outrush of breath. Embarrassed, Elizabeth lowered her eyes, banking her candor.

"Ah," he said. *So Elizabeth is one of those who,* he thought, *determined on the convent at an early age; expected one thing but all too often find another. A common problem.*

Bravely now, as if trying to find just the right words, Elizabeth raised her eyes. "It's- I- there is something... I am not sure, but I..."

Below, in St. James, barely audible, a single yap was followed by the growling briar patch of a dogfight.

Human shouts.

Quiet.

"What expected you to find here in the abbey that you do not?"

Her eyes grew wide. Her cheeks reddened. "Quiet. And calm. Just to be able to sit and..." She reddened. "It seems so selfish."

He smiled. "Doing nothing? Allowing God to surround you?"

She nodded.

Merowald's words came slowly as if he measured his thoughts: "You have been taught, surely, the story of Benedict. Of how he found that sitting alone in his cave did not work. Others came. They needed food, and clothes, and company. And then he found, as you have, that the very presence of company is an irritant. The very nature of togetherness grates on the soul. Hence the Rule, and later, this very abbey and its structure and strictures."

They sat silent. Mercy, the herbarium cat, crouched into the parlor, fur on end, ears back. Another cat bounded in, claws unsheathed. There was a noisy skirmish and the two disappeared.

"Petty feuds," Merowald mused. "First dogs, now cats."

"In the abbey as well." Elizabeth whispered before she could stop herself. "The petty feuds. I heard"—she started to name two nuns but thought better of it— "two nuns, obedientiaries, arguing over a book. A book! They should be grateful we have any books at all."

"We humans fight among ourselves and within ourselves," he said more to himself than to her. "It is indeed peculiar in my mind that Christ called us brothers. Would you like to return home?"

Horror widened Elizabeth's eyes and reformed into a prim propriety. "I have taken my final vows."

"Do you desire the life of an anchorite?"

"An anchorite?"

"They build a cell, a hut—like a wart—on the church and wall themselves in. They hear the Hours and the choir and yet have unending quiet. A protection from the outer world. There is a slot for food."

Elizabeth thought about it, then shook her head and said with conviction, "No, that does not call to me."

Merowald steepled his fingers. "Now and again God speaks to us, but our hearing is faulty. We know we are supposed to do something, but we know not what. Not yet. So, as the child Samuel did, you seem to be hearing the voice of God, but you don't yet know why. This gives you time to prepare, to wait and listen and ask, 'Is this it? Is this what you want me to do, Lord? Is this the person I am meant to speak with?' Listen. Seek. Such openness to God makes everything new and guided. Try to discern not what you want but what He wants. Then we shall speak again."

Merowald rose, pausing to realign his aching knees, took a few steps, and then turned. "Is it true?" he muttered to the wind as he watched Elizabeth walk through the herbarium where a bit of energy had returned to her gait. "Is a spring in one's step the presence of Christ?" Then louder, he mumbled "Aye. If one has no hope, there is neither Easter nor springtime." Merowald loved words, the sound of them, the feel of them on his tongue, the meanings that went back beyond the ancients and yet remained tucked within a word, like the beetles in the streams that glue sand and grit onto their carapaces, and, when the time is ripe, arise to fly. "Indeed," Merowald continued to muse, "if one believes in Easter, in the Risen Christ, then it follows as spring follows winter that joy will pursue one."

He passed two ostlers without even seeing them. They grinned at one another.

"Be easy," one remarked, his eyes following the priest, "to 'ave so little to worriet about. Just God."

The other raised his brows in a long quiet look. A cloud passed over, and drops of freezing rain spattered stray pieces of wood and metal.

Chapter Fourteen

December 15, 1120

The Forest

By the morning of the fifteenth, Isabel could manage the chamber pot. Her splinted leg caused less pain, and Averilla had decreased the dose of poppy. Mind clearer, Isabel sat, hands folded on the counterpane, and again tried to remember.

It was water that allowed Isabel to finally grasp the memory that had so far eluded her. A lay sister, yoke over her shoulders, had brought water into the infirmary from the well and was pouring it into pails. The sloshing sound brought to Isabel's mind *is it a memory—or is the poppy giving me a vision?* She saw a pier and beyond that a breakwater with waves crashing in great fanged onslaughts. The image made her grow cold in horror. She saw jagged rocks rising out of the sea under the path of a full moon, and she felt the grip of terror, though not for herself. Behind it came great sorrow. Isabel probed and knew that this sorrow was not for her sons. Her grief was for someone else, and pain knifed through her mind like shards of frozen water.

That morning, before None, the sacristan swooped down on Averilla, her veil reminding Averilla of a great bird of prey. "Dame," the sacristan began, "we have not gathered greens for the Christmas Mass, and soon I will need to decorate the church. The weather is so uncertain, but have you the strength and will to lead a group of postulants and novices into the forest today to collect greens?"

Averilla blanched, thinking, *Into the forest? Where Ethelind was killed? How can you ask that of me?*

"I wouldn't ask," the sacristan said, "but you alone are familiar with the tracks and paths that cross the forest. You know where to find ivy and holly and fir. I- I realize," she stumbled, registering Averilla's recoil, "that your heart must be raw after… but perhaps the peace of the wood will do you good."

A resounding *no* whirled inside Averilla's heart. It was a given that the nuns themselves must do the gathering, and yes, she alone knew the tracks to take; but to revisit the paths that she and Ethelind had so often trod. And then there was the question of safety. They knew not how Will had come by his wounds or whether the archer who had killed Ethelind was really Isabel's Peter. It might have been anyone.

As if to sway Averilla, the sacristan added, "I have heard that the bailiff and the foresters scoured every inch of the wood."

Averilla too had heard the hue and cry, and the meaning of the sound had sent shivers up her back. Reluctantly, she nodded. Obedience to the request of another…

There was no dearth of novices and postulants eager to traipse into the forest with her. They gathered in the outer court after the midday meal. Their eyes gleamed, relishing the adventure. "But… shouldn't ostlers accompany us?" one of them asked. Averilla glanced over. *Not all of them are insensible,* she thought, and nodded mutely, recognizing that fear fueled her own reluctance to reenter the wood. Will's great size would surely offer protection. The person who had hurt Lady Isabel wouldn't attack them—surely it had all to do with Isabel. Averilla shivered. But Ethelind had been shot.

Dame Elizabeth hurried over from the infirmary with Averilla's bulging scrip. "I think I have packed all you might need."

Averilla heard flatness in Elizabeth's tone, saw dullness in her eyes. A change would do her good. She hadn't responded to Ethelind's need, but here was another chance. "Do you desire to join us?"

Elizabeth gave a small moue of self-deprecation. "It sounds so peaceful, the forest. You know, I have never been. I have stood on the walls and looked at the birds and wished for peace. But who will have charge of the infirmary?"

"No. You must come."

Elizabeth's usually pale cheeks flushed with pleasure. "Really, Dame?"

"Of course. I should have thought of it earlier. We shan't be long, and the more hands the quicker. Fetch your hat and cloak. Lady Isabel is well enough that the lay sisters can handle any need she might have."

THE GROUP OF CHATTERING NOVICES, equipped with an assortment of pruning hooks, and followed by ostlers for protection, passed through the abbey gate and wended their way through the town. Averilla followed with Will and several more ostlers. At the bottom of the hill, Averilla herded them toward the path that led to where she and the abbess had found Will. As she put her foot on the path, she felt the hair on her arms rise.

Past the remembered banks and hedges of burnished holly, and beside a small stream, Averilla felt some relief at the abundance. *We won't have to go any farther, thank God.* After exclamations of delight, the novices, treating Elizabeth as one of themselves, began to pluck and cut, filling the osier baskets. Averilla, with Will standing beside her, sat on a boulder and watched with increasing weariness as the young women flitted here and there gathering greens. Like a flock of blackbirds on a ripe grain field, they meandered slowly into the gaps in the holly bank and onto the nearby deer paths, followed dutifully by the ostlers. Averilla felt her eyelids droop. *The quiet is so soothing.* Averilla's head nodded.

A BRANCH CRACKED, AND AVERILLA opened her eyes. *I must have dozed off.* The weak winter sun was already waning. She looked up and saw, above the trees, the dark of a looming storm. "Time to return," she called, but there were no answering cries. She scanned the glade. Where are they? Irritation seized her. Will was still beside her, resting against his staff. "Where did they go?" He shrugged and made a sweeping motion. "Will? Stay here near this stream. I'll gather the stragglers and send them back."

He nodded.

Thinking about the fickleness of youth, Averilla hurried off. Will took her place; his back against the boulder, he pulled out his packet of bread and cheese and put a tiny bit in his mouth to suck on.

Chapter Fifteen

The Forest

*N*ow, he thought, *be my chance to run.* Will considered the idea. *My body's not healed, but at least I cain walk. Cain probably run, but where to? Some'un 'ud take me on. In a town. For the strength of my back. But with my tongue gone, they'd know. Steward's search'll be wide enough, he'd find me. Fear or coin'd send me back. No, I wot staying with the nuns be my best path.*

His gaze as he mulled these thoughts was suddenly arrested by an unnatural twitching in the leaves on the other side of the stream. It wasn't the shivering of a blade of grass when a mole is gnawing the roots. This movement was higher, within the slight stems of hazel where one leaf's dry movement is not that of a squirrel and more than the quiet shifting of a doe. Will made himself motionless. *A face? Across from me? Others,* he thought. His heart raced. *Those as took my tongue? The steward, Weldon? Found Alcar's body and come looking for me?*

Dropping his food, Will leapt to his feet and raised his staff. *Won't get me again. Not without a fight.* Before he could move further, from across the creek came the hollow sound of a wooden clapper. Fear changed to horror. *Not the steward. Worse. A leper!*

Will took a few tentative steps closer to the stream, the better to see through the denuded branches. Just one person stood across from him, a young woman and very thin. She seemed to have no eyebrows, and there were bumps on her forehead. One raised uneven patch oozed fluid, leaving a leaden blue lump on the rough, fissured skin.

A leper.

Revulsion warred with pity. Will was glad of the creek between them, and would have turned back, yet there was something in the beseeching of her eye, her steady stance, that stayed him. *Gutsy,* he thought. A hempen rope looped round her waist. A wineskin dangled from it as well as a pouch, and *Is that an atlatl?* Curious, he stepped forward. The woman fingered her pouch. *Probably readying her stones.* He stopped. He'd had an atlatl as a boy. It took practice to fit the pebble into the atlatl and fling it forward, but it was an effective weapon. He nodded, appreciating her courage. *Means to use it I wot.* He knew he looked scary, his height alone, not to mention his bulk. He probably seemed to her a masterless man intent on mayhem. Even so, she stayed. *Why?* Then he knew. *Been watching me. Saw the food.* He opened his hands in a gesture of peace, then bent, slowly, so she could see every movement, and picked up the fallen food.

The leper, like all her kind, was inured to any number of responses to her affliction. Most people reacted in terror and fled. Some sneered in revulsion. Rarely did lepers receive pity. It was obvious to her from the length of the silence that, despite his size, Will meant her no harm. He, as yet, had neither fled nor thrown rocks at her. She saw him bend and pick up the food. She felt her saliva pool. She hadn't eaten in two days.

"I be Francine. There be another with me," she said loudly so he could hear her words. "Named Ellen." Her voice was hoarse and low and full of phlegm. She pointed. "Over in them bushes she be. Legs too pained to walk." When Will still didn't respond, Francine shrugged, turned, and limped over to the formless bundle lying in front of the bushes.

Will cringed inside. *What does she expect me to do?* The image of Cecily leaning from her horse and ordering Turgold to help him crept into his mind. He had his food. Odd to have more food than someone else. Inwardly cursing both Cecily and the leper, Will splashed across the stream and into the clearing, in the center of which, Francine stooped and pushed piled leaves off what seemed but a bundle of dirty cloth. Turning to him, Francine's eyes were those of a ruminant, large and wide and infinitely patient. "Sick she be."

Will could see that the wretch's face was spotted all over with purplish patches. A bulbous disfigurement, like a huge boil, enlarged her nose and lips. Francine had said "she," but there was no sense of it being a woman lying there. The hand that protruded from the leaves was wrapped in filthy bandages. Francine repeated herself hoarsely, saying the words slowly so as not to distort them. "Cain't move, and I be too weak to carry her." Her eyes had found the bread and cheese Will still held. He nodded, accepting her need, and carefully laid the food down between them and backed away. She edged toward the food, frowning and suspicious. Keeping her eyes on his face, she grabbed the food, broke the bread, and stuffed part of the larger half between skewed lips.

"We were part o' a band," she said around the bread. Francine's feistiness reminded Will of a robin. He watched as she knelt and tore a bit off the other half. "About fifteen o' us." She shook her head. "One or two 'ad been on Crusade, mayhap. Way back." She swallowed. "That's 'ow they think it came, with Crusaders when they returned." Gently she put a morsel into Ellen's mouth. "But who knows? It just appears, leprosy does. But then, ye see, ye have to flee, for folk be scared. Ye find that first spot of it, or iffen it be on yer face someone else does and points it out to ye. That be the worst. So we flee. Here and there. I wot not where-all." Francine gulped and swallowed.

Will stood, silent and huge, like something elemental, a tree or a brooding great rock, and watched her stuff a hunk of the cheese into her mouth. He was awed. Pity warred inside him with revulsion. The more disgusted he felt, the more fiercely determined he became not to admit to the fear stirring the hair on his arms; to feel the pity the abbess had felt for him. He allowed the fear to bloom until it turned savagely into a righteous anger. *I gave her my food. What else does she expect? Shouldna be in the forest here where honest folk can stumble upon 'er.*

"Finally, she—Ellen be 'er name—tripped," Francine hurried on in the face of Will's turmoil. "Couldna get up. Too weak." She slipped a tidbit of cheese between Ellen's lips. "We were with a band o'…" She shook her head. "Godless they were, those we took up with—but we 'ad no choice, such as we are…." She hesitated, finally noticing the anger in his face, "They—the others—would 'ave left 'er in the forest. She couldna keep up and we 'ad to keep moving. Can't steal from the same village two days in a row. They left her and… and so did I, but I couldna stay away, so I turned back. Not proud of leaving her there alone, I'm not. So- so cain ye help me? Don't 'ave to touch 'er. Just help me build a shelter."

Despite himself, Will's anger dissolved. He'd have to, somehow, tell Averilla.

Will thought, *She doesn't understand why I don't speak.* He opened his mouth and bent forward to show Francine why he was silent.

"By St. Cuthbert!" she gaped.

I cain 'elp 'er make a shelter, but even so, he glanced at the clouds building in the east, *with the storm coming, they'll both die.* He shook his head. *'Ave to tell Dame Averilla.* He held Francine's gaze, ran the fingers over his hand, and then held up the hand in a halting motion.

She cocked her head. "Ye mean to go?"

He held up one finger.

"I should wait? Ye're going to get the nuns?"

He nodded again and leapt back across the stream where Averilla, staring in consternation, stood framed in the bare branches of the thicket.

"Will? Who is it?" Averilla had emerged from the shrubbery and seen him talking to someone, but now, closer, she saw something else in his eyes. *Fear?* "Will?" She heard terror in her own voice.

Will stood, wondering, *How do I do this?* He beckoned Averilla forward, pointing across the creek.

"I don't see—"

Will pushed back a few of the intervening twigs and willow wands. Averilla peered around his bulk and saw a woman, ragged and dirty and... *what? Something was different about her. Her stance? Her face?* Averilla squinted. Francine's disfigurement became obvious. *Lumps. As if she has been stung or has hives.* Averilla froze. *Oh, God, let me... help me to...,* but she could frame no coherent thought. The woman crouched protectively. *Over a pile of leaves? Why? Her food?* The leaves moved. *Another! Oh, Lord. Leprosy. Oh, Lord. You healed them, but I...* Averilla stared at the two women in consternation. *Lepers! Oh, Lord, not now, not me.* Her mind seized in panic. Lepers— right here before her—helpless, vulnerable, and Christ's awe-full love was being demanded of her again. *Please, Lord, not again.* The words bubbled up from her soul. She had thought she was done with recoil and revulsion. *Oh, Lord, take this cup from me. I don't want this. I can't. You can't possibly mean this for me!* Another part of her, a part with ineffable strength, pitied the lepers and tried to will acceptance.

She heard in her mind, loud and living, *Love One Another.*

Left alone, these two will die, I know that. But... objected the other voice within her, *the abbess will... the Chapter... there is no room for lepers in an abbey on top of the hill. And if we put them farther away, they will be helpless.*

"You," she asked holding Will's eyes, "you think I should... what, take them back to the abbey?"

Will raised his eyes to where clouds menaced black above the scrim of trees.

A gust of wind rattled the branches and tugged at Averilla's veil. "I can't," she croaked, her gorge rising. "Surely you must realize that we can't have lepers in the enclosure."

What am I doing? she wondered. A professed nun arguing with a serf? *And not only a serf, someone who has done... something.* She shook her head. As if explaining to a child, she continued, "We would... the nuns would sicken." Inside her heart was telling her that Will was right. *But- but...* "I have to get the novices and the ostlers back to the abbey before the storm. Nor can I allow the community to be infected. You must know that."

Elizabeth had come up behind Averilla. "Lepers?" The word in her mouth held a wealth of possibility, as if it were a treasure to be unearthed and opened. "Oh, Dame." She reached out a hand and gently turned Averilla to her. Elizabeth's face radiated joy. "My whole life I have wanted to help lepers."

Averilla's face screwed up into a wrinkled ball of consternation. "You have?"

"Oh, Dame, we must help them; take them with us. They cannot stay here. Even were we to build a shelter, this storm looks to be long and hard." Seeing the negation, the recoil in Averilla's eyes, Elizabeth pushed on: "We have to help them. We have to shelter them. You know that. Deep inside, you know that." Seeing Averilla's drooping shoulders, Elizabeth's face softened. "You need not worry. I will take charge of them."

Averilla felt herself giving in. *Is this what You want me to do? You are giving me a way to do it. But what then? Once Elizabeth brings them to the abbey?*

"We must take them with us." Elizabeth pursued, feeling Averilla's resistance waver. "They will freeze if left here. They can stay just the one night in the abbey, or… however long the storm lasts."

"Where, Dame, where do we put them in the abbey that will not infect the others?' Averilla felt dread increase within her.

Elizabeth groped for an idea. Then, finding it, she said, "Why not in the tracing house, away from the community? John the Mason doesn't use it in the winter. It will be cold, certainly, but it is a shelter."

"You are mad!"

"I have never," said Elizabeth with a renewed look of eager joy, "been more sane."

"And after the storm? What then? You on your own can't be in charge of them. The responsibility will fall to the infirmaress, and since the infirmaress is gone, it will fall on me, and I don't know what to do." Averilla frowned hearing the words she herself had just spoken. *Before everything, the infirmaress must care for the health of the community.* The thought of what caring for the lepers entailed—pillows, blankets, food, the problem of getting supplies to them—was crushing.

Someone else plucked at Averilla's sleeve. She turned. Flakes of snow now drifted down. One of the novices, fear widening her eyes, said. "Dame, you must take us back. We don't know the way. The storm."

Suddenly, recognizing the storm as a way to extricate herself from guilt and obligation, Averilla turned back to Elizabeth, her voice resolved. "Dame, I cannot do that. My duty is to protect the abbey from ill. I must get the novices back to the abbey before the storm hides the way. I cannot wait for lepers. One of them can't even walk."

To the open-mouthed novices, she ordered, "Come along. We cannot tarry. Elizabeth, I am sorry to disappoint you, but I must bid you come with us."

"I will come, Dame. But I will bring these two with me. Somehow."

"Then," frustration and panic raised Averilla's voice again, "then you must do it alone. I cannot help you with this. Come along, Will."

Will studied Averilla, glanced over to the lepers, and shook his head. As if to underline his intent, he curled his forearms into a gesture of carrying.

"Will, you can't! You can't carry a leper! You would catch the disease, and…"

He nodded.

Something inside Averilla argued, *If you leave them, they will die, and you won't have to defend Will or persuade the community.* With a shooing motion at the novices she said to Will, "I can't help them. Elizabeth, come." She turned and headed out of the glade. A few of the young women looked back as they left, eyes riveted on Francine and Ellen, the ravages of the disease both fascinating and disturbing.

Chapter Sixteen

The Abbey

The gaggle of distraught young women and ostlers struggled back through the wood, lugging their baskets of greens. The wind gusted around them until they reached the edge of the forest, where sleet stung their faces. Averilla seemed oblivious, trying to justify herself to herself. *I am doing the right thing. The novices don't know the way back.*

Neither does Elizabeth, argued the other side. *She told you she had never been into the forest. Even if she remembered the way we came, everything will look different going back, much less covered with snow.*

Averilla reached up to wipe the wet from her face. *Will won't remember either: the snow will blot out and change the landmarks!* reasoned the first side. *Neither Will nor Elizabeth will be able to find their way. They could have built the lepers a hut, given them some food. and left them. One person shouldn't just go off and threaten the whole community.*

What is possessing Elizabeth? Lepers in the tracing house will bring upon me the ire of Dame Joan, the abbess, and the whole community. I don't have the strength to fight this battle. Lord, if this is indeed Your will, help me!

As Averilla continued to put one foot in front of the other in the mounting slush, unbidden and unwelcome came another memory: Mary. The day she had first met the cripple Mary, brought into the abbey by one of the villagers, she had been transfixed by Mary's teeth, all jumbled in her mouth, one overlapping another. Mary's knees bent inward, and revulsion had clambered up Averilla's spine. Unaccountably, Mary had lunged for Averilla, and reacting, Averilla had batted at the grasping hand. *I didn't know what she was going to do.*

Even now the memory brought a blush to Averilla's cheeks. Dame Maud had intervened. She had bent over Mary and caressed her, wiped the drool from Mary's mouth and the tears from her eyes. Not even glancing at Averilla, Maud had taken Mary into her arms and crooned as if she were a babe. When Maud finally turned to Averilla, she had said, "She means you no harm, child. She just wanted to hug you, because you are beautiful, and because she has seen so little beauty in her short life, she wanted to touch it."

I was so wound about my own fear, I didn't give Mary that smallest of recognitions; that she too was a person with thoughts, feelings, and aspirations. I never apologized. Will I never learn? Will I never grow?

Averilla had watched Dame Maud lead Mary to the infirmary kitchen. *There was I with two perfect legs, able.* "Her name is Mary." Maud hadn't turned to Averilla as she tied a cloth around Mary's neck and gave her porridge. Mary had smiled as she managed the spoon, apparently a huge accomplishment. Maud then said to Averilla, "You must ask God to help you erase this… distaste. You cannot beat your will into it. The spirit may be willing, but you will find that the flesh is extraordinarily strong. That, of course, is the key."

"We will pray. Lord," Dame Maud had used a mater-of-fact voice, as if she were an ordinary housewife in the market stalls, asking the fishmonger for a certain rare fish. "Please help this child to ask You for Your help, for it is only when You work within us that we are in any way able to accomplish those things that You would have us do."

Now in desperation Averilla prayed, *Lord, it's the same thing again, isn't it? Just as with Mary, I am revolted by these lepers.* She went as deep into herself as she had the ability to go. *Lord, I don't want to help them. I don't want to touch them.* And then, rebellious—*Why? Why do You ask this of me?*

Is it because You have bidden us to love? And I resist. I don't want to sicken. I don't want this burden. Without Your help, I cannot dissolve these binding coils of self. Help me to love, Give me a heart to love—them.

And with a dizzying bolt of lightning came the words, *You know what you have to do.*

Averilla *did* know: She had to recognize that these lepers— no, not lepers—that beneath the surface ugliness of their affliction, these were women with souls.

Averilla and the novices finally reached the abbey. Just one knock on the slot door in the main gate revealed the somber face of the portress. "Thank God. I have been sore worried. You are to attend the abbess immediately." She peered around Averilla, counting the various heads on her fingers as they filed through the gate. Then, "Where are Will and Elizabeth?"

"They will be along shortly." Averilla's voice was flat. She couldn't meet the eyes of the dear little woman who took the words with a frown.

Averilla dragged herself across the court and up the stairs to the abbess's lodgings. Clayetta gave a low bow and opened the door.

As soon as Averilla set her wet feet in the room, the abbess spoke, censure in her voice. "What in heaven's name took you so long? You were just to gather greens. It should have not taken you—"

The accusation, though veiled, provoked in Averilla a sudden determination to do what was right in the face of certain disapproval.

"My lady," she said. "We found lepers in the forest."

The abbess's eyes widened. "You are not infected, are you? You left them alone, I trust."

"Yes, I did. But Elizabeth—"

"What? What about Elizabeth?"

"Elizabeth insisted we bring them here."

"Here? Lepers? Surely not." Cecily rose, aghast.

"Neither Elizabeth nor Will would leave them." Averilla lifted her hands in resignation. "I couldn't force them to come with me."

"You left Elizabeth in the forest? With this storm brewing? With lepers? Oh, Dame, this is indeed too much to countenance, even for you. It is getting darker, and the snow…" Her voice trailed off. "And Will too? Sick and tired? Does either of them know the way back?"

Averilla shook her head miserably.

"Send someone with a torch to retrieve them. Have that person insist that they leave the lepers behind."

"I will send Wat with a torch." Averilla heard a new defiance in her voice. "But Elizabeth will not come without the lepers. And she is right. We cannot knowingly leave them to freeze."

"If they are in the forest now, surely they have been there for days. They cannot come here. The health of the abbey must be my first consideration."

"Is not this the same situation as that of the good Samaritan? We cannot walk by and do nothing."

Cecily looked as if she had been slapped. "Dame, you forget yourself. Again."

Outside, the last bell rang for Vespers.

Cecily rose. "Vespers, Dame. Now as the Rule bids us, it is time for Vespers. Nothing must distract us from our duty to praise God."

"But they will freeze."

"Not during Vespers. Come."

Averilla bowed low and, disobeying years of obedience, turned her back on the abbess. "I will," she said over her shoulder, "have them put in the tracing house for the length of the storm." Reaching the still-open door, she elbowed past the open-mouthed Clayetta and almost ran into the bulk of Dame Joan who looked furious. Averilla realized Joan would have overheard the entire conversation.

Chapter Seventeen

The Forest

ill and Elizabeth watched Averilla and the novices disappear down the path and looked at one another blankly. The early dusk of the storm was replacing the glimmer of light with a howling wind and the start of an incessant rain. Will was worried. *No protection from the abbey in these woods, and surely by now, the steward be seeking me for the murder. And now the rain.* It might have been possible to build some kind of shelter before, but not in the rain. He thought of the stump in which they had found Isabel but didn't think he could find it in the dark.

Elizabeth's voice trembled, "I don't think I can find the way back. I wasn't paying attention. Can you?"

He shook his head and stumbled wearily to his feet.

Francine looked up, a glimmer of hope softening her eyes. "Aye, then. Ye'll really take us?

Will nodded grimly.

A tear joined the rain on Francine's face. "You would do that?" Then fiercely, "Ye wot, I cain't leave Ellen. She would die."

Again, Will nodded. *Freeze, most like,* he thought. *Naught to eat. No shelter. Beasts.* He looked around, gauging the twilight.

If I leave them, it will be two more that I have murdered. I'll have to take them to the abbey, which means I have to touch Ellen. His face contorted at the thought of touching the filthy pile of rags that was a person.

How much worse was it for the abbess to touch you, filthy and bloody as you were?

And, he completed the charges against himself, *don't forget, Lord, I'm a murderer.*

Francine watched the emotions twist Will's face. She was used to such reactions. Always disgust at the leprosy. Disgust was usually followed by sorrow, and sometimes pity. Few could ever bring themselves to touch a leper. She rubbed her arms.

Straightening his shoulders, and full of reluctance, Will crossed to Ellen, pushed his hands under her, and lifted her onto his shoulder. She was lighter than many sheep he had carried. He took a step onto the path he hoped was the one on which Averilla had brought them.

Francine trotted along behind or beside him, quiet for once. She wasn't strong, and Will's strides were long. "Taking us to the abbey?" she panted. "Fine kettle of fish that'll be."

Will grunted, and Francine took it for a yes.

Elizabeth straightened her shoulders and followed.

Even if Ellen was but skin and bones, her dead weight was a burden for Will. He had been hiking in this bitter-cold forest for an entire—and seemingly endless—day. He was tired. As the four of them thrashed down the sides of yet another berm, he saw a hollow in which a fuzzy yellowish moss still glowed in the twilight. Low branches overhung the small hollow. He stooped and placed Ellen on the moss.

Rooks and crows clunked above the bare trees.

Francine shivered, and her voice trembled. "Be full dark ere long. Know ye the way in the dark?"

Will shook his head and pointed to a nearby fallen log. As Francine sat, he ripped curls of dried bark from a birch stump. Elizabeth, not understanding what he was about, dug her hands deeper into her sleeves and watched. As Will gathered dried needles and twigs, Francine rose and scuttled close, craning her head over his shoulder. *Like a fox,* he thought, smiling, *with her sharp little nose and chin and the wisps of red hair.*

"Ach, o' course. Ye be making a torch."

Will rose and wandered off, looking for something.

Eyes never leaving him, Francine said to Elizabeth, "So why be ye with us? What be we to ye?

Elizabeth lifted an eyebrow, gave a rueful smile, and said, "Salvation."

Francine cocked her head. "Ye believe ye can be saved by helping us?"

"No, not exactly. I saw lepers when I was a child, and it seared something inside me. I kept thinking how lonely I would be if I were as they were, hungry and cold. I believe that each person is called to something, and when they find that thing, it is like, like a sword in a sheath. It just fits."

Will had returned with a sturdy branch. He hacked it into an arm's length, curled the bits of slightly damp bark around the top, and filled the opening with the dry lichen and needles so that the hollows were interwoven with but held apart by the dried tinder.

"A torch, ye be fashioning," Francine said. "Then ye be needing a tie." Francine proceeded to gnaw a rip in the hem of her tunic and tear off a strip. Will hesitated, reluctant to touch it, then took it and tied the cloth around the tinder-filled bark.

He elbowed out of his sheepskin and handed it to Francine who took hold of it, eyes questioning. Will reached over pulled out a few tufts of the matted fleece, then teased them apart so the fibers looked like a dandelion. Francine nodded and, rather like dog worrying a foxtail from its pelt, plucked and pulled until she had a generous fluff of wool. Will placed that on the ground with a gentleness belied by his huge hands, fumbled his flint from his scrip, and slipped his eating knife from his belt loop. He placed knife to flint and struck them together. A spark sank into the fibers, producing only a dispiritingly frail plume of smoke. Careful not to smother the struggling spark, he picked up the fluffball and wafted it, forcing the spark to gorge itself on air. When a flame emerged, he held the burning fluff under the torch head and grunted in satisfaction as one by one the curls of bark caught and lit. The torch wouldn't last long, for he had no fat to prolong the flame, but he could fashion another, and at least he wouldn't have to spend time striking another spark.

With grave courtesy he handed the torch to Francine, hastily wrapped his sheepskin over and around Ellen, picked her up, and nodded to Francine.

"Ye'd 'ave me lead the way? But where, which…?"

With his chin, Will gestured toward the far side, remembering a rock formation that, even wet and limned with snow, seemed familiar. Going was tough. Trails were numerous, mere trickles in some cases; others were well trodden by feral swine and masterless men. Small rocks, half-hidden by the snow-purpled torchlight, became stumbling blocks. The looming dark gave the scene an eerie gravity, hiding or outlining one aspect of each landmark.

They tramped on. Each time they came to a fork, Francine paused until Will nodded a direction. Their footsteps were muffled except for the soft snap of the occasional twig.

If Francine was confused, Will was only a bit less so. He knew little more of the landscape than she did, having never returned to the abbey from this direction by himself. He was tired, and still grinding within him was the vision of returning and replacing on his own body a sheepskin that had been in contact with a leper. Elizabeth had gone deep within herself in prayer. To Francine, it seemed she was barely there.

As they trudged, Will held, in the back of his mind, the hope that they would stumble on old Madge's lichen trail. He trusted the old woman, not just because she had supplied the tincture that had cured his fever, but because there was something about her, some wisdom that inspired trust. Mayhap everyone felt that way, and that was why Madge prospered. What she had explained to them was so incredible that he thought it just might be true. He'd seen enough weird things in his lifetime to credit most anything a wise woman told him, but he had no way of knowing if the lichen was in this part of the forest. It wouldn't have mattered had he been alone, or if he had had only Francine and Elizabeth to care for. They could have probably hunkered down and lasted out the night, but Ellen was frighteningly frail. Would she still be alive if they made it back?

Chapter Eighteen

Abbey and Forest

verilla left the abbess, trying to erase the images of Will and Elizabeth lost in the sleet, icicles furring their eyelashes, hands blue lodging in her mind. Head down, she hurried not to the church for Vespers as bidden, but to the stables, eager to elude the tongue-lashing she knew Joan itched to deliver. *What was I thinking, leaving Will? Those who took his tongue could come! We know someone hurt Lady Isabel and murdered Ethelind. "He," whoever he was, could still be out there. And I left Will, exhausted and maimed. Obedience to the rule means I should wait for the abbess to change her mind or bring it to Chapter, but loving my neighbor means sending for them—now.*

Men sat within the door to the stables with a small brazier for heat, laughing over some joke. "Wat?" Averilla called, spotting him just under the eaves. Wat scrambled to his feet, apprehensive. "Dame?"

"I need you to go back into the forest. For Will and Elizabeth."

His face paled.

"I- I shouldn't have left them. Neither knows the way back." Her voice thickened. "Would you take a torch and show them the way?" Sensing rather than seeing his resistance, she said, "You needn't touch the lepers."

Wat nodded, his jaw working.

"You'll go?"

Again, he nodded, eyes widening at something behind Averilla.

Averilla turned. Joan loomed behind her.

Joan hissed, "I heard you talking to the abbess. I heard you just now telling Wat to go fetch the lepers. How dare you? The abbess never gave you permission. She did not!"

Wat, now near the door of the stables, the hood of his jerkin shielding his face, a lighted torch in one hand, looked from Joan to Averilla, uncertain.

Joan said, "The abbess did not give her permission. As sub-prioress, I forbid you to leave."

Lifting his chin, Wat said, "I mun follow the orders I be given. I cain not disobey." He turned his back to her and trotted toward the main gate.

Joan shouted, "Wat, come back here right now. You will not go. I forbid it."

As Wat disappeared in the twilight, Joan turned on Averilla, her voice rising to a screech, spittle flying. "Think you to show compassion by this deed? What compassion? You give no thought for the women in this community, who will surely sicken. The abbess gave you not permission to bring them back. She gave you no authority. I have been enjoined to keep this abbey safe, and I say the lepers cannot come here."

Averilla shook her head, lowering her voice in dismay at her defiance of Joan. "I doubt he will find them." She started for the church, but Joan managed to keep up with Averilla's longer stride.

Joan wasn't finished. "Dame, have you lost your wits? Will is a murderer. You have compromised the safety of this abbey by bringing him into it, and now…"

Averilla turned her head, but Joan would not be ignored; she grabbed Averilla's arm, forcing her to stop. Joan's face was bunched in fury. "So busy being the holy helper of the infirm and the poor that you don't think about those nearest to you."

"We don't know that he is a murderer."

"Why else cut out his tongue? You are compounding your trespass against those of us who seek peace and God. If Will does not murder us in our beds, we shall catch leprosy and die. And don't tell me you can use your precious potions to cure leprosy. There is no cure."

Joan brought her face close to Averilla's. "As always, so engrossed in your own selfish concerns that you managed to get Ethelind killed in the forest!"

All color drained from Averilla's face. She opened her mouth to speak, but the words were like a knife in her heart, burrowing deep. Joan continued, sensing victory: "Had it not been for you, Ethelind would still be with us." Turning her back on Averilla, Joan marched into the nave.

Below the steps to the choir, Averilla fell to her knees and again prostrated herself on the freezing flags. *Oh, Lord,* she prayed, but could form no further thought. Her mind was a maelstrom, swirling around the burr of truth in Joan's words. Tears welled. *Oh, Ethelind, had I but spoken a kind word. Had I just listened. Ethelind made her own decision, but if only I had listened to her when she asked me for help. Oh, Lord.*

Averilla put her head down and felt herself dissolve into the red behind her eyes.

Brow bunched in worry, and squinting into the swirling snow, Wat crossed the Bimport and slipped and slid down Tout Hill. He was confident only of the way through the verges of the forest. By the time he reached the rock where earlier they had entered the forest, the wind was howling. What in daylight had been a path was, in the night-blurred snow, invisible. Wat stumbled over unseen rocks and roots that rose up from nowhere. He turned once, thinking the path jogged to the right, and ended up sprawled in bramble canes, their thorns still sharp. The sleet made everything more difficult. He overstepped into the stream and landed in shin-deep water. *Was this the stream they had followed?* he wondered. If it was, he had missed the clearing where they left Will and the lepers. He backtracked, thought he had found the place, but found it empty. He wiped the rain from his face and spewed a spate of Anglo-Saxon swearwords both virulent and diverse. *They've started back*, he decided. *And yet I didna pass 'em, so no way to follow 'em. Don't know which way they took, do I? Any path I take, I'll just be mucking farther into the forest and will get myself lost.*

After Vespers, Averilla slogged back to the infirmary. She glanced around. Lay sisters were serving an evening meal, which Lady Isabel seemed to be enjoying. There were few patients now, and the hall seemed cold and bleak without Ethelind. Averilla's mind was a gyre. Thoughts of Elizabeth and Will and the lepers elbowed each other into confusion. In her mind she could see them struggle, trying to find their way through the snow. Would Wat find them? It all seemed futile.

Miserable, she moved down the infirmary aisle. Scholastica's raspy voice came to her as if from a deep well. "Averilla, remove your cloak, my dear. You are dripping." The old nun patted her bed. "Then come sit down here, remove your boots, and warm your feet in front of the hearth." Averilla dropped her cloak, and, newly aware of her feet, which were indeed very cold, untied the thongs on first one then the other boot.

"You look unwell," Scholastica said. "What happened?"

"We found lepers in the forest." Tears seeped from her eyes and she brushed them away irritably. "Will found them, and he wouldn't leave them to fight the storm by themselves. And Dame Elizabeth agreed."

"So Will found lepers. How many?"

"Two women. One could no longer walk. He wanted me to bring them to the abbey."

"Will told you this?"

"Er, yes. With his hands. Motions."

"Why, that is wonderful. Think you not so? He is thinking and caring and communicating. But I interrupt. Elizabeth agreed with Will, you say?"

"Yes. She refused to come back with me. She said that she and Will would bring the lepers back and put them in the tracing house until the storm passes, so I left them. I had to." It was a plea for understanding. "I had to get the novices home before the storm's full rage hit. It was getting dark. They didn't know the way back, but, but…" Averilla hung her head, "neither do Elizabeth nor Will."

"The novices? You got them back safely?"

Averilla nodded. Then, "I am so afraid for Will and Elizabeth. He is ill and she is not strong."

"Nonsense. You take too much on yourself. You brought the novices home. Elizabeth made a choice, as did Will. They are both strong enough to withstand the storm. Should the lepers die, at the least, Will and Elizabeth will have let them know that someone cared." Scholastica made a huffing noise in her throat. "Mayhap you could send someone for them."

"I did. I sent Wat."

"Then why the tears? The world is in God's hands. You have accomplished that for which you had responsibility. What else did you do when you returned?"

Averilla told her all, omitting only what Joan had said. That conversation was too raw.

Scholastica leaned back against her pillows. "You know, child, the devil works in devious ways. Know you what he is now doing?"

Averilla shook her head dumbly.

"He is distracting you from the good you do by letting you see only your faults. You brought the young ones safely back, but instead of thanking God for that mercy, you worry about a decision that others made, one that you could not, in fact, have prevented. You have a calling in which you excel. Keep your eye on God and what you can do for Him and for your fellows in your own calling. But you can do nothing if you don't obey God's commandment to rest. You are exhausted, and when we are tired, none of us can fulfill God's will for us in the way we should. Go to sleep and wake refreshed, and lest you put too much emphasis on your vocation, remember it is never our actions that make Christ love us. It is His free-will gift accomplished at Calvary. You cannot earn His love. It is His will to love.

IN THE FOREST, A FOX barked, once, twice, and again. The hope inside Wat curled up and closed. He loved Dame Elizabeth, and something about Will called to him. He shook his head in frustration and backtracked along the forest path, stumbling and restarting, and repeatedly losing his way. Suddenly a pale ribbon of light glinted through the trees to his left. He squinted. When he again opened his eyes, the trees still glowed, and by that gentle luminescence he could make out moving shadows, one of them lifting high a small torch. "Well, I'll be—Madge's path of light is real!"

"Will," Wat shouted, cupping his hands around his mouth. "Will. It's me, Wat." He clomped toward them. "Ye must be fagged, man," he said when he reached them. "Let me carry 'er." Hearing his own voice, he backed up a step, appalled at what he had offered. He would no more get himself that close to a leper than embrace an adder.

Will shook his head tiredly.

"Then I'll carry my torch behind Dame Elizabeth. More light that way."

AVERILLA CREPT TO AN UNOCCUPIED bed in the south aisle and slept. The bells for Matins and Lauds woke her momentarily, but exhaustion overtook consciousness. Somewhere in the dim hours before dawn, she dreamt.

When first she saw Him, the Man was working His way down the great green hill of the chalk giant, the spring grasses ruffling around his knees. Behind him there were pockmarked standing stones. The stones began to sway, just slightly, as if with the breeze, into a sort of ranking march, an ordering. Averilla began to see the pattern. It was one of the complicated dances country folk do when the harvest is gathered in. They, the stones, wove in and out around the Man, as if in pleased response.

He passed beyond the stones to a great lake. Where the water met the land, He continued walking, as if to Him there was no difference between form and formless. She could tell it was water, for His feet sank a little, and small waves curled and foamed around his feet. A child came from the shore, called by Him, called by a word she couldn't hear. The child looked dubious, but tentatively took a step, then another. The water held, and the child ran across the surface and took His hands. Others now followed the first, skipping and jumping over the waves. He, laughed. Then He started to dance. His feet did something complicated. The children saw and copied.

When they reached the far shore, the man herded the children before him. They turned and Averilla saw that the children had changed. Their faces were sore and disfigured; oozing and scabbed; their noses half eaten away. Some had no hands. Others, without feet, hobbled on crutches.

Averilla felt tears well. He was looking at her. His gaze sent a deep shiver of awe through her body; the strength of the ages leashed by compassion. He said three words: "Bandage my lambs." He held out His hands to her, and on them she saw the unmistakable marks of the nails.

He moved again, and suddenly the children's rags were gone, the sores healed. She felt joy surge, send gooseflesh up her arms. The soft voice of sweetness was suddenly replaced by thunder.

These are souls I have made.
Care for them.
If you but knew the beauty of one
Immortal soul.

CHAPTER NINETEEN

DECEMBER 16, 1120

THE ABBEY

It was before Prime; in the east, the sky had lightened into a bleak smudge, and the fury of the storm was easing when Will, Ellen in his arms, trudged up to the town gate, a weary Francine hanging on to his tunic. Elizabeth was now beside him. Wat was keeping his distance. The gate was not yet opened, but from the gatehouse there came a desultory trail of smoke. Will, his arms full of Ellen, kicked the gate.

"Who goes?" bellowed from inside, as an eye peered through the slot. "Gate don't ope 'til the sun be well up. Who be ye?" Will, of course, couldn't answer, so Wat closed the distance and stood in front of the small gatehouse. "It's me, Rogan. Wat. Open up."

"Ach. Wat. And be this Will? Heard about ye." The door scraped open, and the man, like a turtle, stuck out his head. Seeing Elizabeth, he bowed awkwardly. "Dame." He shook his head and disappeared back inside. They heard the metallic grating of a key, then a rumble as the bar was pushed through its housing.

The gate inched open and the gatekeep peered more closely. He studied Francine's face and recoiled. "Ye bring a leper? No, by Saint Swithin, ye will not bring 'er into my town."

Elizabeth said. "It is my doing, Rogan. You need not fear."

"Dame! Do you know…," he protested. Suddenly realizing that Will most probably carried another leper, his eyes narrowed, "Does the abbess know?"

"I believe Dame Averilla told her. She sent Wat here to us."

"Never would 'ave thought I'd be letting lepers into the town." he moaned. "But iffen ye say so, Dame. Never would 'ave on my own. You tell the abbess that. I'll ope the gate, but back up and wait 'til I get back into the hut before ye come through. Don't know what is possessing ye. Just wait 'til the townsfolk hear o' this."

They staggered through the gate and slogged behind Wat up the High Street to the Bimport. This time it was Wat who knocked. The portress pulled back the grill in the slot gate and peered out. "Ah, Wat. Saints be praised, ye be back. But…"

Behind Wat stood Will, exhausted and soul weary, Ellen on his shoulder. On glimpsing Francine's face, the wide black hat, the clapper, the portress gasped. Her eyes widened and her mouth gaped. "Dame Elizabeth? What are you bringing into the enclosure?"

Elizabeth didn't answer her directly. "We are putting them in the tracing house for the length of the storm. To Wat she continued, "Thank you for finding us and leading us back. We will manage from here."

Wat gave Elizabeth a worried smile, bowed briefly, and scuttled back to the stables.

Will lurched in behind Elizabeth, and followed her to a little stone hut on the infirmary side of the forecourt. Nuns on their way to Prime, along with the masons and carpenters, took in Francine's black hat and the clapper that drooped from her hand. They stood dumbfounded or muttering.

"This is the tracing house," Elizabeth said, pushing the door open. "The master mason uses it to draw his ideas for the new church on the packed sand of the floor."

DAME JOAN HAD BEEN RESTLESS with affront the night through. Finally she had risen, and tiptoed down the night stairs to her office to be ready when Elizabeth and Will returned. She heard the gate open and the protest of the portress. Joan's mouth drew into a grimace of outrage. Lepers! How dare they!

Will and Elizabeth waited for Francine to sidle in behind them, and then Will kicked the door shut. In winter, because of possible damage to the mortar by the change in temperature, no masonry was worked. Therefore the little tracing house was empty, except for the wooden patterns for corbels and plinths stacked against one wall. The sand floor was devoid of any tracings. It was very cold.

Will laid Ellen down on the clean sand and smiled at the look of awe on Francine's face as the latter stood rubbing her arms. Will nodded, then stumbled out.

Averilla also wakened before Prime, and so heard the portress's shout of dismay. *They made it,* she thought. Elation rose in her heart. She had already tied her shoes and donned her veil. Quietly, she went to the store shelves and grabbed two coverlets, then hurried through the herbarium and across the court to the tracing house, knocked at the door, and pushed through.

In the dim light of dawn, Averilla saw that Ellen, still in Will's sheepskin, was lying seemingly comatose on the sand. Francine stood shivering, eyes huge in her sunken face. Averilla took the coverlets to Francine and laid them down, careful to avoid contact.

"Thank ye." Francine smiled, but it was the hurt smile of someone who recognizes a snubbing about which she can do nothing.

Averilla blushed and turned to Elizabeth. It was as if a bonfire burned behind Elizabeth's great blue eyes. Remembering her dream, Averilla probed her heart. The fear had gone, replaced by compassion.

"We found a path." Elizabeth was not only wet but disheveled, veil askew, smudges on her face. "Oh, Averilla, we made it. Thank you for letting us bring them here. Thank you for sending Wat. We wouldn't have got back without him." She paused, remembering. "There was a strange glow. A path it made. We followed it and it led us home." Her brow puckered. "Surely witchcraft."

"No. 'Tis not witchcraft," Averilla explained. "As a young woman, Madge discovered a lichen that reflects light. Over the years she has draped it in the trees to make paths that the peasants can follow in the night, or with torches if the night be moonless."

"Oh. How knew Will of it?

"Madge told me, and he overheard."

"Will made a torch. We got lost for a while. Then Wat appeared."

"I had given up hope," Averilla said, vaguely watching Francine cocoon herself in the coverlet.

The second bell for Prime tolled.

"We must attend the office. The abbess needs to see that you have returned. I told her that we were going to use the tracing house. She wasn't pleased."

Elizabeth nodded.

"After Prime, we can bring broth and food. More coverlets. Water. Clean tunics. But for now, we must be in the church."

Francine looked bleak.

Following Averilla to the door, Elizabeth touched her arm. "I want to care for them from now on."

Averilla whirled around, shocked, abandoned, dismayed, voice rasping, "You would leave the abbey with them? You would tend to them?"

"If it came to that, yes, I would. I thought about it all the way back."

"But…" Averilla frowned in consternation. "But why?"

"I can't just send them back into the forest. They will die. I can find… someplace. Perhaps the tithe barn in Tisbury."

"But how would you get food and heat and, and everything?"

Elizabeth's voice was firm. "To minister to these women would give me the quiet I have been seeking."

"Were you to tend them, you would not be able to return to the abbey. You do understand that? The contagion. Have you any concept of what you are suggesting?"

"Some. But neither had I any idea what life in the abbey entailed. To be very honest, it has not been what I had hoped."

"We cannot, I cannot… oh, Elizabeth." Elizabeth closed the door softly, and Averilla stared at it blankly for a moment before she turned and trudged through the dirty snow, thinking, *To not see Elizabeth ever again? First Ethelind and now Elizabeth? I can't do this all on my own. I need Maud back.*

As SHE CROSSED THE COURT, Averilla saw the abbess descend from the lodgings. Cecily reached the bottom stair, where Dame Joan stood waiting.

Averilla couldn't hear what was said, but guessed from Joan's face and gestures that she argued against lepers being allowed inside the enclosure.

AFTER PRIME, AVERILLA RETURNED TO the infirmary and gathered worn tunics. On the way across the court, she stopped a lay sister and asked her to bring two buckets of water to the tracing house. The girl's eyes widened like those of a horse who has spied a snake, but she bowed and headed reluctantly toward the well-house. Even the lay sisters had heard about the lepers!

Averilla then veered to the kitchen. Cook was preoccupied with Christmas preparations, and the Kitchener, wimple askew, red in the face and short of temper, glared at the interruption. It wasn't unusual for the infirmary to retrieve broth. What *was* unusual was for Averilla to come for it herself. The cook huffed, but nodded and stepped into the hearth, ignoring the fire around her, and ladled steaming broth into a rope-handled pot. Furtively, Averilla slipped bread, cheese, apples, and two wooden tumblers into a scrip she had brought for the purpose. She thanked the cook, then proceeded to the tracing house, where she tapped on the door. "Elizabeth, I…"

Elizabeth opened the door. "Oh, Dame." Seeing the broth, she grinned in relief. "I feared you might be here to tell me…" She broke off. "Is that broth? And tunics. Oh, bless you!" From outside, behind Averilla, murmurs washed into the hut.

"They are afraid," Elizabeth said. She looked worried.

Trying not to stare at the two lepers, Averilla shrugged off her scrip. Francine's fingers twitched as she ogled the pot of broth. Averilla handed the bulging scrip to Elizabeth, who pulled out the crusty loaf of bread. At the sight of it, Francine sighed. "Wheaten bread? For us? Not plain maslin, but wheaten?"

Elizabeth explained to Averilla what Francine had told her of how the unfortunate pair had come into the forest.

Francine added, "So, I mun bide with Ellen, 'til she dies." Her eyes fixed on Averilla. "I know we can't stay here—"

Elizabeth held up a hand. "I hope that will not be so. After Mass, the community has a Chapter meeting where we discuss such things. I am hoping to be able to establish a lazar house."

Averilla blinked and caught her breath. "Dame, may we speak outside while these two break their fast?"

Elizabeth slipped out the door behind Averilla. "Dame," Averilla hissed, "you are giving them false hope. The abbess will never agree. They will die. And you will be a leper. "

Tears brimmed on Elizabeth's eyelids as she held Averilla's gaze.

"Oh, Elizabeth, why?"

"They are helpless. On my way here, with Winifred, my nurse. I had, what, ten winters? The cart was clumsy, and I was used to riding a horse, but my father insisted, because he said that was how a nun would be conveyed. I think he was punishing me, for he hated the idea that I would leave them. My mother was distraught." Elizabeth looked aside, remembering; her eyes narrowed as they rested on a building outside the abbey wall. She shook her head.

"We passed a line of lepers. The first I knew of them was the sound of a cracked bell and the dull clack of clappers. I pushed my head under the cart's curtains and there they were, huddled alongside the road, their arms, legs, and feet covered in filthy cloth. One poor wretch's head covering slipped, and where his nose should have been, holes gaped, and his lips were misshapen, drawn up on one side into a snarl. He opened his mouth and rasped, 'Unclean, unclean.' His tone was resigned, like that of a tinker calling, 'Pots and pans, one a penny, two a penny, pans for sale.' There was no hope in his voice."

Elizabeth now focused on that roof outside the abbey wall. She cocked her head and nodded, then, eyes alight, turned to Averilla. She paused to collect her thoughts. "I tried to make the ostler stop the horses, but Winifred wouldn't let him, so I started to throw the gifts we had brought for the abbey onto the road—a round of cheese, two hams, my nightdresses and blankets—all went over the side.

"Winifred finally wrestled me to the bench. I believe she was afraid I would jump out. 'Child,' she said, 'you have done what you could. Perhaps more than you should have. Even our Lord healed not every leper he saw. In the abbey you will be able to pray for them. Be not distracted from the prayer and meditation you have chosen. You can't save them. Alone with them on the road, you could not help.'"

"But now, Dame, I *can* help—and pray as well. Will you help me persuade the others?"

Averilla flinched, bewildered. "Oh, Elizabeth, how? Even if they agreed, where would you put this lazar house?

Determined, eyes again suffused with the holy brightness, Elizabeth pointed over the abbey wall. "It just came to me. The workmen's lodgings are perfect. They are far enough away, and food and stuffs could be sent from the abbey. Will you help me, Averilla? Please."

Averilla pondered the request, sorrowing for herself, but in light of her dream, vowing that, in the unlikely event the community agreed, she would not stand in the way. "Elizabeth," she said finally, "let God's will in this be done."

Great Dunstan tolled over the abbey.

When it stopped ringing, she said, "But first there is Mass. We need to pray on this. But I… I will not stand in your way.

CHAPTER TWENTY

The second bell for Mass and Chapter sounded over the outer court and drifted in eddies around it. Averilla saw with dismay the huddle of nuns standing midway between the brode hall and the church. Snatches of talk came to her on the wind, the sound an irritated hiss.

"Can you smell…?"

"She had no right."

"We will all sicken."

"Brought right into the center of the community."

A stronger voice, hidden within the crowd, called out, "Surely you took not tunics, good abbey tunics, to the lepers." Dame Joan stood defiant in their midst, eyes daring Averilla to speak. *Joan intends to force my hand during chapter*, thought Averilla.

Elizabeth faltered at the sight of the clusters of nuns, and Averilla's heart saddened to see the fear in her eyes. The young nun's face drooped in submission as she made her way toward the throng. Averilla felt antagonism wash against them. She shouldered her way through. But Elizabeth hesitated, then bowed low, for from behind, the abbess had appeared beside her and taken her arm.

MASS WAS HALTING. EMOTION ROILED through the nave. The nun's priest, John of Avranches, intoned the Latin with drawn-out vowels and split sibilants. The abbess's voice quavered at first on the psalm, but finally the cadence of the familiar words and the solace of the Mass calmed her. One by one, the other nuns quieted.

When Mass ended, the nuns processed through to the cloister and into the chapter house in grim determination. Chapter opened with the usual reading of the Rule and the necrology. Most of them were poised when Cecily bade them speak about the "affairs of the house." As she had done in bringing Will into their midst, Cecily had again made a unilateral decision on behalf of the community by not sending the lepers packing at first light. Averilla was glad she had done so, but wondered at the heavy-handed behavior. *Will this just make the community more resistant?*

Ignoring the glowers coming from those on the tiers below her, Cecily began, "We believe leprosy came to England with the pilgrims returning from Jerusalem. The Bishop of London contracted it and died. The horrid disfigurements frighten people, yet our beloved Queen Matilda caused St. Giles Leper hospital to be built. She even invited lepers into her home and kissed them."

The ensuing silence crackled with shiftings as each nun parsed Cecily's words and her own fears, deciding if she should be the first to speak.

The prioress, usually the most easygoing of souls, spoke. "Should we? Should you? I- we can't, Mother, for—"

Cecily said, "Dame Elizabeth has made a request. She asks that we allow…" Cecily paused trying to marshal her thoughts, "allow her to minister to the two lepers who arrived last night. They are very ill, but they could be housed in… the place where the unmarried workmen sleep outside the abbey western wall.

Averilla's mouth rounded in an 'O.' *Elizabeth did speak to her, and...*

The simple solution took the nuns by surprise. They remained silent, eyes blank, as they absorbed the thought.

"That shelter in which they live is far enough from the enclosure and cloister that surely no contagion can spread. The sewers reach there. The workmen could construct another building, on the town side, to replace their loss. We could provide them—the lepers, that is—with daily provisions."

Eyes returned her gaze, unconvinced.

"A leprosarium! Here!"

"I marvel," said another.

"But why do you want this, Elizabeth?" asked the nun nearest in age to Elizabeth.

Because Elizabeth had been in contact with the lepers, she was seated on the floor near the door. She rose, smoothed her tunic, and adjusted her scapular. As she moved to the pulpit in the center of the circular room, those on the lowest tier ostentatiously pulled back their habits. Elizabeth's hands were shaking, clutching one another in anxiety. She cleared her throat.

"The lady abbess has broached this subject and requests an affirmative decision, not for herself, but for me. I need Sabbath." The hostile silence weakened, becoming confused. "I need the quiet that comes not only from a lack of speech but from a lack of activity. An anchorage is not my desire. It is for some, I know, but I would serve the poor and needy as well. As St. James cautions us, 'What is faith without works?' I ask, of my own free will, to be permitted to bide with these two lepers and minister to them. If I sicken, I will have the long Sabbath of each day in which to pray and be with my Lord."

"You will sicken," whispered Dame Emily, the novice mistress, and particularly attached to Dame Elizabeth. "I know you will. We shan't ever see you again." Her eyes teared.

Questions of health and fear erupted. Numbers too were mentioned. In the end, one of the novices, asked her opinion, as was customary of the youngest in the community, said, "Won't other lepers come, and then Dame Elizabeth will never get the quiet she seeks?"

After more discussion, the community decided that the lepers should have their own council, a ruling council, when and if there should be more than the two. How many to allow was debated. Seven was decided upon. "Is not seven a sacred number?" had come from somewhere—none knew who suggested it. Father Merowald would be asked to write a Rule for the lazar house, "Like our own, but different, of course."

"But how shall we support them? We have barely enough for ourselves."

The answer had come from an unusual quarter.

"Could not each of us fast one day a week, and that portion be given to them?"

"The number of lepers we can accept must be consistent with how many are willing to fast?"

"It has to revolve amongst us."

"Renunciation is good for the soul."

The nuns amazed themselves.

Dame Emily looked across at Elizabeth, her grief unassuaged. "It will be hard to lose you."

The cantor, in charge of the nuns' singing, looked bereaved. "Your voice," she bleated. "I will lose your pure voice."

Face reddened, Elizabeth hung her head.

ON HER WAY BACK FROM the chapter house, alone with her thoughts, Elizabeth nearly collided with Father Merowald.

"Dame?"

How does he appear just when he is most needed? Elizabeth wondered. She bowed low and then explained what had transpired. About how the others seemed to feel betrayed by her decision.

"I didn't mean to hurt them, Father."

"Of course you didn't. Remember you our earlier conversation?"

Elizabeth nodded dubiously.

"Yours is a special calling. You require silence. Seemingly, God has called you to this ministry."

Elizabeth said, "But it is hard for them."

How to explain holiness to one who is holy? By definition, a holy one can't comprehend her own holiness, he thought, one side of his mouth turning up in affirmation. "Your spirit is ambrosial" he continued. "It draws others to you."

"She—Emily—draws on me." Elizabeth hung her head, ashamed of her shrinking.

"That is her problem to manage. Her longing may never ease."

"But I?"

"Cannot be a slave to her longing. Because your spirit is sweet, if left to themselves, the others would swallow you. You must protect yourself."

"You agree that I need this?"

His eyes warmed, and his mouth turned up on one side. "Did I not say earlier that you should ask God for an answer. He seems to have answered."

There was silence between them as they mused on this. "Now, you must put your mind to practicalities. For instance, you will need an extern sister to move between the abbey and this new lazar house. A messenger if you will. She will provide a distance from the disease and protect the nuns. You two must not meet or touch, but have a place for putting, for the transfer of food and so on, and to ensure that the two of you do not interact." He squinted in concentration. "Remember, you alone are choosing illness. It would be wrong to infect the whole abbey. There are some cases, I am told, of those who seek illness, leprosy in particular, as a way of expiating their sins. I am persuaded that it is not so with you."

ELIZABETH CONTINUED BACK TO THE tracing house, shut the door softly behind her for fear of waking Ellen, and pointed to the bucket.

"I have water for you to bathe."

"Er, so what said the abbess? 'Bout us?" Francine sounded as if she had a cold. Her crooked jaw and the congested phlegm distorted her words.

Elizabeth responded slowly, giving herself time to understand Francine's garbled words, "They won't let you stay here in this building because the men will need it and the contagion will spread."

Francine glanced down at her filthy rags and grudgingly withdrew one arm from her tattered tunic. She paused, one elbow over her head, and gazed around at the sand floor, the shelves, and the open plan of the building. She said, rather bravely, the rags dropping to a pile in front of her, "We knew we couldna stay, but we thank ye kindly for this night and this food and the clothes."

Elizabeth shook her head. "No, no, I didn't mean that you had to go away from here. The abbess intends for you to stay, just not in this house. You are to have another place."

Francine. puzzled, gave Elizabeth a skeptical look.

Elizabeth moved one of the buckets toward Francine, and held out a slippery mess of soap, gray from ashes and tallow. "The workmen's lodgings, on the other side of the abbey wall."

Francine dipped the soap into the water, hesitantly, as if it might bite her, and dabbed at her hands and face. Then, at a nod from Elizabeth, she rubbed the soap over the rest of her body, avoiding the bandaged left foot and leg. Elizabeth said, "There is a hearth, and a big room, and two windows with shutters." She waited to give Francine time to absorb her words. There was something so entrancing about her enthusiastic innocence in the face of her disfigurement that Elizabeth did not wish to hurry her.

Francine sloshed clean water over her arms and body, then picked up a well-worn linen undertunic, and, shivering, slipped it over her head, rubbing the coarse fabric against her body to dry it. Not willing to let herself believe in this miracle, Francine said, trying for cheerfulness, "Cold. Cold but clean. 'S been a long time."

She stopped half in and half out of the habit. "She'd do that? The abbess would? For us?"

"She would," said Elizabeth.

"Forever?"

"For as long as I am alive, for I will tend to you. The abbess said something about the queen, her reason for giving you shelter."

"What queen?"

Elizabeth shuffled through the Abbess's former words. "Queen Matilda."

"Ah, Queen Mold, as was. Saint she be. Took in lepers her own self. We all 'ave 'eard about 'er."

"Yes, well, the community hasn't worked it all out, but it is settled that I am to stay with you."

Francine snuggled into the overtunic of black wool, then plopped down onto the sand and unbound the pus-encrusted cloth that bandaged her leg and foot. The leg was swollen to a shapelessness that lacked ankle and calf. There were reddish-blue swellings, and ruptures that oozed. The disease had eaten away two of her toes, and the room reeked of the caked bindings. Francine again took up the gray mess of soap but did not flinch as she scrubbed her abraded toes.

"It don't hurt," she said, seeing Elizabeth's horrified gaze. "Numb, more like. Makes me stumble. No toes." She sloshed clean water over her feet. "Ellen…" she continued grimly. "Ellen 'as pains some'ut awful. Deep down, it aches, cruel-like."

Elizabeth rummaged through the scrip and pulled out strips of clean linen for bandaging.

Francine concentrated as she rewrapped her leg, wincing now and again, and finally going around and over and over her foot. "Why would you… want this? For it will get you, in the end, leprosy will."

"I- I need quiet," Elizabeth said. "I long to have time to meditate without interruption."

Francine said, "I've 'eard nuns are that way." Her eyes took on a curious look.

"You wouldn't have to be quiet with Ellen or any others who might join you. Just not loud. Allow me to just be… unless, of course, you need me."

"You, er, want to be with God?"

Elizabeth sighed. "Only for certain times during the day. Other times I'd be with you, work with you. Think t'would do?"

"'Twould be a marvel!" A tear trundled down near the sore on Francine's cheek. "To be where no one can…" she glanced at Elizabeth, blushed, and continued, "get at us. To be safe, and warm. But we've naught to pay ye with."

"Aye, we know that. We decided that two of us nuns would fast for one meal a day, and those meals would be given to you. 'Tis little enough."

Momentarily, Elizabeth's eyes clouded as she wondered if she would be able to sustain what she had taken on.

Chapter Twenty-one

After Chapter

Long after the midday meal there came a rough pounding on the main gate, and a preemptory shout that effectively broke into the concentrated whispering of some of the nuns, still muttering over what Elizabeth had thrust upon them. The gate was dragged through the slush to admit a party of horsemen. Their mounts circled restlessly in the forecourt as the portress, habit flapping and veil askew, bustled down from the gatehouse. An accomplished horsewoman herself, she had no fear of the prancing hooves, and grabbed near the bit of the lead horse, her habitual calm broken into impatience. "Your name, sir?"

Will, in front of the stable brushing the abbess's palfrey, turned to look. His face blanched. *Oh, Lord.* He bent down, ostensibly to brush a fetlock, effectively hiding his great height. *The steward! Master Weldon. Has to be him! Same black leather tunic. Same sword. Same spurred high boots. Knew he'd come, didn't I?* Panic seized his heart. He kept brushing, mind in turmoil. *'Ave to run. But, 'ow cain I leave and not be seen?*

Despair blanketed Will's mind. He had known that eventually they would begin to cast a net for him, but he had hoped, when nothing came amiss during the long days of his convalescence, that mayhap…

"My name?" Weldon shouted as if the portress were deaf. He dismounted and stood, removing his gauntlets, arrogantly surveying the courtyard. "I will see the abbess," Weldon declared.

"The abbess is a busy woman," said the portress. "If I might tell her ladyship your name?"

Will sidled toward the rump of the abbess's horse.

"I will have to give the abbess a name," persisted the portress, still clinging to the bit.

It was into this confrontation that the abbess suddenly appeared. The gathered nuns parted, veils bending as she passed. "I am the abbess. You would speak to me."

"My lady." Weldon bowed, subservient and arrogant at the same time. "I am Master Weldon. I seek one Isabel FitzRolf, wife of my liege lord Gervase FitzRolf, and daughter of Robert de Geroi."

Cecily's face went blank, disdaining Weldon's haughtiness, but at the same time seeming prettily confused. "Wife of Gervase FitzRolf?"

"Surely ye wot who I mean. The manor is but ten miles away!"

"Aye, I have met her." Cecily widened her eyes in a naive little-girl guise. "Why would she be here?"

"The bi-… she ran away."

"Ran away in midwinter? Surely not."

"She took off with one of the serving men, a lad named Peter. But that matters not. Be the woman here?"

Will heard their words. *Not after me?* Surprise and relief inched into his heart. Then, *E'en so, cain't let 'im see me.*

Cecily shook her head and said firmly, "We have no guest of that name."

Perhaps it was the authority in her voice, or more likely the lack of workmen in the courtyard, that emboldened Weldon.

He'd noted that the castle, the only obvious garrison, was farther down the Bimport; had seen that the ostlers were mostly young, and that it being winter, the masons, glaziers, carpenters, and hod carriers were—all except Wat—in the workmen's new, hastily erected lean-to beside the church.

Weldon said, curling his lip, "Mayhap she bides here despite your knowledge or command."

The abbess blew a puff of derision at the idea.

Then, "Despite your protestations, Lady, we believe that she is being… given sanctuary, so by your leave or no, we will search the premises."

"You," the abbess's voice still seemed mild, "have no authority to search."

Will risked a glance.

Ignoring the abbess, Weldon turned to survey the area for possible hiding places, and glimpsed Will as he sidestepped around the mare.

"God's blood!" Weldon bellowed. "There—the murderer! The runaway! Get him!"

As Weldon's men hurtled from their horses, Will thrust the brush into Wat's hands and pivoted into the darkness of the stable. Reaching the rear stalls, he clasped a beam with his knees, shimmied upward, grabbed the lip of the hatch, and swung his body through the opening into the hayloft. There he crawled over and into the narrowest part of the eaves, ripped into the moldy thatch, and burrowed like a dog after a badger. In seconds he had gouged a jagged hole through the side of the thatched roof. He struggled through the hole, paused to get his feet under him, and vaulted out onto the Bimport, landing arms akimbo in the dirty snow.

Weldon, behind his men, skidded to a halt in front of Wat, who trembled beside the mare.

"This man is not the man I just saw," Weldon blared, pulling the hempen fabric of Wat's tunic tight against his throat. To the abbess, who was closer behind him than he had anticipated, he bellowed, spraying spittle onto her habit, "You were hiding my serf."

Cecily's eyes iced, her chin rose, and her voice took on a timbre of command. "Unhand my stable lad. Wat has worked for this abbey since childhood (she had no idea). Her jaw was clenched. "Be clear, man, are you searching for your master's wife or for a lost serf?"

But Weldon was not to be sidetracked. Ignoring her as he would a gnat, he pointed into the dark stable. His men thundered past him with the eagerness of pillage, unsheathed their short swords and stabbed through the heaps of hay, moved tools, frightened horses, and finally climbed up into the loft where they dug like ratters through the humble bedding of the ostlers.

The deliberate loudness of the abbess's voice, however, had finally had the desired effect. From the east gate, Turgold had heard her and responded immediately with a piercing whistle meant to alert all the men within earshot. He then corralled a village urchin, one Ferghal by name, and sent him scurrying down the Bimport to alert the bailiff. Workmen in the lean-to beside the church heard Turgold's whistle and immediately picked up whatever implements presented themselves. Luckily, the smith, customarily at the forge down the High Street, was in the mason's lodge gathering blunted tools for sharpening. A shepherd, just seeing to the penned ewes, stuck his head out, saw Cecily's distress, and hefted his iron-tipped crook. Masons with their hammers, hod carriers, and carpenters emerged from the lodge to answer the call.

The first of Weldon's men reappeared from the stable, "'E's gone. Up inter the loft. Hole in the thatch."

Weldon's mouth twisted in a grimace of fury. He turned around, only to find a motley line of abbey workers blocking his way. Lips taut, he thrust his face so close to Cecily's that she smelled the acrid odor of rancid breath and unwashed body.

"Well, lady." He spat the word "lady" in such a rage that his words disintegrated into the dialect of his upbringing. "He may 'ave got away, but now I know you 'ad 'im and ye mun 'ave known it. Lying…" He didn't say "bitch," but it was on his breath. He snatched his reins and put a foot in the stirrup. "'E won't get far, and when I catch 'im, I'll be back, with 'is dead body acrost my saddle-board, to take a closer look for FitzRolf's lady." He mounted. "If Lady Isabel be found here…" He never finished the sentence.

The abbey workers made a narrow path across the courtyard to the main gate, narrow enough and bristling with so many sharp implements that Weldon's men were happy to remount and clatter out the abbey gate.

WILL'S TRACKS LED ACROSS THE Bimport and disappeared into a sliding slash down the north side of the mount, the icy, steep path on Tout Hill. To get to him, Weldon and his mounted men had to ride back along the spine of the hill and down through the town gate on the other side. Let loose in St. James, the horses stretched into a gallop.

By the time they rounded the mount, only a few huge footprints marred the snow. Will's trail soon petered out in the stubble. Weldon stared, mouth a frustrated gash, eyes on the distance. He raised a gloved hand. The men gathered round. When Weldon was through talking, they trotted off in pairs, each headed in a different direction. To those left, he said, "Without FitzRolf we can no more get Lady Isabel out of that abbey than get a horse to fly. FitzRolf himself has to tame that abbess. But at least now we know where his lady bides."

WILL HAD KNOWN HE WOULD be no match for men on horses, but panic had propelled him down Tout Hill where he had floundered across the snowy field. The thawing, soggy soil clung to his boots and dragged him down. He tripped on a rock and fell face first into an icy furrow. When at last he reached the edge of the field, Will was panting, a deep, almost bestial growl against the back of his scabbed tongue. *Verily, not much more than a beast be I without a tongue.* He blundered instinctively into a leafless willow thicket, dense and high, denying any concealment. The snow beneath the bush had melted, but farther out there were traces of animal footprints thawed into elongated grooves. Just so would his footprints lead Weldon's men to him. *'Ave to move so they cain't see where I go.* Trying for silence and keeping well within the concealing fringe of low growth, he crouched his way to the south until he reached a thicket of holly. Feisty little birds clicked and wing-flapped among the branches.

AVERILLA TOO HAD SEEN WILL FLEE INTO the stable, watched Weldon's headlong pursuit, and heard the abbess order the gate closed and bolted behind them. Fear for both Lady Isabel and Will scorched a hole in her stomach. She hurried back to the infirmary. *Why,* she asked herself, *fear I so for Will? Is it because I found him? A stray serf. Brought him here? Tended him?*

She slipped inside. "FitzRolf's steward!" Averilla hissed to Sister Blythe, trying to keep her voice down, "A Master Weldon, came for Lady Isabel! He recognized Will. Called him a murderer. Will, it seems, worked on a FitzRolf manor. Apparently burrowed through the thatch, so Weldon's men went after him out the gate."

"May God protect him." Perplexed, Blythe asked, "Down Tout Hill?"

"No, I don't suppose they could. Not on horseback. Weldon would have to go through the town gate and around the mount. It will give Will time to reach the forest."

Averilla glanced over at Isabel who hadn't reacted at the reference to the 'FitzRolf manor.' "How is she?"

"She continues to improve. Worries about her sons, but," the girl paused, "her worries have no fangs. The poppy, I wot."

Averilla nodded, then made her way down the aisle to sit next to Isabel's bed.

The movement next to her roused the woman, who smiled and stretched her arms. Poppy still swam behind her eyes. "I was dreaming of my husband, Bernard."

Averilla took Isabel's hand. "No, my lady. You must remember now. Remember you that Bernard died? Remember you that at all?"

Isabel looked confused, and after a moment, as if someone had slapped her, her face dissolved in grief. "Oh. Oh." She closed her eyes. "I hoped it was all a dream." Then, "Bernard died?" Her eyes beseeched Averilla to shake her head and say no.

Averilla's eyes softened. "We were told his horse threw him. A number of years ago."

"There was something… more." Isabel concentrated, eyes blank as if reviewing a scene only she could see. She shook her head. "I remember now. Oh, Lord, I remember." She gagged the next words into the silence between them. "I married his brother! Against all law and nicety, I married his brother."

"My lady, apparently Gervase received a dispensation."

"As if that could erase the sin!"

Averilla bit her lip.

Isabel, watching her, said, "There is more, isn't there?"

Feeling the urgency press upon her, Averilla blurted, "Gervase's steward is here. A Master Weldon. Looking for you."

Isabel's eyes narrowed and she nodded. "An ill-jointed piece of work."

"He said you had run off.

"But I didn't. I wouldn't. It is all coming back to me now. The hall and Gervase."

Isabel shut her eyes. After a while, she opened them and said determinedly to the blank wall in front of her, "I shall try to be candid. 'Tis hard. Secrecy has been my favorite weapon."

Isabel looked down at her blue-veined hands. "I resist this telling. To admit what my husband is—must be—to blame myself."

After a while, Isabel lifted her head and continued as if no time had intervened. "I overheard them talking, FitzRolf and others. I know not who. I was descending from the solar. Something they were saying. I- I can't remember exactly. Something tells me I thought it treasonous. I imagined what the king would do to my sons after such a betrayal. What was it? I don't know. But it was enough to cause me to sway and miss my footing."

Averilla allowed her glance to stray to the leg swaddled beneath the coverlet.

"No, 'twas not broken just then. I would have surely expected something like that from him. Our union, mine with Gervase, had become like a dried-up puddle in a parched wheat field, but he had never yet laid a hand on me. Except in lust." Isabel's eyes drifted as she remembered something painful. "He thrust his face close to mine. I could smell the drink-laden breath, hear the fury in his voice.

"FitzRolf bade Peter kill me; said, as he sent us off, that he would put it about that I had run away." Isabel let her head loll back onto the pillow. "My lack of love for him was well known. He could not risk an obvious murder at home—a knife, a tumbler of poison, a fall—for that would bring my sons, who hate him. He would not risk their ire.

"In the end, Peter couldn't. Kill me, that is." Her eyes widened in memory. "Peter was told to, but… so he risked his own life in allowing me to live." Again, Isabel shut her eyes, struggling with the horror. Finally, she whispered, "FitzRolf bade him use a knife. 'Slit her throat,' he said. 'Quickly. Just do it!' Did I tell you they tied my hands? I was thrust on a horse, in front of Peter, and we rode. Somewhere. Finally, before moonset, Peter slowed, to kill me, I suppose. Dawn was breaking. Did the sun pick out the rotundity of that great old stump? I know not, but as the night's mist dissolved with the last of the moon low on the horizon, in that greenish black that presages the morn, his eye lighted on the stump crouching there in the dell.

"He prodded me forward and scrabbled at the bark seeking an opening. It was my one chance. I fled. 'Twas but a few steps before he caught me and pushed me through an opening in the stump." She shuddered. "The sun, just rising, gave light to the inside. Peter's eyes fell to his shoes as he fingered the knife and saw the stout limb lying there. He lunged, swung it, and broke my leg. The rest you know. Still I live. And FitzRolf found out and has sent someone to fetch me. So you see, Dame, your abbey is at risk, and I would not have any other innocent death on my conscience. I will let him take me."

Averilla held up a calming hand. "No, never. But certainly not now. Weldon has left. He recognized a runaway serf. The one we call Will. Will saw Weldon and fled, through the stables and over the wall. Weldon went after him but said he would soon be back. I suppose he means to bring FitzRolf."

"You must send for my sons."

"Your sons?"

"Gaston and Michael. By my first husband, Bernard. They are in Winchester, with the king. My sons want only a reason to battle their stepfather."

Averilla rose. "A messenger will be sent."

"Dame underestimate him not. FitzRolf can be… daunting."

"The abbess showed no love for this man Weldon. Dame
Joan will be told to send a messenger. We have, I imagine, little
time. I need to think of a place to conceal you."

Isabel closed her eyes, trying to forbid fear.

Chapter Twenty-two

Averilla patted Isabel's hand, grabbed her cloak, and started toward the offices. She pushed open the door, and Dame Joan greeted her with the merest nod. Averilla tensed, knowing what would likely ensue.

Joan began to rant, spittle flying, "What mischief now? You fill the court with murder and contagion. Dumb Will might slit out throats. Lepers in the workmen's lodgings is much too close. Even Queen Matilda's hospital of St. Giles is out in the country." My duty is to protect the abbey. To make certain all the rules are obeyed, to keep the community from harm. Everyone—absolutely everyone—dreads leprosy!" Her mouth tightened into an unpleasant line of triumph. "It matters little to those who catch it that the queen kissed a leper. My duty is to keep it from spreading in this enclosure. Cecily needs nobles to stay and bring gifts and benefices! They will shun the place when they learn we harbor lepers.

"And then there is the mute giant," Joan continued. "Weldon confirmed our suspicions. You heard him. Called Will a murderer! It is all your doing. Your selfishness has poisoned Cecily's mind."

Averilla put both hands on Joan's table and leaned in, beseeching. "Dame, Will was the abbess's choice; the lepers were Dame Elizabeth's. Both those things are beyond my control and duty, but Lady Isabel is in my charge. She avers that FitzRolf and Weldon are threatening her life. Could you, would you, please ask the abbess to send for Lady Isabel's sons to untangle this mess? She says they are with the court at Winchester. She is very frightened of her husband. Don't you think it is our duty to help her?

Something dark moved behind Joan's beady eyes. "Lady Isabel isn't even a guest. We can expect no gift. What in the name of Saint Swithin do we really know about her? Like as not she *did* run away from her husband. Joan paused as if coming to a decision, then said, as one granting a boon to a petitioner, "I will tell the abbess. When it is convenient."

FEELING DISPIRITED AND HELPLESS TO overcome the obstacles Joan was throwing in her path, Averilla dragged herself back to the infirmary, where she hung up her cloak. *So tired. Ethelind. Oh, Ethelind. What will I do without you? And Will now alone and hunted? Elizabeth taking on leprosy? And now, oh, Lord, where can we hide Lady Isabel? Forgive me my weakness, oh Lord. And my fear for them and of them. Please bring Maud back."*

"Dame Averilla!" The voice was soft and hoarse, but somehow managed to slide under the coughing and quiet murmurs of the infirmary. *Scholastica? Oh, please, no, not now! I just can't take anymore.* Wearily, grimly obedient, willing herself to be kind, Averilla headed toward the bed nearest the hearth.

"My dear," Scholastica reached out a veined and spotted hand and patted the bed. "Sit down."

"Dame, I- I have to…"

The hand clenched. "Dame." It was a command.

Averilla perched, like a dog waiting to be loosed.

"The world is too much with you. I can see it in your eyes." Averilla's shoulders slumped. "You must go, now, my child, to the brode hall. Sit and meditate—at least until the bell rings for Vespers. Longer if you need to."

"Dame, I cannot."

"I know. I am old and perhaps fey, but I order you to rest not on my own. It is the same order Our Lord gave to His apostles when they came back exhausted from preaching and healing. Besides," the kind voice subtly hardened. "Remember you your vow my dear," the aged face forced a smile. "Remember you the third step of humility," Scholastica repeated, "which teaches us to submit ourselves 'in all obedience' to our superiors?" Averilla heaved a great sigh and lowered her eyes. "So, as your superior, if not in command then at least in age, I send you to the brode hall. Sit there in silence and let the Holy Spirit minister to you. Allow Him to ease the weight of this yoke that is burdening you and is of your own making."

"But… but I have to—"

"Remember Mercy."

Thinking Scholastica meant "God's mercy," Averilla bowed her head.

"No, not *that* mercy," the old woman huffed. "Although that mercy must always be in our minds. No, I speak of the herbarium cat. When you caught him, that tiny ball of gray fluff you held in your palm, would immediately relax, lie on his back, soothed and calm. Try to be like Mercy in God's hand."

They held one another's eyes, and then Averilla rose, simultaneously beckoning to Sister Blythe. Her instructions to the latter were given in a breathy un-Averilla-like voice. The bell for None rang from Mary Minor, a bell smaller than Great Dunstan, that tolled for the minor offices. *I will miss None,* Averilla thought. *I should—*

As if reading her mind, Scholastica said, "Yes, you will miss None, perhaps even Vespers. You have been too busy. You must rest. You need Sabbath, more than anyone else in the abbey. Remember, my child, that God himself rested. And our Lord went away to be quiet and to speak to God. And child"—reluctantly, Averilla turned—"I will pray for you. Remember, the devil delights in our moments of despair and uses them."

Averilla looked at Scholastica's hands, now calmly lying on the coverlet, seeming all knots and veins and bones, and thought, *Scholastica has been in the abbey all her life. She will know of some obscure place where we can hide Isabel.*

"I will go," she said finally, "but first I have a question.

Scholastica's eyebrows rose in a disapproving smile. "I will answer if I can."

"Know you of some secret place in the abbey where we might conceal Lady Isabel?

Scholastica eyes retreated into memory. "Aye, indeed I do. The treasury."

"But the men searching will make us open it."

"Mayhap, but there is a secret in the treasury. We all know that the abbey plate is stored there in the crypt, protected by an iron grille, but behind those shelves, hidden by the silver, is a false wall that leads to a small tunnel carved into the rock. Isabel could be hidden there. No one else remembers it, so no one else would know."

"But if I go now, who will get her to the crypt?"

"Weldon will not return before morning. There will be time to move Lady Isabel when you have come back."

THE SODDEN THAW OF THE afternoon was firming into ice, and the evening shadows were extinguishing the last glimmers of day. Will tensed, listening, but there was no sound, neither of horses nor of men. The few winter birds had resumed their preparations for night. Nothing unusual disturbed them. Will attempted to stretch his left leg. He had bruised the knee badly in his headlong rush down Tout Hill. Now, without warning, his right leg cramped. He was stretching through the agony when he heard them.

Hoofbeats. Slow. Weldon? One of his men? Will waited, deliberately slowed his breathing, stilling as he had seen rabbits do when a fox neared.

The sudden screech of a nearby crow sent cold fear down his back. Will shut his eyes to hide the shine of their whites. The crow, now more strident, was joined by its fellows, and, frantic with ire at the territorial trespass, the entire murder rose with a noisy clacking of wings. As the birds flew off, Will caught a whiff of the horses, could hear the creak of the men's saddles, and the cricks of a hoof against a stone. *So close. Know they I be here?*

A muttered word. "Footprint?"

I should 'ave brushed out the tracks.

"Naw. Snowmelt around a cone."

Leather creaked against leather. "Iffen 'e went in there—well, you go look. Too close to night for me."

"Too close? For what?"

"Masterless men. Worth your hide to go in there alone."

"But Weldon will—"

Weldon's not going in there, is he? No. Need dogs for that. Or more men. Any rood, need to get back by the time FitzRolf arrives. 'Tis him we answer to, not Weldon. Weldon won't know what we did or didna do."

With a clicking of tongues and the sound of horses trotting off, they were gone.

Chapter Twenty-three

eldon was impatient by the time the last of the scouts finally arrived at the assigned meeting point. He turned to one of them, a man named Thord, who was not only huge but was as close to a snake as anyone Weldon had ever known—wily and completely without conscience. Weldon had seen him do unspeakable things in the course of a day, and what Weldon wanted of him now would bear hard on the conscience of a normal man. He fixed his stare on the distant trees. "You know what to do. When it is done, meet us back by the path to the hermit's hut."

As Weldon and the others cantered off, Thord studied Shaftesbury on its hill, surrounded by the sharp, angled stakes of its wooden palisade, and nodded. He turned his horse onto the track leading back into the town. To do as Weldon had asked, Thord needed to examine it while there was still light. He cantered around the other end of the mount and up to the town gate. The gateman had heard what had happened to Will earlier, and was leery of Weldon's intent, but as Thord was alone, the gatekeeper confined himself to a glare.

Thord was well aware of furtive looks from the cottages as he paced the huge, black horse along the High Street, his dead eyes restless, probing. He came to a market in front of the eastern abbey wall where another street fell down the hill. He assessed its potential: Too steep and too much in the open to be of use to a man on a horse. The abbey wall, unlike the palisade that wove along the entire perimeter of the mount, was of stone. Almost invisible, on that side an iron gate was fixed. Instead of staring at it, Thord studied the abbey roofs protruding above the wall, an uneven line of varied materials from thatch to tile to wood. He walked the horse farther down the Bimport to the front of the abbey, passed its main gate—now firmly closed—and continued as far as the unprepossessing stone and wooden castle. He didn't speak to the guards, just turned his mount and headed back, scanning for loose stones along the wall and paying close attention to the slope and construction of the roofs abutting it. His attitude was casual, a man admiring the view. He paid particular attention to the steep drop of Tout Hill opposite the abbey's main gate. Here too a palisade of sharpened poles protected the summit, but it was in ill repair and he knew it for the place the murderer had escaped. Thord finished his reconnaissance before the bell for None finished tolling. He trotted down the hill, chuckling to himself at the thought of the grim report the gatekeeper at the town gate would give. They had no idea. Not yet.

At the bottom of the hill, Thord turned north, cantered back around the mount, and on the other side, brought his horse to a halt inside a small copse. This part of the year, this time of day, there was no one to see him. He tied the horse to a tree, flipped open his saddle bag, removed a handful of oats, and opened his hand to the soft nose of the horse. Thord flung his waxed-cloak onto the frozen ground in a clear spot, wrapped his mantle around his body, crossed his legs, and sat. Here he would watch until the full winter dark had descended.

As Averilla dragged her feet across the courtyard, she thought of all the things she had let go of, all the things she should be doing. She started to pass the tracing house and stopped—she should check on the lepers and Elizabeth. She knocked on the door. After a moment, Dame Elizabeth whispered, "Who is it?"

"'Tis I," said Averilla. Elizabeth opened the door a crack and pulled her inside.

"Dame Scholastica has sent me to the brode hall. To pray and rest."

"I think that will be hard for you."

"Does everyone know that? Everyone but me?"

"Mayhap keeping yourself busy keeps you from being with God. Is it possible that instead of loving Him you focus on yourself, on whether or not you are doing something worthy? He loves you. He wants you to open yourself to Him."

Averilla's eyes opened wide. "If everyone else sees it, I wonder that I do not."

"That is what you must talk to Him about."

A loud pounding shattered the calm. Francine jumped and ran protectively to Ellen and crouched over her. The pounding got louder. Averilla drew the bolt and cracked the door. Before her loomed the bulk of John the Mason. With no salutation, nod, or bow, he pushed the door fully open, crossed to the shelves, and shoved the small model of the finished church under his arm. Remembering himself, he nodded cursorily to Averilla and Elizabeth, and, eyes straying momentarily to Francine, nodded again and left. Elizabeth stared, astounded by the unusual lack of civility.

"Fear does that," muttered Francine, noting Elizabeth's bewilderment. She hobbled back to retrieve her coverlet, wrapped herself in it, and, running a hand over the old wool, said, "It don't mean aught toward us. Just fear."

Elizabeth looked at Ellen, still asleep, warm in her own cocoon-like coverlet, and said, "I suppose we need to wash Ellen?" It was a question. After seeing Francine's leg, the idea of revealing Ellen's devastated body made her spirit falter.

Francine gave a huge yawn. "Not now. It be late. Hard, coming through the forest, and difficult getting all that food in. Leave 'er be." Before Elizabeth could think of anything more to add, Francine sank down, curled herself around Ellen, and went to sleep.

WILL DIDN'T KNOW WHAT HAD wakened him. The sky was the blue-black of a winter's evening, the bare tree limbs mere scrawls against it. Moonlight filtered through the gnarled branches. Had there been a crack just now? Some sinister sound not right for the forest at evening? Will's whole body tensed. The sound came again. No, not a crack. Just the bark of a fox. He could imagine the feisty little fellow, his red coat grayed with winter. So if there was a fox… one that barked… then there was no man nearby. While he dozed, Will had come to a decision: Now was not the time to run. Night would freeze and encase his massive footprints in ice for Weldon's men to find and follow. Even if he kept to the forest paths, there was little to eat in a winter wood. The edible berries had shriveled and gone. The nuts were rotten or hidden, and the animals were burrowed too deep.

No, the abbey was his only choice. The time to go back was the present, when he knew exactly where Weldon's men were, and that for the time being they had given up looking for him. He must accept the abbess's offer of sanctuary, get behind the altar or wherever it was this church had attached the sanctuary ring, and stay there for a year and a day. He was so tired. The thought of just lying near the altar in the quiet of the church was strangely appealing. He unfurled himself and stood, waiting for his aching knee to ease, his mind's eye searching the fields for the best path back to the abbey. There was no cover. He pushed through the clump of holly, lengthened his legs into a stunted sprint, and stumbled back across the furrows. He knew he was slow. He knew he'd have to enter through the abbey main gate before the office of Compline ended and the gates would be locked for the night. His knee felt as if a leather thong connected his calf to his thigh and clicked and stabbed at each step. It was all he could do to move ahead. *Will they let me in, now that they know I be a murderer?* The moon alternately darkened and brightened with scudding clouds. Will cautioned himself: *If I can see, I can be seen.* He kept his head down, relying on the camouflage of hair and beard, the dun color of the (new to him) sheepskin, and slogged on. *Them in the castle. Bound to see me. A murderer. Be their duty to take me.*

He headed for Tout Hill, which he had earlier hurtled down. At the bottom he paused, his breath rasping against his mangled tongue. It had been easy to slide down Tout Hill. Going up was a different proposition altogether. The path was steep, and now slick with ice, and his knee threatened to give out. He placed one foot horizontally across the incline and immediately slid back. He tried again, digging in with his good knee. The footing seemed secure, but then his foot slipped. Grappling for foot- and handholds, he clambered his way upward, using his elbows and good knee. As often as he rose, he slipped backward, his hands losing their tenuous grip. Partway up, his hand gripped a rock. He bent his good knee, and, placing all the tension on his bad one, crooked his foot. The injured knee collapsed, but the rock held. With the last of his energy he boosted himself up using only the strength of his arms, muscles aquiver. As he teetered there near the edge of the precipice, the sound of a whinny came from somewhere behind him. *Weldon?* The sound of the horse was enough to give Will the energy to lever himself the last few feet to the top.

He grabbed the bottom of a stake, one of the uneven teeth in the palisade, lay flat, then slithered his way first under and then between the crossed poles. There he stilled, listened, and tried to see sound, willing the muffled whinny to come again. He was just bringing his feet up when he lifted his head and saw, standing above him, one—no, two—no, three—men-at-arms from the castle. His body froze. *They must see me.*

Nothing happened.

Why do they wait?

Chapter Twenty-four

verilla left the tracing house. *Bless Dame Elizabeth*, she thought. *Helping the lepers will give her time for God, but...* She skirted the nun's graveyard on her right but was dragging her feet as she neared the brode hall. Scholastica and Elizabeth were right: Averilla knew that she was exhausted, emotionally and physically, from the chaos of the last week. She knew she needed to take out her thoughts, examine herself and why she so avoided giving herself wholly to God, but she feared to unleash a whirlwind.

The brode hall stood before Averilla, empty and dim, only the glimmer of light from the pottery vessel that kept the coals alight overnight, peeped through the shutters. The brode hall was where ornate liturgical vestments were embroidered for abbeys and priories the length and breadth of Europe. The work was called English work, and the garments embellished in Shaftesbury were much sought after.

Averilla pushed open the door and felt her way inside, letting her eyes adjust to the dimness. She plopped onto a near bench and inhaled deeply the smell of warmed wool and silk. In the gloom, the intricate swirls of mesmerizing gold on copes (bishops' capes) and chasubles (tunics) still gave off a faint gleam. Nor could the shadows entirely veil the bright-colored silks, linens, and wools—red for martyrs, green for growth, purple for penitence, and whites for purity of the Christian year—that waited to be cut, sewn, and embroidered. Looms of varied sizes stood along the back wall, their warping thread holding either black for the wool habits, or coarse, off-white linen intended for shifts and undergarments. One smaller loom was used only for the innumerable altar linens such as burses, veils, and purificators.

Averilla relaxed into the caress of the quiet. Tentacles of grief tiptoed into her calm. She felt tears brim. Her mind vacillated from one emotion to another. Impotent rage at Ethelind's murderer dissolved into guilt. *I didn't speak a kind word when I had a chance.* A recognition of her own selfishness followed. *I was paying attention only to myself.* A bleak loneliness pounced and dug in its claws. *Maud. Dear God, send Maud back to me.* Fear lashed her into alertness. *Will. What will he do now? Where can he go?*

Averilla bowed her head. Just as she closed her eyes, she caught a glimpse of her folded hands in her lap. She peered closer, then held her right hand in front of her. Her hands no longer trembled! A frisson of awe crept up her back and lifted the hairs on her head. So, Madge and the Living Water had…? Could that be true? Averilla released her held breath. *Thank you, Lord God.* She shut her eyes and gazed on the red behind her lids until her breathing slowed and she knew peace.

WILL WAITED FOR THE MEN to call and haul him upright. But no! Unaccountably, the bailiff's men continued unaware of his nearness. *How is that possible?* One of them spat, loudly, and mumbled something. The others laughed, then all three sauntered back to the castle. Will waited for the space of a paternoster, then boosted himself into a crouch and crabbed across the Bimport to the gatehouse. Fire baskets flickered, one on each side of the gate. There was a squeak as a rat scuttled and disappeared. *Let*

the gate not be locked, he prayed, then leaned against the gate and gave two weak blows. *Let me in. Oh, God, let the portress let me back in.* There was an interminable wait, but then movement. *Some'un still 'ere. Let it be a nun.*

The grille slid back and the portress peered out. "Benedic—" but her formulaic greeting stuttered into "Will—you're back!" She slammed the grille. His heart sank. He heard her bump and fumble until finally came the rasping grind of metal as she jostled the key into the lock. *Oh, Mother Mary, thank you!* Will stumbled through the slot gate, jerky and drunk with fatigue.

"We were so worried." She seemed almost angry.

Worriet?

"You must get into the church, to take sanctuary! Hurry! One of them came back, riding along the Bimport. Not long ago. He might return, so you must be in the church. To the altar. The Sanctuary ring is there. Behind it. I'll tell the abbess. She told the bailiff earlier you were not to be harmed. Saw you his men?" She peered at him, concern wrinkling her kind face. "You are so tired." Then coaxing, "But you must be in the church. I'll send for Father Merowald" She lifted her skirts and hurried in the direction of the stables, seeking an ostler to summon the old priest.

Will leaned his head against the gatehouse wall waiting for the stitch in his side to ease. Each inhalation was a razor on the nub of his tongue. He could taste new blood. *Scabs must 'ave opened.* He looked across the court to the church, then slid down the wall and slumped onto his hocks, A rising wind lifted his hair. An owl hooted. *First get my breath. Just a short jog, but…*

Chapter Twenty-five

uring the winter, because of the shortness of the days, Compline followed quickly on Vespers. For most nuns, the office of Compline was beloved, especially in winter. The summer's nights always tasted humid, but in winter, as they waited in the cloister under the stars, the air was sharp with cold, and brittle with the piercing winds. So when they entered this night, the dark held the sweet, thick smell of old beeswax and stone must and the warmth of the braziers at their feet. It was homey, comforting, and full, and as the nuns glided silently into the dark, the cellarer's candle overpowered the gloom—the power of just one candle against the dark. As each nun lighted her candle from the nun ahead of her, the light bloomed and strengthened, probing the dim recesses of the church. When they had settled, the cantor's voice rose in the antiphon.

When the bell for Compline clanged, low and deep, Will had jerked into wakefulness. Nothing moved across the flags, and the western door of the church remained resolutely closed. Will had not permitted himself to enter the church during his days of convalescence. Dread had stayed him. *Blasphemy. A murderer in the church. But… cain't confess without a tongue. How repent*

and be shriven? He hardened his jaw, which caused another searing pain to shoot through his mouth.

Suddenly a pinpoint of light gleamed through the horn windows. Then another. Finally, the many flickers merged into one warm glow. *Nuns got into the church. 'Av to try to get in now while they be busy.* Will slowly rose. The old parish church at the manor where he had grown up had had a small hall, right inside the main door, a place for folk to stamp the snow and dirt from their feet. *Be a place to hide 'til they stop singing. The portress was kind, but others may not be as glad to have a murderer in their midst.* He tensed, crouched, keeping as low as possible, and with his last ounce of energy crabbed across to the church. *Please, God, let the door be open.* The great ring that served as door handle turned easily, and as he tugged the iron banded boards open, one voice, low and rich and full of color, soared on the night.

"The Lord Almighty grant us a peaceful night."

The full-throated answer from myriad voices, "And a peaceful end," covered the grate of the latch and the creak of the door as Will stumbled inside. He pulled the door into place but did not slam it for fear of the sound. Then, slowly, alert to any hesitation in the chant, he edged to the right, one step at a time. He had heard the nuns' voices before, faintly from the orchard, but never had he been so close to the ethereal sounds—light and pure and piercing—that floated aloft and echoed around the nave, bounding back and forth from stone wall to stone wall. The words were Latin, but it didn't matter to him. Tears ran down his face as he again allowed his body to slide to the floor.

THORD WAITED ON THE GROUND across from the mount, dozing, yet aware of the noises around him. With amusement he watched Will stumble across the field. *Weldon would be glad*

to know where the churl was holed up. That would be for later. Thord had other orders.

When he heard the bell for Compline, it was full dark. He rose, stretched, shook out his cloak, and stood listening. Hearing nothing untoward, he loped across the field to the bottom of Tout Hill where he had watched Will struggle to the top. Thord snapped his whip upward and it looped over a palisade stake. He yanked, not trusting the sturdiness of the chosen stake, having seen the ill repair of the entire rampart on his earlier reconnaissance. He mounted with the stealth of a man determined, testing each handhold, easing his foot onto each rock before putting his full weight on it. He had earlier decided against entering the abbey compound by way of the hole in the thatch that Will had earlier created. Ostlers probably slept in the loft; most likely had already patched it. His earlier investigation had revealed a long, low building with a tile roof and an open smoke hole—his chosen destination.

Thord snaked through the stakes of the palisade and darted across the Bimport. He hunched from shadow to shadow, keeping close to the abbey wall. At the slightest sound, he stopped. The stable was obvious from its odor. Where the roof tiles of the embroidery hall protruded over the wall, he listened, glanced around and, placing his hands flat on the tiles, leapt, flipping his legs up so he lay parallel to the edge, tense in case someone had heard the thump of his landing. After several long moments, he rose and crept along the spine of the roof. From the corner of his eye, he saw a movement. He stopped. There, beside the gatehouse, someone was running low across the court to the church. Thord clenched his jaw, and then, recognizing Will—*So, heading for the church*—relaxed.

Thord slithered along the roof spine until he reached the hole that vented the hearth. He grunted in satisfaction. The flap was propped open and the hole was large, which would make it possible for him to slide through. He thrust his legs into the hole, swiveled his hips, drew his arms together close over his head to make his torso as narrow as possible, and let go. He landed like a cat, then stilled, breath shallow, waiting, probing the dimness with his mind. Yes. Over to his left. An outline. A lone nun, as silent as he was, immobile. He smiled. *Pure luck, that.* He pulled one arm out of his wool gorget, a combination of cape and hood, and after a moment the other, finally pulling the whole thing over his head. With his eating knife, he sliced the hood from the main body of the cape, below the ties. Holding only the severed hood, he put the toes of his left foot down, relaxed his arch, and brought his right foot forward, step by deliberate step.

AVERILLA, HAVING DESCENDED TO THE very depth of her soul, barely breathed. She didn't register the strange thump on the roof, nor did the faint shuffling along the roof spine do any more than deepen her sense of peace, the sense that here in the abbey she was protected. Troubles occurred and violence happened, but still God was with her. The louder thump on the hearth, the ripping of fabric, brought her up but not out of her prayer. She slipped back down, down.

A huge hand closed around her windpipe. She opened her mouth to scream but could only emit a choking gag. She felt herself being hauled backwards. The pressure on her throat increased. Her mind shuddered. *Will? Oh, Will, did I so misjudge you?* The pressure was suddenly released, and Averilla dropped to the floor. She gasped for breath and fumbled for her throat. *Oh, Will.* Her hands were yanked behind her and tied. With a strap—leather—*a whip?* Veil and wimple were ripped from her head—*the cold, vulnerable nakedness of it.* A slight sound came from outside. A hand was clamped over her mouth.

She bit down. Hard.

Her assailant swore, long and low.

It took Averilla a minute for it to register. *He swore?!* Realization banished disappointment. *Oh, thank God. The man speaks. So he isn't Will!*

Chapter Twenty-six

A hood, dense, smelly, and suffocating, dropped over Averilla's head. Thord smiled grimly. He had got himself a nun sooner than he had expected and with much less trouble. Averilla braced herself and fought back, scratching and kicking like a cat in a sack. She was unprepared for the power of Thord's fist as he slammed it against her hooded head. Pain bloomed red against Averilla's eyes, and she slumped to the floor, unconscious.

Thord sucked at the oozing blood on his hand. Having her unconscious would make everything that much easier. He shook his head, silently cursing Weldon's decision to pursue the runaway serf. They should have just snatched a nun when they first arrived, as FitzRolf had commanded. He went over, pushed open the door, and peered out. How was he going to get her out of the abbey, across the field, and onto his horse?

Thord was a cautious man; wouldn't have been alive were he not. Warily, he studied the outer court and graveyard. His pale eyes fixed for a long moment on the sides of the church; inside, the nuns chanted, oblivious to the violence against one of their own.

But not all of them. Prioress Aethwulfa, mid-chant, paused, frowned, and looked around as if suddenly aware of something amiss. She counted her chicks. Prioresses were universally referred to as "Mother," but here at Shaftesbury the term was applied with deep reverence, for Dame Aethwulfa was as truly beloved as the most loving natural mother.

She counted again, alarm growing. Averilla was missing. Aethwulfa realized that, because of her work in the infirmary, the infirmaress was required to attend only one of the two evening offices, but, and this was what concerned Aethwulfa, Averilla had attended neither. And Averilla caused Aethwulfa particular worry. The strange illness that had beset Averilla just the year before made any deviation in her activity a cause for scrutiny. As the other nuns started to sing the middle hymn, Aethwulfa rose, bowed to the abbess, and made her way out through the southern door. Her abrupt and unheard-of departure caused a hesitation in the singing.

That break in the rhythm, that faltering, startled Will from the deep drowse he had fallen into. He felt the disturbed air as another door opened and closed. *Mayhap the abbess heard of my coming, and now knowing that I be a murderer, sent some'un for the bailiff? Won't want 'er nuns with a murderer at their backs? Or mayhap some'un sent to fetch Weldon? But if I be at the altar, cain 'e still take me?*

Aethwulfa hobbled through the outer court and the snow-pillowed bushes of the herbarium, then, without knocking, opened the infirmary door.

"Dame Averilla," she panted to the nearest lay sister.

The girl, startled by the opening door, belatedly bowed. "Er, not here, Mother. Dame Scholastica sent her to the brode hall around None. For quiet. Sabbath."

The prioress glanced over to where Scholastica lay asleep. Surely Averilla would have returned by Compline, wouldn't she? Aethwulfa bowed wearily to the girl, squared her shoulders, and, grasping the door lintel, wobbled outside. She trudged back through the herbarium and shambled over the icy flags of the outer court, her corns and the unfortunate swelling on her big toe, as she had feared they would, strenuously objecting to the unaccustomed exertion.

THORD FINISHED PROBING EVERY ELL of the courtyard. Leaving the door propped open, he hoisted Averilla onto his shoulder. He was just maneuvering her through the door when he spied, across the court, a nun, old if he could judge by her walk, heading from the shadows into the flickering light of the fire baskets. Since he could see her, she could see him.

AT THE GATE, THE PORTRESS had been shifting from foot to foot like an impatient urchin, eager to tell the abbess about Will's return. Finally someone—was heading toward her. *But the singing hasn't yet stopped! So who?* She squinted. A long veil, so certainly *a professed nun*, but the plump, limping figure crossing the outer court and backlit by the fire baskets wasn't the abbess. *The prioress?! Was the abbess ill?* The portress stepped down and hurried across the intervening distance. "Benedicte, Mother."

"Benedicte, Dame. Has Dame Averilla—?"

"Aye. Oh, aye. To the brode hall, around None."

"And you have not seen her return?"

"Nooo."

The prioress sagged in relief. "Oh." Then, "Good. I will go to her. Just to make sure."

The portress blurted, "Mother! Wait! You need to know. Will has come back."

"Will? Here?"

"Aye. Before Compline. Went toward the church. Seeking sanctuary. But you saw him not there? I saw him go in myself. Right at the beginning of Compline."

Aethwulfa frowned. "No. No we saw him not in the church, but... how can Will ask for sanctuary? He can't speak."

It was a nicety the portress hadn't considered. Her mouth rounded in an "O" as the thought stumped her for a moment. "But certes, we would all understand. He would have only to take hold of the ring."

THORD AGAIN PEERED OUT THE door. His brow narrowed into a deep "V." Used to getting his own way by dint of size and strength, he was frustrated to the bursting point. The damned cow was now headed straight for them. *Looking for this one, most likely. Why else come here while all the rest sing?* He carted Averilla back to the looms and placed her down almost gently, afraid to wake her. Shoving her beneath the loom, would be sure to rouse her. Assessing, he looked around, chose the safety of dimness, and grabbed a length of black fabric. He tossed it over her, and hid himself behind a bishop's cope that hung beside the loom. He heard footsteps hesitate outside, and wondered whether he had left the door ajar.

AVERILLA LEFT THE DOOR AJAR, Aethwulfa thought irritably, *and let all that blessed warmth escape.* She entered hesitantly, pulled the door firmly closed, and squinted into the shadows. "Averilla?" she hissed. "Are you here?" Aethwulfa thought she detected a faint rustling near the looms, and craned her neck. She didn't want to investigate for fear of stumbling in the dark. She turned around and studied the door, finally deciding that

Averilla must have gone back out. *Surely that is it. Someone came and got her. Someone sick in the town? Turgold will know. She will have told him. But why not tell anyone else? But everyone else was in the church—I am sure of it—so Averilla took no companion.* That thought alone, the lack of a companion, made the hair on the back of Aethwulfa's neck rise. Had Averilla lost her sight again? Had she never reached the brode hall? Had she stumbled into the graveyard and fallen, or gotten lost? "Oh, Lord!"

Prodded by fear, Aethwulfa gritted her teeth, for the pain in her foot was now a sharp stabbing that went up her leg, and she hobbled out the door.

WHEN COMPLINE ENDED, THE ABBESS detached herself from the procession bound for the night stairs, and hurried into the shadowed outer court to lock the gate, worriedly fingering the swirls on the ornate iron key tucked in her sleeve. She had been stunned when Aethwulfa had gotten up in the middle of Compline and headed out the door. *To leave in the midst of an office! Unheard of! Where did she go? Mayhap the portress will have seen her.*

The portress had descended the steps and was now outside the gatehouse. When the abbess was nearly across the court, the portress hurried to greet her. "Benedicte, Lady Abbess, I—"

Cecily raised her brows. The rule of St. Benedict was clear. There was to be no talking after Compline.

"May I speak?"

The abbess nodded.

"The prioress was here seeking Dame Averilla. I told her I saw her—Dame Averilla that is—enter the brode hall before Vespers. But Averilla never came out. And neither has Aethwulfa!"

Cecily glanced toward the east gate. "You told Aethwulfa about Averilla? And she went to fetch her?"

"But, my lady, neither has returned." She twisted her fingers together and, like a child needing to tell all her news at once, blurted, "But Will is back."

"Will?"

"Aye. Horrible tired he was. I sent him to the church for sanctuary. I sent Brach from the stables to tell Father."

WHEN AETHWULFA CLOSED THE BRODE hall door, Thord relaxed. He had nearly panicked when Averilla's arm slid off her body and hit the floor, but the old biddy hadn't heard, or if she had, had dismissed it. It was absurd, these comings and goings in an abbey at night. Easier, he told himself, to have taken the nun while we were all together and in force. Time had been wasted looking for the serf. Soon, men from the castle would undoubtedly come to guard the main gate and the side gate for the night. "The side gate!" He hefted Averilla back onto his shoulder and stuck his head out the door. Looking right and left, he saw the old nun limping toward the east gate to fetch the gatekeep. Not back inside. He'd be trapped. The gatekeep would look closer. By the flickering torchlight he made out the shapes of tombs, just across from the brode hall. Among the smaller slabs loomed one larger than the rest. He crouched across the cobbles and laid Averilla, again gently, onto the frozen ground behind the large tomb. She moaned. He held his hand above her mouth, ready to stifle any sudden sound.

"DAME AVERILLA NOT IN THE brode hall?" Turgold peered in confusion at Aethwulfa who was now panting and clutching her side.

"But I saw her enter." He glanced over the gate into the corn market, then pulled his sheepskin from its hook. In the court, torchlight glazed leftover patches of snow but revealed no movement.

"No, she is not. I did look." Aethwulfa, who never was perturbed, sounded worried.

Turgold twisted a torch-head into the brazier. The pitch-soaked reed fiber caught instantly.

"Why went she to the brode hall? At night? Surely…"

"Scholastica sent her there. Poor thing has been fraught, what with Will and Ethelind and Lady Isabel. Enough to exhaust a saint. And Averilla…" But Aethwulfa didn't finish. "Dame Scholastica wisely saw that Averilla badly needed to rest. But do you suppose—the blindness—I mean, could she have stumbled out and—?"

"I would 'ave seen 'er," Turgold said. Everything in him rebelled against leaving his post, but if Averilla had hurt herself… *It will take but a moment,* he told himself, *and the men from the castle will be here soon,* then shut the door to the little hut, checked the bolt on the gate, and, putting a hand under the prioress's arm to steady her, hurried toward the brode hall. When they reached it, he pushed the door open with his foot and, holding the torch high, stepped into the warm room. Turgold's search was quick and thorough, the thought of the unguarded east gate gnawing at his mind. He pawed quickly among the hanging copes and chasubles, patted the huge bolts of black and white wool, and paused as he passed the hearth. When he got to the looms he again hesitated. There, near what the nuns referred to as the loom's cage (he had learned the word putting one of the wretched things together) was a puddle.

"She may have been 'ere," he said grimly, his northern accent so broad Aethwulfa could barely understand him. "An' so was some'un else."

Chapter Twenty-seven

From his position behind the tomb, silently cursing Weldon and all his ancestors, Thord watched while the nun and gatekeeper went into the brode hall. They exited quickly—*too quickly. I must 'ave left some sign.* He watched them hurry toward the main gatehouse. Thord smiled. The side gate was now unguarded.

THE EYES OF THE PORTRESS wandered distractingly from Cecily's face to stare at something over her shoulders. Cecily turned. Two figures hastened—albeit one with a pronounced limp—arm in arm from the brode hall. Cecily grasped the arm of the portress. "Why is Turgold not in his place at the east gate?"

Turgold, still some yards away, yelled, "Some'un was in the brode hall. Mayhap Averilla, but some'un else too. There be wet under the big loom."

"Someone else was in the brode hall?" Cecily asked, "And is not there now?"

"I saw a footprint in the ashes on the hearth. A man's. A big man. And a bit of water" he repeated, closer now. "Melted snow, near the loom."

"Who could want a nun? It must have been someone who was ill. But they would have asked at the infirmary and entered through the gate, and you would have seen them."

"I went there first," interrupted Aethwulfa, "and was told that no one came to the infirmary begging help. Averilla was sent to the brode hall by Dame Scholastica."

"You are telling me that there might be a strange man in the enclosure?" The abbess's voice rose. "Send someone from the stables to the castle." Then, "But who was it? Could it have been Will? He came back. Mayhap… Turgold, ring the bell. Torches. We need torches to search. Every nook and cranny of the enclosure. We'll do what we can until the bailiff arrives."

THORD AGAIN SHOULDERED AVERILLA AND lurched toward the east gate. The key was easily found, and when he inserted it the well-oiled latch opened with ease. With his burden, he slipped out the gate and into the concealing shadows of the abbey wall. Thord went along the Bimport, staying within the shadows and ignoring the sounds of panic from the other side of the abbey walls. The nun's body bounced against his back as he ran. At Tout Hill he bent and lowered Averilla, holding onto her waist and one limp arm. He let go of the arm and pushed, watching coldly as the body rolled and bumped and then lay still. He followed, feet sliding. Averilla moaned. Disregarding her, he whistled softly for his mount. The horse now beside him, Thord propped Averilla against his leg. Then, Thord drew back his arm and slapped Averilla's face. One eye half-opened. She looked at him uncomprehendingly, trying to focus. He pulled her upright and, clasping her neck in his huge hand, dug his thumb beneath her jaw, his sour breath harsh on her face. "On the horse. No guff." When she nodded blearily, he tightened the gag and made his hands into a stirrup. Averilla drooped, a rag doll. He forced her bound hands up so she could grab—reflexively—the pommel, then shoved her up in front of the saddle board. He was up behind her in a bound.

In his hut next to the church of St. James, Father Merowald made his few preparations for sleep. His cottage was blessedly quiet, a refuge and sanctuary from the busyness of the abbey. He usually spent the time between Vespers and Compline—and often long afterward—in contemplation and prayer. In the summer and fall he would kneel before the altar in the church, allowing the dark sanctity to surround him as the gloaming deepened, but in winter he stayed in his hut before a measly fire. It wasn't that he was afraid of the snow. It was, he had convinced himself, selfish to put himself in the way of illness. His bones hurt in the cold, and if he caught a mortal chill, his parishioners would be without a priest. *Still,* he now thought, *I am taking warmth when my parishioners often have none.* He swept a coal absently back into the dying fire as his mind pursued the thread of this quandary.

Bursting into his mind, like a swollen ember, a thought bloomed: *Averilla.* This happened to him now and again; thoughts came with the suddenness of command. It was not his voice speaking, not really a voice at all, more like the insistent nudging of an impatient sheepdog. This thought was fully formed; having little or no connection to his previous meandering meditation, it was rounded and perfect and clear. It came again. *Averilla.*

Well, yes, I am concerned about Averilla. We all are. There is that strange blindness, and of course her grief over Ethelind, and then her worry about Will.

Averilla.

Groaning, he rose.

Before long, the enclosure was alive with running figures, their silhouettes angular shadows against the walls. Torches moved rapidly here and there as frantic ostlers searched randomly. Men from the castle soon joined them. Robert Bradshaw, the bailiff, ordered them into groups to search methodically, building by building. The abbess watched with increasing anxiety as stables, ewery, wellhouse, kitchen, infirmary, and officina were lighted and searched. Fruitlessly.

All but the church. "We were all there. We would have noticed."

Bradshaw raised an eyebrow, then shrugged.

When the last note of Compline swirled into the darkness, Dame Joan had led the community, docile but anxious, dutifully keeping the Great Silence, up the night stairs to the dortor, making sure there were no stragglers.

All had neatly folded veils and wimples and scapulars on the ends of their beds, removed their shoes, and climbed beneath the covers.

Even the most sleep-befuddled of the nuns was aware that something was badly amiss in their world. First Aethwulfa had, without permission, left in the middle of Compline. Then the abbess failed to accompany them to the night stairs but rushed off. They heard the halloos from the outer court. The tumult was distressing, but not to know why made everything worse. Eyes roved, and met, signaling to one another confusion and dismay and in some cases terror. Joan too lay awake staring at the roof beams. *The abbess will handle whatever it is now that the bailiff has arrived. No. The real threat to the abbey is the presence of lepers in the enclosure. Does no one else realize that? The workmen's lodgings might "possibly" be far enough away. But the lepers are inside with us now.* She felt the hair rise on her arms, as repulsed by the thought as if a nest of vipers had appeared and was slithering through the dortor.

Joan well knew that community decisions were unwieldy in practice. There were bound to be further discussions, "concerns," "hindrances," and, therefore, "objections." Something would need altering about the workmen's lodgings. The workmen would postpone and put off, and in the end the move would take such an unconscionable time that leprosy would make inroads into the community. Always Dame Averilla. Such hypocrisy, really, leaving it all to Dame Elizabeth. And Dame Elizabeth… well, Dame Elizabeth was just making a spectacle of herself, pretending to love lepers! Dame Averilla was thinking more about the lepers than the safety of the community. Joan pursed her lips, decided what she must do, and fell into a restless sleep.

IN A COPSE ON THE far side of Shaftsbury, Weldon and his men awaited Thord. When they heard, faint at first and from the north, the trot of a horse, heavily laden, they all straightened. Thord appeared, Averilla slung in front of him. Weldon cantered over. "A nun. Well done!" He appraised the drooping Averilla and smirked at Thord. "Alive as FitzRolf wanted. We'll take 'er to the hermit's hut and await FitzRolf."

Thord responded, voice low. "Serf's back in the abbey. Saw him go into the church."

Weldon's head jerked up and his eyes narrowed. "Is that so. Be able to kill two birds with one stone when FitzRolf arrives.

They spurred their horses into the forest.

Chapter Twenty-eight

December 17, 1120

Between Matins and Prime

One of the bailiff's men reached the east gate and found it pulled to, but close inspection revealed that, though the bar was down, the lock hung open, the key still in its hole. "Ain't guarded either. 'Ere," he yelled. "They went 'ere. Out the gate."

Two of them ran back to alert the bailiff and abbess. "East gate, my lady," the first panted. "Key in the lock. Looks as if someone…" he stared accusingly at Turgold.

Turgold's face blanched. "Lady, I—"

The abbess made a gesture of impatience. "What else could you have done? Let Aethwulfa flounder and perhaps fall in the snow and compound the problem? It was closed and barred when you left to accompany her?"

Turgold frowned and nodded.

Cecily shook her head as if at a gnat. "You had no choice. You were guarding the gate against someone coming in. No one would have imagined someone going out."

"Proves that someone was here," added the bailiff. "Could 'ave taken Averilla. But why take her?" To Turgold. "You are sure you saw wet under the loom?"

Again, Turgold nodded.

Then, "But who?" And why?"

"There was a footprint in the ash near the hearth. Did I tell you that? So someone must 'ave got in—through the smoke hole."

And you are sure Will is in the church?" The bailiff turned to the portress, who again nodded, but her eyes darted, unsure.

AFTER LAUDS, BUT BEFORE THE first rays of a reluctant sun had peeped through the shutters, while the morning was a luminous indigo-green, Joan rose, donned scapula, wimple, and veil, picked up her shoes, and tiptoed out of the dortor and down the night stairs. She went through the outer court, ignoring the clamorous hue and cry outside the walls.

Joan rapped loudly on the tracing-house door. The three, sleepless through the hours of turmoil, lay rigid. Dame Elizabeth fought her way out of her coverlet, stumbled to the door, and whispered, "Deo gratis?"

A woman's voice answered. Elizabeth unbolted and peered worriedly around the edge of the door. Dame Joan drew her mouth into a thin line and said, "Obviously, I have considerable worry about contagion."

A deep flush suffused Elizabeth's face.

"You will remove to the workmen's…"—she couldn't bring herself to classify it as a "lodgings," but "hut" seemed malicious—"as soon as you finish breaking your fast. That pot," her voice overrode the objection she saw in Elizabeth's eyes, "you are to keep for cooking in the new lazar house. In the stables there is an old barrow, which you may use to carry the

one who cannot walk. When the lepers are settled, you are to
return here and remove the sand where…" Joan motioned at
the recumbent forms of Francine, yawning, and Ellen asleep,
"they have lain."

"Dame, you can't mean…" tried Elizabeth. "Is it safe? The
hue and cry!" She lowered her eyes to avoid seeing the unat-
tractive black gleam of triumph that glinted behind Joan's eyes,
and bowed.

"But mayn't it be in two or three days' time? Or the morrow? Ellen…" Elizabeth gestured to the blanketed lump, "is
very ill. You see, the phlegm collects and—"

"All the more reason," Joan interrupted, "to remove her to
someplace where others—innocents—will not be infected by this
dread phlegm. You are to do it. Now."

Elizabeth bowed her head. "Do convey to the abbess and to
the community our deepest gratitude."

Without bowing, Joan left. Elizabeth shut the door softly.

"Dame?" said Francine. Joan's loud voice had wakened
Ellen, who pushed a shaking elbow under her body and leaned
on it.

Elizabeth studied Ellen's tattered face. The lumps on her
forehead were pronounced, giving her an angry appearance.
The left side of her mouth canted down in a snarl that showed
her teeth. Her left eye slewed, showing the white as she peered
blearily out. Ellen muttered something, but the hoarse nasal
sounds slurred together. Francine interpreted: "Ellen said she
feels alive, and thanks ye for it." Francine would have said more
but another knock came from the door.

From the other side, a male voice said. "I've brung ye the
barrow, Dame."

"Deo Gratis," said Elizabeth.

"What's that word?"

"What? Oh, 'tis Latin, Francine, from church. We speak
in Latin much of the time, being an abbey. Those words, 'Deo

gratis,' mean God willing or God be thanked, which I am, for you." To Francine's bewilderment, Elizabeth rose and, crossing all taboos, hugged her.

THE THUNDER OF HORSES HEADING off had earlier waked an old woman in St. James from the thin sleep the nights now gave her. Most folk knew her as Robin's widow. She had a name, certainly, but married to Robin, a dour man, her personality had over the years been subsumed into his. She was one of those who live life by plucking tidbits from others' lives and passing the information along. Gossip was too kind a word to describe the practice, for a certain malice pervaded her curiosity and infiltrated her need to pry into and dissect the lives around her. Questions now kept her awake. *In the middle of the night? And riding away from Shaftesbury?* Deciding that someone *surely* needed to know, she struggled upright, threw a thin cloak over her shoulders, peered out the door toward the laundry, and forced her aging body outside.

BRACH, FINALLY REMEMBERING to fetch Father Merowald to be with Will, also heard Weldon's men canter off. At the bottom of the hill, across from the church, Robin's widow, hair hanging down, skimpy clothes askew, accosted Brach. She reached out a claw, and with amazing strength grabbed his arm, her nails biting into his flesh.

"Ach, what the…!" Brach raised his arm preparing to strike her hand away, when "It be just me, lad." He tensed for the inevitable meander. "I heard galloping," she said.

"Aye. As did I. Who do ye—?"

"I wot not now, do I, so swift they went. Like the hunt."

Brach frowned. She was right. Who could have been here and then galloped away? No one from the abbey. He would know. He was an ostler wasn't he? Going through St. James from a manor nearby? But whose? He leaned close. Robin's widow was small and withered, bent with age, but now she was mumbling, and he couldn't understand. He shook his head and gave up. He had been sent to find Father Merowald. Maybe the priest could sort out Robin's wife. "Auch aye," he said, for want of anything else, and sidled around her. In front of the unprepossessing wattle and daub of Merowald's hut, he pounded on the door. The flimsy wood—it was wood, not just a leather curtain—trembled. He should have hit the upright.

FATHER MEROWALD HAD JUST FINISHED tidying the coals when Brach pounded on and then opened the door. "Ah," said Merowald, his voice barely a croak. "Will is back."

Brach nodded, wondering how Merowald could possibly know that. "The portress sent me to fetch you. To be with 'im in the sanctuary." Brach followed Merowald outside where they found Robin's widow waiting where Brach had left her, still muttering.

"'Tis you, is it, Hilde, outside on this cold night?" Merowald's voice was calm, and it was this calm that brought the old woman back to herself and her mission.

She grabbed onto his cassock, her fear palpable. "Did ye hear 'em? Horses galloping, as if the devil be at their back."

"Were there?" Merowald asked, frowning. He racked his brain. Had he too heard something? While praying, mayhap? Nothing had registered, but then, snow may have muffled the sound. "Which way, daughter?"

"Going away. Can I go back now you know? She trembled and drew her meager cloak close. "Someone needed to know."

He patted her shoulder. "You've told me, Hilde. Now some-one knows. I'll tell the abbess." Privately, he agreed it did seem strange, what with the murder of Ethelind, the discovery of Lady Isabel half dead in a tree, and Will apparently chased back into the abbey from the forest. Had someone followed Will? He gave her a reassuring smile. "Well, Brach here tells me that at least Will is back." Merowald reached up to pull his cloak closer, then remembered that he hadn't put it on when Brach knocked. *Well, a little cold won't hurt me, Lord. Your mother was cold on the ride to Bethlehem.* "Brach, I would be much obliged if you would you see Hilde home and see to her fire. Take some of my wood. I would consider it a great favor."

Elizabeth gave a last look around the tracing house, gritted her teeth, snatched up one of the coverlets, and hurried outside, eager to be gone before Joan returned. Her whole body was shaking. She laid her scrip in the front of the barrow and placed the coverlet into it as padding.

Back inside, she waited as Francine propped Ellen into a sitting position and forced her arms and head into the other tunic.

"How," asked Elizabeth, brow knotted, "do we move Ellen? I can't ask the men to infect themselves."

Francine gave her an odd look. "They wouldn't, Dame, not even iffen St. Peter done the asking. No matter. I done it before. Takes two, though."

She cocked her head at Elizabeth, who took in a deep breath and said gamely, "Show me."

Francine knelt and placed one of Ellen's arms around her own neck. "You do the same as me."

To Ellen she said, voice gentle, "Try to hold on."

To Elizabeth, on the other side, she commanded. "Put yer arm around her."

Elizabeth again breathed deep, but knelt and did as she was told. They rose together and hauled Ellen up between them. Her feet scrabbled for purchase as they maneuvered her out the door, eased her down into the padded hollow of the barrow, and threw the second coverlet over her. Francine went back and then returned lugging the pot, which she nestled beside Ellen in the barrow.

CECILY WAS ON THE LOWEST stair to the lodgings when Father Merowald came, half running, from Laundry Lane, almost tripping on his cassock. She bowed, then said, in answer to the question in his eyes, "Dame Averilla is missing."

"Oh." Then, piecing it together, Merowald said, "Oh, dear. Robin's widow heard horses galloping."

Cecily stared at him; the implications too dread to be taken in.

"Horses? More than one?"

"Brach and Hilde both heard horses galloping. " Merowald reiterated. "Most certainly no longer here."

Cecily paled. "It must be those who took Averilla! No one abducts a nun!"

The bailiff had drawn near. "We will need to tell the sheriff."

The abbess glanced at the office door, and seeing a dim light, wondered if Dame Joan was inside. "I will have Dame Joan write to the sheriff. And the king. I will find her."

FATHER MEROWALD WATCHED THE ABBESS enter Joan's office, and, acutely aware of the despair this turmoil must be creating in Will's mind, made his way through the darkened court to the church. There he found Will where he expected, face pinched, hands gripping the sanctuary ring. The priest put a hand on his shoulder. "You can let go. If someone comes, then you can grip it. You heard the men outside?"

Will nodded, eyes terrified.

"Not looking for you, lad." Merowald folded himself down, bending awkwardly like an unstrung puppet, onto the cold tiles beside Will, "Nay, lad. Not you be they looking for. Something else entirely. Dame Averilla was abducted."

Will's eyebrows bunched together, then he firmed his lips and bowed his head.

"The bailiff's men searched the abbey precincts for her and now check the town. The bailiff suspects the man who was here earlier. Man called Weldon."

They sat, each in his thoughts. After a moment, Merowald cocked his head and said softly, "I think mayhap Dame Ethelind's death weighs heavily on your heart."

Will's face tightened, and he looked away.

Merowald waited. "I would find a way for you to speak."

Will's eyes remained on the north wall of the choir. Wearily, he nodded, a light thing, a mere jutting of the jaw. Then, surprising Merowald by its simplicity, Will bent his fingers, palm upright, in a beckoning motion.

"You would have me speculate on what you are thinking? Then you can nod yea or nay in response?"

Will raised an eyebrow, then nodded.

"I think that this death of Ethelind and the abduction of Averilla angers you."

Will looked into the distance and then bowed his head.

"Such violence against a woman destroys a value you hold sacred?"

Will looked unsure.

"Cecily told you that you were to protect them?"

Will let out a sigh, almost a groan, and then again offered the beckoning motion of the hand. Merowald stilled, not praying but thinking, bringing all his hard-won knowledge of the human spirit and of God to the fore. After a moment, he said, "Master Weldon said you committed murder."

Will's face contorted in grief.

"You did murder a man?" Merowald's eyes narrowed.

Will hung his head.

"I wonder perhaps if the person you murdered was hurting someone—like Ethelind—who was vulnerable?"

Will widened his eyes in surprise, then, nodding, closed them.

"Understand you the enormity of your sin?"

Will hung his head and rubbed his hand over his eyes.

"Do you repent?"

Will raised his head. Merowald saw a flicker of hope burn behind the saddened eyes. With an exaggerated gesture, Will slowly crossed himself.

"In the name of Jesus Christ, your sin is forgiven. Your penance is to pray every day for the soul of the miscreant you killed."

Chapter Twenty-nine

Two of the bailiff's men beside the stables eyed Elizabeth and her charges warily, but seeing Francine's clapper and hat, were all too eager to let them pass. Elizabeth kept her head down and pushed the barrow. The previous night had been cold so that the slush had refrozen and was not only slick but treacherous. The two men guarding the main gate were embarrassingly eager to remove the bar in the face of the lepers, and opened the gate just enough for Elizabeth to judder the barrow through the narrow opening. The two pushed and jostled out the gate, turned left onto the Bimport, across the hardened snow, and then left again onto the lightly trodden path behind the abbey's western wall. As they struggled toward the workmen's lodgings, the barrow hit a rock. Elizabeth, forehead beaded with sweat, had to back up and veer around it. Francine lagged wearily.

When they finally reached the hut, the two stood, uncertain. The building, with its wide brow of thatch, was about fifteen feet long and eight wide, and had been built with a stone plinth for a foundation. Seeing the stone soothed some deep anxiety in Elizabeth. *A cornerstone, a rock the builders rejected. And the hut has a door. Thank God!* She saw that the wooden door swiveled on the stone at the base and was fixed firmly to the frame. "The door looks… sturdy," she said encouragingly"

A lone workman left in charge of the lodgings peered out at them, puzzled that anyone was near the hut, least of all a nun wielding such an odd conveyance, but when he noticed Francine's hat and clapper and Ellen's bulbous swellings, he took a step back.

"God be with you," Elizabeth said. Her voice could never be considered piercing, but she was exhausted, and so her words were even softer than usual. Despite the white of the wimple and the black of the habit, the cold had brought color to Elizabeth's cheeks; her ineffable aura of complicity with God arrested the young man's retreat.

She continued, "I hope you were warned… of our need."

With not the least idea of what she was talking about, the man gaped, eyes rapidly veering from the ethereal beauty of the young nun to the ravaged faces of lepers.

Elizabeth said, "I regret… the abbess—I hate to invoke her name as if to make you move by dint of her will, but indeed it was her decision"—(he heard nothing but 'abbess') "asks that you take pity on these women, these lepers, and allow them to take up residence in your… home."

The men had heard about the lepers the previous afternoon. Rumors had been rife about what was to be done with them. He frowned. "Oh, Dame, not now. Ye cain't throw us out in the cold, nigh on the birth of Christ."

Chapter Thirty

Thord, Weldon, and the others trotted into the verge of the forest. The gallop from St. James roused Averilla who, trying to stay upright, clutched the horse's mane. Insensible to her surroundings, she knew only that they were in a wood, and was acutely aware of grinding pain and engulfing fear. *What can I do to help myself?* She tried to count. *Eight men?* It was hard. Her head throbbed. Every muscle quivered with each jangling hoofbeat. *I was hit.* There was a shooting pain in her ribs. *Mayhap broken? No, no, I can breathe. No fresh blood in my mouth.*

It seemed to Averilla as if an eternity of pain had elapsed when, finally, the horses turned off the well-beaten track and onto a deer trail. The stench of Thord's body and breath inundated her. Before long, a small shape emerged from the gloom. *The hermit's hut!* It had been abandoned, unused for years.

"Get 'er off the horse and put 'er in there," Weldon ordered. "FitzRolf'll be here anon." Thord dismounted, hefted Averilla down, and half-carried her into the shelter. He pushed her, and she landed heavily on her shoulder and couldn't stifle a groan. *FitzRolf, did he say? Lady Isabel's husband? What could FitzRolf want with me?* Something sharp lay beneath her hand. It felt like a tiny bone. She shifted in revulsion and felt a rock dig into her side.

With her one good eye, Averilla vaguely made out the dim interior. Cobwebs clung in banners from partial walls. The thatch drooped. She inched her body off the rock, wincing as her rib objected. The cadence of conversation from outside changed into a wicked chuckle and manly hoots. Thord appeared in the doorway. His smile was one of power and possession and malice. Averilla pressed herself against the wall, pushed back with her heels, and brought her knees up protectively. "Feisty one ye be." He bent to his knees and lifted the hem of her habit, fumbling through the layers of fabric. As he forced her onto her back, she rubbed her face on his shoulder to work off the gag, opened her mouth wide, and again bit down, this time on a soft spot on his neck. His shout of rage preceded his punch to her mouth, the force of which slammed her head into the wall. Momentarily dazed, she thought she heard hoofbeats vibrate through the wall behind her. Thord made to hit her again—then hastily rose, adjusting his breeches.

The muffled pounding ebbed into the whiffles, shuffles, and thumps of arrival and dismounting.

One loud voice rose. "You brought a nun, I hope?" Then, "Well done."

The doorway darkened as a man appeared, silhouetted against the dawn light. He was not as tall as Thord, who now stood beside him. Averilla could make out the trailing sleeves of court clothes, as if FitzRolf—*It must be FitzRolf*—had just risen from a meal and come hurriedly. He took one long stride toward her, hauled her up by the neck of her tunic, and forced her against the wall. "Where…" the word ground out from between gritted teeth, "is Isabel?" Averilla shook her head, silent. He flung her back down. Her ankle turned and she slid to her knees.

FitzRolf stood, raking her body with his eyes. As if to himself, he muttered, "Short hair. Like a man's."

Averilla felt naked.

As if no more needed to be said, FitzRolf turned and shouted to Thord, "Get her up." Then, "Isabel must be in the abbey. You searched the abbey?

Averilla heard Weldon hesitate. "Not all of it. We found—"

"No matter. I have decided on a barter. My wife for a nun."

"I wanted a nun so that if the abbess balks at releasing Isabel, I will then suggest blinding this nun, or giving her to Thord as a plaything. That'll likely sway her."

FitzRolf reached over and took Averilla's face between his hands, forcing her to look at him. "How would you like to be blind? Probably not a hindrance."

Averilla shook her head, her one open eye huge in terror. *Not blind, dear Lord, please.*

A half smile skewed his lips. "King Henry took the eyes of one of his daughters for a lesser infraction. You could serve your God as well without sight. Probably enjoy being a martyr. We shall see what your abbess thinks of such a transaction."

CHAPTER THIRTY-ONE

ecily was back in the church by Prime, at the end of which she exclaimed, "You all heard the disturbance in the night. Dame Averilla is missing." She saw no need to tell them that Averilla had gone without a companion or that there was a footprint in the ashes or that the east gate had been left open and unguarded. "Men have been searching for her."

A WEAK SUN FINALLY PEEKED through glowering clouds as the nuns exited the church. They stood, darting glances at the main gate and whispering.

"They say someone took her."

"Would she have gone else?"

"Mayhap called?"

"Unheard of!"

"From the fury of the Norsemen," said a junior, parroting the great litany.

"But they are not Norsemen," said a novice, taking the other literally.

The usual sounds of sheep and the few cows left from the autumn slaughter were suddenly overwhelmed by the thunder of horsemen riding hard. One of the younger nuns ran to peer over the wall toward the small hamlet of Cann. A dozen or so mounted men scattered geese and children as they hurtled through the village. The horsemen swerved around the fishpond, overtook a wood cart, and shouted imprecations at the town gatekeep.

Cecily paused on the lodging stairs and waited for the young nun. "Horsemen, my lady. Coming fast." The novice put a hand on the aching stitch in her side.

"Colors?"

"I couldn't well make them out. Blue, I think, and red. A dragon rampant."

"FitzRolf." Cecily had met the man once or twice at court, and the memory still made her stomach turn. She remembered the broad chest and bandy legs of a rider, and the swarthy, pocked skin. His wide, bulbous nose had sported a black mole and a bush of hair, as if he had inhaled a mouse.

My lady?"

"Yes," Cecily snapped, forgoing, in her fear, all pretense of civility.

"There is a woman with them. A nun, I think. From the black."

Cecily paled. "Averilla?"

"I know not. No veil or wimple."

"Averilla," Cecily muttered. Skirts gathered, she started down. "The gates are still barred, are they not? Send someone for the bailiff."

"But lady, Bradshaw and his men are…"

They were defenseless.

Sister Clayetta, the abbess's maid, watched from the top of the stairs. She dashed back inside, then reappeared almost immediately, the abbess's silken wimple and veil clasped in her arms. The abbatial pectoral cross (the one inlaid with diamonds) dangled from her hand. Cecily now stood midcourt, a group of nuns behind her. Clayetta ran down the stairs and elbowed through the throng. "My lady."

Cecily glanced over, nodded, tore off her woolen veil, held out her hands, and tilted her head. Clayetta laid the heavy chain over her shoulders and arranged the silken veil on her coif. "Clayetta," Cecily's voice was terse, controlled. "Run to the infirmary. Isabel must flee."

"But where, my lady?" asked Clayetta. "She canna walk?"

"She can. A bit." As Clayetta adjusted the folds, Cecily muttered, "Averilla said something about two bones in the lower leg, and the leather binding. Isabel shouldn't, but she can if she must. Now, she must. With a stick. Tell those in the infirmary to take her to the treasury in the crypt. Scholastica can tell them where. I will keep FitzRolf talking for as long as I can."

ELIZABETH AND THE LEPERS STOOD speechless in front of the leper house. Francine bowed her head. "I knew it was too good to be true." The bleak look on Elizabeth's face stopped whatever excuse the young man had been ready to give. He wiped his mouth, for his ill-timed words had brought to his mind the image of a virgin denied shelter at an inn in ancient Bethlehem.

Sheepishly, he recovered. "Aye, Dame. As ye will. I'll be out o' here in a trice."

Elizabeth inclined her head, embarrassed by her vulnerability. A tear brimmed.

The workman gathered his few possessions and stepped out of the building, but seeing Ellen, legs akimbo in the barrow, and Elizabeth, unable to steer over an icy rut in front of the door sill, hesitated. Cain I help?"

At her nod, and careful to hold only the handles, he pushed the barrow inside, where Francine removed the blanket that covered Ellen and laid it on the far side of the central hearth. The young man's eyes weren't wild, but they were wary. He couldn't bring himself to offer to carry Ellen. Francine motioned to Elizabeth, and, using the earlier lopsided arm hold under Ellen's frail shoulders, maneuvered her out of the barrow and onto the coverlet.

Puffing, back aching from the barrow and the long, arduous trek, Elizabeth turned to express her gratitude to the waiting man, but her eye caught the door sill and she frowned. "This threshold has no stumbling block?"

"Nay." The man scratched his thatch of blond hair. "We 'ad no need." Then, relieved to be able to help, "I cain do that easy eno'. At least some'ut I cain do to help." He sidled over to the neatly stacked pile of firewood Elizabeth had eyed covetously while hoping he would leave, and pushed aside two logs before grasping a timber about two feet in length and a handspan in diameter. Upending it on another round left as a chopping block, he hefted the ax. In four deft strokes he produced a squared beam of about a hand's width on each surface. He laid it across the outside of the threshold. It didn't quite fill the gap, but there was only a triple-finger's width between the beam and the door sill. He cleaned his ear, gazing at Elizabeth and blushing furiously, his gaze beseeching.

"Thank you," she said. "'Twill make my heart easy to know 'tis there."

"But I mun fit 'er in a bit more."

"That would be good. Bless you for your kindness," she gestured around herself, "with all of this."

While the man tended to the chore, Elizabeth gazed around. The building was framed in the usual way of such peasant houses. A series of crucks, curved oak timbers, upheld the roof. These were joined along the roofline by a ridgepole. The walls were framed by horizontal beams, infilled by ash struts around which had been woven osier or rye. These were then covered with daub, a kind of plaster, now blackened with soot. Similar struts crossed the oak beams overhead, and thatch peeped through.

A hole, a wind eye, was carved through the thatch to allow the smoke to escape.

The two windows that gave onto the north and west sides were unglazed but had inside shutters, hinged with hide. Various implements still hung on wooden pegs—a tub, three hoops, a rake, and a hayfork. Two benches, boards for a trestle table, and a tripod over the hearth completed the bounty. Elizabeth would need to get rushes and beg heather and ticking for mattresses. She sank onto one of the benches, ashamed that she had assumed she could take on such a task by herself. Her eyes focused on a water tub that sat next to the door, beside which stood two pails and a yoke for carrying them back from the well.

Water, she thought, gladdened. She closed her eyes and turned her mind to Christ as living water. Whose yoke is easy; Whose burden is light. She couldn't do it alone, but with Him, with Him anything would be possible.

Clayetta threaded her way between the nuns, ran across the inner court, and slammed open the infirmary door. A voice, raspy and old, came from a bed near the hearth. "My dear, perhaps you ought to talk to me. I am afraid there is no one else."

Clayetta scanned the room.

"I am over here, dear. That's it, close to the fire."

Near the central hearth, a bed with more coverlets than any other held a frail body and beckoning hand.

"Dame Scholastica. Who is in charge? I need—"

"For the moment, odious as it sounds, I am," repeated the hoarse voice. "Dame Averilla and Dame Elizabeth and dear, dear Dame Ethelind… well, 'tis done and… suffice to say that you may as well tell me." Then, amused, "Everyone is now listening anyway."

"Lady Isabel needs to be hidden. Her husband is riding up from Cann! The abbess said to take her to the crypt! Something about the treasury."

"I remember, dear. 'Twas I myself who told Abbess Cecily of that place in the treasury. You said Cann? And riding? The crypt won't do now…." The old voice trailed off, and Clayetta despaired of Scholastica's sense.

"No," Scholastica, continued, voice strengthening. "'Twould take too long to cross the court. She is too frail to go quickly, and they would see her. But I think, yes," and raising her voice called "Lady Isabel. Lady, your husband…"

Isabel had listened to the entire exchange. Her hands on the coverlet trembled.

"…is approaching. There is a chance for you, I think. If you so desire?"

"Please."

"I imagine the abbess will stall him—or try. You need to get to the lazar house."

"The lazar house?" Isabel swallowed.

Impatient now, "Lady, can you stand?"

Hesitantly, "Aye."

"Can you walk?"

"I will have to." Isabel's voice was grim. She pushed off the coverlets and slid her legs over the side of the bed. She swayed. Sister Hope rushed over and forced Isabel's head between her knees. After a moment, Isabel sat up and scooted her bottom forward on the bed to get her feet under her on the floor. Sister Hope, fumbling with the leather thongs, jiggled Isabel's shoe over the swollen foot. Isabel was sweating.

"Would one of you" Scholastica asked, "be kind enough to fetch an old habit? Might as well be mine, I have no more use for it."

A habit was lifted from the store chest and slipped over Isabel's nightdress. An old cloak, green with age, was taken from a peg. "A wimple would be good, and I wonder if we could find a veil?" One of the other nuns tore off her own wimple and veil. She looked shorn without them.

Because the women hurried, the veil went on at a slant, and inevitably the last shoe was dropped. Gamely, Isabel tested her good leg and took a hesitant step, winced, clenched her jaw, and weaved toward the door.

"Sister Hope, your arm around her would help, I imagine." Scholastica's voice was determinedly polite. "Please."

Speaking through gritted teeth, Isabel managed. "No. I can walk. I must." As she took another step, she muttered querulously, "You said 'husband,' Dame. He is not actually my husband. I never said the words. The priest pronounced it so, but I never said the words."

"And, and a stick, please."

A walking stick was placed in Isabel's left hand.

"Never one to be stymied, I see," murmured Scholastica. "Sister Hope, heard you my words? Assist Lady Isabel if you would." Then the old voice wavered in uncertainty: "But how will you get to the lazar house if the men are at the gate?"

"Through the herbarium to the pilgrim's lane?" Clayetta suggested.

"But if nuns and servants and everyone in the abbey is heading into the outer court, and we three hurry in t'other direction, won't it be obvious who we are?" Sister Hope's voice was tentative.

Scholastica, still preoccupied with practicality, said, "It would be easiest with one nun on each side. Clayetta, might you take the other side of Lady Isabel?"

"Dame, you mean not that I should go. Surely—"

"I did mean that." Scholastica's voice managed to sound amused and despairing at the same time.

"But…" Clayetta's eyes started to water. Her lower lip trembled. "The lepers. If there is contagion, my habit—the abbess. Sister Blythe would mayhap be…"

The old eyes saddened, understanding Clayetta's fear. "You would rather that Sister Blythe and Sister Hope took Lady Isabel?" Scholastica's eyes met those of Sister Blythe. "And you? Will you go to the leper house, or does it scare you as well?"

Blythe said politely, "I am younger, mayhap stronger. But won't they see us?"

"Probably." Scholastica gazed at Lady Isabel's white face as if the woman were a sack of grain for sale. "You will have to go right through them—the men, I mean—and out the main gate. You will have to hide in plain sight, rather like an oak moth."

Scholastica smiled gently at Sister Clayetta. "We all have different gifts, my dear, and different fears. It is no shame. If you would go into the outer court and ask the nuns there to shuffle and mill about so the movement of these three becomes unremarkable to the casual glance. They will appear to be merely three more nuns upset by the uproar. Can you do that?

Oh, yes, Dame."

"Afterwards, hie you to the church. You know the space behind and within the altar?"

"Yeees."

"Tell Will to hide there. Pull the altar cloth down over his back. The men won't know enough to know there is a space beneath. Then go down into the crypt and tell John the Mason about FitzRolf. He'll know what to do."

Clayetta, embarrassment reddening her face, bowed, glad not to have to be near the lepers.

Chapter Thirty-two

From her place in front of Thord, Averilla heard the hesitation in the voice of the portress as the grille slid open.

"Deo gratis." The portress managed, although Averilla could hear the fear in her voice.

FitzRolf ignored the courtesy. "The abbess."

The portress responded ingenuously, "The lady abbess Cecily FitzHamon?" Her eyes widened as she glimpsed Averilla, who—gagged, bloody, eye swollen and dirty, wimple and veil gone, hands tied—sagged in front of a second rider. The portress swallowed.

The lead rider nodded, "Yes, the abbess Cecily FitzHamon. "Who shall I say?"

FitzRolf's look indicated that she should know his identity from the standards held behind him, the way he sat his horse, and the distinction of his very demeanor. He said "FitzRolf," the arrogance of the Norman French giving not only his lineage but his right to admittance. "If you don't open the gate, I will slit the throat of this, your sister, and send my men over the wall to retrieve what is mine."

The portress looked behind her for direction. Cecily, mid-court, firmed her lips and held out the key. The clank of the chains and locks as they were unfastened was loud in the silence. Two ostlers pulled back the massive beam.

CLAYETTA BROKE INTO A STILTED run outside the infirmary. She raced through the herbarium, hitching up her habit and clutching it in front of her. She could hear the sound of the men outside the main gate. She paused to whisper to several of the nuns at the back of the court, "Mingle and move around. We must slip Lady Isabel past these men. Tell the others."

Clayetta entered the church, bowed to the rood, and tiptoed forward as her eyes adjusted to the gloom. Will sat in front of the high altar, a pallet, a sheepskin, and an earthenware jug of water beside him.

"Will. Quick. Horsemen. Coming here. They have Averilla."

Will's eyes widened in fear.

"A party of horsemen," she repeated slowly, enunciating as if he were deaf as well as mute. "Come." She sidled behind the altar and beckoned to him. "There is a space to hide you."

Obediently, Will crawled, wincing at the pain in his knee. The back of the altar had indeed been hollowed out. He wouldn't have dared explore around the holy altar, had assumed it was solid, as would FitzRolf's men. Clayetta lifted the heavy brocade frontal that pooled at the corners, and Will squirmed his great frame inside the opening so he was lying on his back. Slowly, painfully, he pulled his injured knee to his chest. She thrust the jug into his hands.

Clayetta pulled the altar brocade so it covered the hole, checked the folds, half-ran through the transept, and opened the door to the circular staircase. Her leather shoes made a platting sound as she hurried down. The master mason had been surveying the walls of the old church these several months, pondering the foundations of the new church Cecily intended to construct. The few small lamps John had lighted illumined only a small portion of the undercroft. "John, John the Mason," Clayetta

whispered hoarsely, hurrying through the grove of squat pillars.
"Quick! Horsemen! Armed! The outer court! Tell the others."

Although Clayetta did not say "Norsemen," in John's mind
the words *horsemen* and *Norsemen* collided, bearing with them
brutal images of pillage and rapine. The familiar words of the
litany—"From the fury of the Norsemen, good Lord deliver
us"—echoed within him. A stone cutter behind him picked up
the divider they had been using to gauge the stones of the old
foundation. In his other hand he hefted his hammer.

Above them, Will unfolded himself and crawled out from
beneath the altar.

BLYTHE AND HOPE HAD DECIDED to wear hats. "It's winter, by St.
Steven, and hats keep the snow off. We will seem just nuns off
to gather greens."

"If all the other nuns have no hats and you do…" came
Scholastica's querulous voice.

"If we carry baskets?" Hope asked.

Scholastica shook her head. "Too obvious."

Isabel hesitated on the second stair to the door, then stepped
up with her good leg, allowing it to carry her up and over the
sill. The two nuns put their arms on either side of Isabel's waist,
and together the three of them hobbled into the herbarium.
Isabel bent over the stick and tried to mimic the shuffling gait
of an old woman.

IN THE CHURCH, RAGE AGAINST the Normans in general and
Weldon in particular ignited in Will's mind. He unfolded his
long legs and grabbed a fold of the brocade altar cloth to steady
himself. He heard the brass candlesticks atop the altar topple

and clang onto the floor. He managed to scramble to his feet and stood, hand on the altar, momentarily dizzy. A ray of winter sun gilded one of the recumbent candlesticks. *Make good weapons,* he thought. *Heavy. Shoulder one of 'em and…* But no. The no was a conscious decision, an inner sense of rightness that forbade such use of something dedicated to God. Will turned, bowed low to the rood as the priest at his old village had taught him, straightened his shoulders, and limped, dragging his bad leg, toward the western doors. In the narthex, the little hall in which he had first rested, stood another candelabrum, this one of iron. *Good.* He wrenched the candle off the center spike and shouldered the massive piece.

ISABEL ESSAYED A QUICK GLANCE at FitzRolf as she and the two beside her joined the gathered nuns. Her lip curled in disgust. Her second husband in his splendor. Suddenly into her mind bloomed memory: She was standing on the poop deck of the king's ship on that ill-fated night in early December. She saw again the lap-sided White Ship readying to follow, sails luffing as the south wind began to fill them. The prince and all the young courtiers aboard it seemed very drunk. She heard them make catcalls at the priest on the quay who tried to bless them. As Isabel watched, she saw FitzRolf run up the gangplank, chivying a sailor who was rolling another barrel of wine up to the revelers. Someone was with FitzRolf. *Who? Yes, Stephen of Blois, the king's nephew!* She observed aghast as they gave orders, and drink was ladled out to the rowers and sailors. *Giving them more drink? Why would he? Crossing the channel was chancy at the best of times, but with this wind…* Then, instead of staying with the young party, FitzRolf and Stephen of Blois jumped off, leaping from the gangplank just as it was being removed. Isabel had shaken her head. She remembered watching as the lights on the following ship began to fade. She had then thought, *They have veered off course!* Later, she thought she heard screams. At the time, she told herself, *Surely it is just the wind.* It wasn't until the next morning that she learned that the *Blanche Nef* had run aground on the Catterville rocks, and all aboard had drowned. Deep suspicion had gripped her heart. *Had FitzRolf, this second husband, deliberately caused the accident?* The certainty that that was exactly what had happened now brought tears running down her cheeks

WILL EASED OPEN THE LEFT-HAND door of the church and slipped into the morning light. His hair stood wild around his head like that of an Old Testament prophet. The courtyard roiled with men and horses. Workmen were running out of the lean-to beside the church. John the Mason pushed past him, heavy hammer in his hand. Above all the heads, Will saw Weldon, and then Thord with Dame Averilla bound in front of him. He jutted his jaw. His eyes lit on another figure, resplendent in the trappings of power. FitzRolf. *That's the man as took my tongue!* In his mind he again saw FitzRolf trot into the glade in which Will had spent the night after killing Alcar. Will had not known then that the man before him, in all his bullish bestiality, was the noble who owned him. He'd never seen the man before except in the far distance. Hidden beneath the hazel bough, he had watched them dismount and had memorized the face and listened to them talk, not understanding most of the Norman French. Will had moved then, just slightly. The men had turned, as one. Will had fought, but the three had overwhelmed and hogtied him. Then FitzRolf had unsheathed his eating knife, intent on killing him. One of the others had stayed FitzRolf's arm, saying something in French. FitzRolf had paused, considering, nodded, and bent over Will. Will had smelt the fetid breath, looked right into the piggy eyes. In English, FitzRolf had said to Will, "Indeed. Like killing an ox. It would be a loss. This way you won't be able to repeat anything you have heard this day." Will had opened his mouth to yell, "No!" The one in a blue coat had grabbed his tongue, and the last thing Will saw was the flash of sunlight glinting off the blade before FitzRolf slashed his tongue. After that, Will knew no more until he had wakened in the stable. Will now strode forward, barely seeing anything beyond the crimson of his ire.

FITZROLF'S HORSES MILLED ABOUT THE court, splattering slush. Cecily straightened her back. FitzRolf scanned the sixty or so nuns and then allowed his eyes, condescendingly, to meet Cecily's. Neither spoke. Cecily's eyes flashed.

Lazily, FitzRolf surveyed the precincts, resting on each building, assessing. He seemed to dismiss the workmen who sifted into the court carrying the tools of their trades as of no more import than those in the pages of a psalter, innocuous things, things of the day's work, the masons their hammers, the carpenters their saws, the hodmen their bricks. The tools could conceivably be effective in one-on-one combat but would be useless against mounted men.

Blood seeped from Averilla's temple. Will noted that she was filthy and was gagged, *but she is alive!* Averilla's one good eye looked ineffably sad. Will saw Cecily's mouth turn down as she took a step toward Averilla.

FitzRolf wheeled his horse between them.

"You block me from my nun?"

"Mayhap, lady." Condescendingly. "But this nun is in my possession, just as my wife is in yours. So, you will return to me my wife, in trade for this your nun."

Cecily's voice was an exhalation of anger. No man, not even the king, had dared order her thus. "Wife?" she spat, her jaw thrust forward, forehead creased. "You tell me you know not where your wife, the Lady Isabel, is?"

A small muscle on the side of FitzRolf's mouth twitched.

One of those lolling behind him made a sound that could have been a laugh.

The wind ruffled Cecily's habit.

The pause was long enough to force FitzRolf to speak first.

"Something dark moved behind his eyes. "She herself chose to run away." FitzRolf's voice was emotionless. "She is my wife. She left...."

"And you didn't follow?"

"They lost us. Not my part of the forest."

"Indeed."

FitzRolf's men were still astride, languidly lounging on saddle boards, amused to see a woman best their despised master.

"All that should be of concern to you is that she is my wife and I am here to fetch her."

Cecily's voice held haughty sarcasm. "No concern for her? She had been abused, and there comes from you no outrage, no horrified questions of her well-being. I mistrust, sir, your... forthrightness in this tale."

"Enough, woman! Your words tell that she is here." He gestured vaguely behind him toward Averilla. "As I said, each of us has something to offer the other. I have your nun. You have my wife. Surely some... arrangement can be agreed upon. It is all so very simple. I have come to retrieve what is mine, a chattel you... appropriated and now harbor within your walls. And I have something that you would, presumably, like to see returned. Or..."

Movement, not just restlessness in a crowd, but deliberate movement among the gathered nuns, caught Averilla's eye. It was subtle. She focused as best she could. Three nuns were moving along the edges of the outer court. *Isabel?* The other nuns were, as if wafted by the wind, milling among themselves, seemingly trying to conceal Isabel and get her through the court unseen.

Does Cecily know? Is she stalling?

Cecily's voice had lowered. "You have been admitted into our outer court because we are bidden by our Rule to welcome the stranger, as we know not when we might be entertaining Christ. Since the Gospels mention no time when Christ tied and battered defenseless women, you are obviously not the Lord and therefore due no courtesy. Release my nun."

FitzRolf's brow lowered. His hand went for his sword. "Toy not with me, madam; you well know I am here to retrieve what is mine, and my patience grows short."

"Everything here belongs to God alone."

"I am the Lady Isabel's husband, given by the king at her widowhood, legally wed in the eyes of God and man. She was given no leave to depart from me. You say everything belongs to God, but to belong to God, the owner must first relinquish the item to Him. The lady was not so relinquished."

Cecily faltered, then came up with a half-truth, surprising herself: "And I tell you, we have no person by that name residing in the precincts of this abbey."

Averilla heard the murmur of unease from the nuns. *The abbess is deliberately misleading him. Isn't that the same as lying? Isabel is almost out of the court but still...* thought Averilla, *but still....* Knowingly disobeying a commandment, even for good, condemned a soul.

Hearing the disquiet behind her, Cecily faltered, then plowed on. "You, of course, may search these precincts if that is the only way for me to retrieve my unfortunate nun from your clutches. Will that satisfy you?"

Averilla frowned in consternation. Cecily must know and is trying to delay him.

FitzRolf gestured languidly in a circular motion.

The men, Weldon among them, quickly started to dismount. It was a mistake.

JOHN THE MASON ELBOWED OUT from the crowd. He lunged for Averilla's leg. Thord slewed his horse, pulled back on the sagging Averilla with one arm, and grappled for his sword with the other.

For Averilla the scene broke into a thousand fragments. It was all she could do to stay upright. She saw FitzRolf sneer, lift his left arm, grab the top of his trailing knotted sleeve with his right hand, and swing it in a wide arc, using it like a mace. The sleeve swung heavily, as if weighted. John dodged away as Will—*Will?*—charged forward from deep in the crowd, brandishing an iron candelabrum like a lance before him. The sleeve whirled. Will veered and thrust upward. The iron spike caught on the midsection of the sleeve. Will wrenched upward with a twist, pulling and tearing the bottom length of sleeve clean off. The rock concealed between two of the lower knots flew out and thumped to the ground.

Suddenly more mounted men swept into the outer court. *The Bailiff's men?* Averilla thought, but no, the man in the lead was on a destrier, and the huge horse shoved—as it was trained to—through the roiling mass of fighting men. It took Averilla a moment to discern the colors and recognize, with relief and confusion, that the graying man astride the stallion was the sheriff. *Where had he… why was he…?*

Nuns squealed and backed away. Abbey workmen, masons, ostlers, and even what looked to be the smith, unheeding of the new arrivals, were battling with FitzRolf's dismounted men.

Within the gatehouse arch, Sister Blythe and Sister Hope flattened themselves against the stones as the horsemen passed.

Then they hoisted Isabel under her armpits and broke into a hobbling jog.

The riders surged into the roiling melee within the court. Two horses reared, fearsome in the enclosed space, and in the ensuing chaos, Averilla lost sight of the fleeing nuns. Her heart plummeted. *Had one of FitzRolf's men seen and stopped them?*

Chapter Thirty-three

Inside the lazar house, Francine had built up the fire and was holding her hands to the blaze when she heard shouting on the other side of the abbey wall. Her first thought was that the townsfolk, enraged at the presence of lepers, were demanding their removal. She hurried to the door and peered back toward the Bimport. Instead of an onrushing mob, she saw two nuns supporting a third, making their way—with urgency—along the lane. *Why?*

"Dame Elizabeth," Francine called, "Some'ut amiss. There be nuns coming this way."

Elizabeth peered over Francine's shoulder and saw two sisters supporting another slogging through the snow. She frowned, unable to discern who it was. At just that moment, the nun in the middle, head down, stumbled and would have fallen but for the supporting arms. Her veil slipped. Elizabeth could now see that the middle woman was gray, and in pain. *Lady Isabel? Dressed as a nun?!*

In the outer court, as one man after another recognized the sheriff and the ominous presence of his well-armed men, the melee quieted. The sheriff dismounted and then, slowly, to give himself time to assess the situation, eased his gauntlets off, one finger at a time. The men parted to let him through. He bowed to Cecily, nodded to FitzRolf, and then his eyes locked on Averilla, who was still bound and gagged. He turned to FitzRolf.

"FitzRolf." It was a neutral greeting yet held in its tone grim authority. Neither man offered a hand.

Turning back to Cecily, protected between a glowering Will, scraps of FitzRolf's torn sleeve dangling from the candelabrum, and John the Mason, hammer by his side, the sheriff said, voice raised to carry over the shuffling men, "Word has come to me that" he turned to FitzRolf, "your lady wife has been abducted, and that she is perhaps being harbored in these precincts." To Cecily he continued, "'I received the message from one of your nuns. With your seal."

Cecily looked confused, "With my seal? But I did not—"

"'Tis all well and good, my lady, to aid a woman in distress, but I understand that you are keeping her from her husband. This man has right on his side and..."

A gleam of malicious triumph flicked behind FitzRolf's eye.

Cecily said angrily, "The Lady Isabel was found by one of my nuns, beaten and left for dead. And the nun who found her, my lord, was later found dead, killed with a FitzRolf arrow. The lady Isabel requested sanctuary from us."

FitzRolf sneered and said, "The lady abbess earlier said my wife was not here. Now she avers that Isabel requested sanctuary."

"My lady," the sheriff's eyes held a note of warning and he held up his hand.

FitzRolf said simultaneously, "In the infirmary? Natural to place her there."

He gestured. Two of his men began to move.

"FitzRolf, hold your men!" The men stopped.

Ignoring the sheriff, FitzRolf shifted his gaze to the offices and lodgings and kitchen. "There would be many a place, I imagine, to hide someone in this rabbit warren."

Cecily put her hands in her sleeves to stop their shaking. "You will not find her in the abbey precincts."

"On the other hand, FitzRolf," interrupted the sheriff, "I am at a loss to understand why…" He turned toward Thord, "why a nun would be trussed like a Christmas fowl and tied on one of your horses. Surely a nun can have done no harm to a man of your… stature?"

FitzRolf's lips drew into a narrow line. "We found her and are bringing her back."

The sheriff's voice was as hard as Damascus steel. "Bound and gagged? I think not. The plight of this nun gives credence to the abbess's words about your lady wife. Untie and release the nun."

Sneering, Thord raised his arms in mock surrender and let go of Averilla. Too abruptly.

Averilla felt herself list sideways. She began to fall. Her hands had been retied so she couldn't grab the pommel. She tried to lean back, but she had been placed awkwardly on the saddle. She felt a push from Thord's body, a tension that nudged her sideways, and then that final ultimate loss of control. How long is it between knowing you are to fall and hitting the ground? Yet consciousness catalogued the various outcomes. Even so her mind didn't expect or foresee strong arms around her torso. The smith had lunged forward, caught her, and, steadying her with his arm around her waist, propped her against the side of the horse.

"Take your nun." FitzRolf spat at Cecily. Fury skewed his face into loathing. "And relinquish my wife. She is my chattel. I can do with her what I will."

DAME JOAN, ON THE EDGE of the aghast nuns, latched a spidery hand onto the sleeve of one of FitzRolf's men who, despite FitzRolf's order, was slipping toward the infirmary. The man whirled, glaring, and slapped at her hand.

Joan said, "I will tell you a secret. She is in another building. A leper house. On the other side of the abbey wall."

The man wrested his sleeve from Joan's grasp, gave her a queer look and nodding, elbowed his way toward FitzRolf. "My lord," he said, not bothering to lower his voice. "There be another house, t'other side of the wall. 'At's where she's hid." His voice took on a menacing timbre. "A leper house!" The word "leper" stilled all movement.

Cecily blushed.

FitzRolf's eyes narrowed in outrage. "Is there indeed?" He turned to the abbess. "You! You," he glared at the abbess. "You speak piously of my dealings with my wife, yet you place her in a leper house?"

The sheriff glanced from FitzRolf to Cecily. "Lady Abbess, is this true?"

Cecily faced the sheriff, mustering as much dignity as she could. "There is indeed a leper house. It lies on the other side of the abbey wall. It served until recently as lodgings for the workmen." She raised her voice. "Lepers were yestere'en rescued from destitution and were placed there, as we could not have them within the abbey walls. We sent Isabel there only this morning for fear of the harm FitzRolf would do to her, if he found her." Cecily went on. "It is little more than a cot, this lodging…." She faltered, not wanting FitzRolf to be privy to the fact that there were but two lepers. "If you wish to see the lazar house—"

"We will indeed see for ourselves. It would be good to question Lady Isabel in this matter. Lady Abbess," the sheriff inclined his head, his courtesy intact. "Would you be so good as to guide us there so we can ask the lady herself?"

"We must go this way, through the pilgrim's gate." Cecily motioned behind them toward the back of the abbey. "It is the shorter way. We shall have to walk." Reluctantly, FitzRolf, Thord, and Weldon dismounted.

Chapter Thirty-four

ecily is delaying, Averilla thought. *Taking them a round-about way.* She nudged Cecily's arm and croaked through her split lip, "My lady, I would come."

Cecily's eyebrows drew close. "Can you? Can you walk?"

Averilla nodded, "That I cannot go at speed might help."

Cecily turned. "Will, would you give Dame Averilla your arm?" Cecily led them through the inner court and then to the narrow pilgrims' gate. It was the most circuitous route, and the slim arch forced the men to go single file. They turned up Magdalene Lane on the other side of the gate. There were no footprints on the snow leading to the lodgings. Cecily gestured vaguely toward the thatched hovel. Will plunged ahead, his great frame making a path through the snow. They all stopped, well clear of the entrance. There was neither perimeter wall nor withy fence around the little building. The workmen hadn't needed one.

Despite the sheriff's restraining hand, FitzRolf elbowed his way forward, pushed open the door, and peered inside. The noxious reek of Ellen wafted out to him. Dame Elizabeth, the white of her wimple brilliant against the dim interior, hands calmly tucked into her sleeves, face serene and serious, stood before him. Hand to his nose, FitzRolf said, "I seek the Lady Isabel. My wife." The others crowded behind him.

Elizabeth's voice was low and somber. "Not yours, I think. And no longer wife."

Neck reddened, eyes slitted, FitzRolf growled, "I will have…" He lunged forward. Elizabeth stepped back. Averilla put her hand to her mouth, expecting both Elizabeth and FitzRolf to go down. Instead, FitzRolf alone tripped. *A stumbling block?* Averilla let out her breath.

FitzRolf fell, his arms outstretched, feet scrabbling for purchase.

Will took a step forward and extended his arms, effectively blocking FitzRolf's men from following.

Isabel, who looked taller in the black habit, limped out from behind Elizabeth. Her lip curled as her eyes lit on the prostrate man.

FitzRolf scrambled halfway to his feet, face contorted. "Wife, you will return to my hearth and my bed."

Isabel put a hand in front of her stomach.

"I," she said, "was never wife to you."

Pain flitted across FitzRolf's face. His jaw hardened. "I loved you, but you would not…" He reached out and grabbed Isabel's leg.

With a growl of rage, Will lunged, hand outstretched, through the doorway. Before he could reach FitzRolf's arm to break the hold on Isabel, something—it turned out to be a rock the size of a thumb—slammed into FitzRolf's temple. The nobleman staggered, then stumbled over the pile of firewood and crashed forward into the fire, his head striking the hearth.

Will's eyes widened as he recognized the atalatl in Francine's hand. There was a complete cessation of movement.

"Where did that…?"

Averilla, knees weak, body sore, pushed unsteadily beside Will, propelled by her instinctive determination to follow her vow to attend the ill or dying. She bent over the unconscious man, pushing his head off the hearth, and placed her hand to his neck to feel for the throbbing of lifeblood. FitzRolf's voice was weak, "Tell my liege lord that… what I have done was always for him." Then, like a waiting snake, FitzRolf grabbed Averilla's wrist and pulled her down, curling his elbow round her neck.

The sheriff unsheathed his sword. Will wrestled it from the sheriff's grip and aimed at FitzRolf's heart, but Averilla was in the way, caught to FitzRolf's chest. Francine, seeing that all eyes were on FitzRolf, Averilla, and Will, nudged the tripod over the fire with her foot and sidled back. The heavy iron pot atop the tripod tipped precariously, overbalanced, and crashed onto FitzRolf's head. The sound was the hollow thump of a rotten stump hit by a hoof. A tremor lifted FitzRolf's body, and then he lay, limp and unmoving, eyes open but forever unseeing.

There was a shocked silence. Averilla felt the sudden relaxation of the arm around her neck. *How did that happen?* she wondered, and then saw, in memory, another brazier tip and fall. She looked around. Francine was now tending to Ellen, and Elizabeth was on the other side of the room.

"It must have jostled. When he fell." Elizabeth's voice was serene.

ON THE EDGE OF THE onlookers, Thord slashed at the arm of the man closest to him and took off toward the Bimport, but John the Mason, who had never taken his eyes off the scoundrel, had his hammer out of its loop, hefted it, and threw. The heavy missile somersaulted through the air and struck Thord right behind the knees. He crumpled and fell.

Bailiff Bradshaw and two men only now appeared at the Bimport end of Magdalene lane as the sheriff's men piled atop Thord's chest and began pummeling. Thord tossed them aside like a bear fending off dogs. He tried to rise, but the hammer had hit something vital, and his legs wouldn't hold him. He tried again, but only managed to scuttle, legs useless. He rolled over and sat at bay, brandishing his sword at the circling men. While they feinted in front of Thord, Wat came from behind and, gripping the wicked curved knife that had been his father's, slashed an arc across the naked throat from one of Thord's ears to the other.

Standing near the leper house door, another of the sheriff's men was the only one to notice Weldon slip from within the throng around the hut and edge back toward the pilgrim's gate. A workman's shout came out in a strangled gargle as he leapt in pursuit. Weldon was too far ahead, but the cry had alerted another mason who stood farther down the lane and carried a lever, an iron bar five feet or more in length, used for hefting huge blocks of dressed stone. He crouched, holding the lever low, and tried to trip Weldon, but the latter leapt cleanly over. A hodman aimed his final stone and threw. It hit Weldon in the middle of his back, and he went down.

Chapter Thirty-five

he sheriff, face grim, entered the lazar house, nudged FitzRolf with his toe, and asked, "Dead?"

Averilla nodded. The sheriff turned to Isabel. "Lady Isabel." She nodded. Their gazes held. "Madam, I have not the folly to assume you are bereft at the loss of your husband, and I will not be so unwise as to speak to you of grief. My duty here has been satisfactorily completed. I will convey news of this… event to His Majesty, when he has come out of mourning for his own son."

Cecily's voice was tight. "What will you tell the king?"

"That it was an arrow miscast in the chase." The sheriff's voice held no irony, but he raised an eyebrow. "It happens. Why, even in his majesty's own family I believe three of the sons or grandsons of the Conqueror have been so killed. Besides, there was some suspicion—nothing that could be proved, of course—but some suspicion about the death of the Atheling, young Prince William. FitzRolf's name came up." He tilted his head.

But surely, my lord," Isabel's eyes were terrorized, voice pleading, "If the king should hear the rumor about FitzRolf, will he not then take his fury out on my sons. A son for a son?"

The sheriff raised his eyes and squinted into the middle distance. At length he bent his head to her and said, voice kind, "I very much doubt the king will give credence to such a rumor, for it involves someone else much closer to his heart. If FitzRolf is suspected, so is Stephen of Blois, and such a betrayal by his beloved nephew, he will quickly discount."

At a signal from the sheriff, two of his men carried Isabel outside and gently lowered her onto the bench affixed to the front of the leper house. The sheriff followed. Someone went to fetch wine.

"Lady, can you enlighten me as to why FitzRolf would treat you thus?"

"My lord, you are right in your earlier suspicion. I overheard him speak of their plot, and for that I was sent to my death." Isabel dipped her chin, pointing to where her husband was being borne away. It was…" she shook her head as if to see the scene clearly, and then the words, until now dammed behind her lips, poured out. "FitzRolf was just returned from London." She held the sheriff's eye for a moment, then looked at Will. "Methinks you, Will, might have been able to tell us something, but now I have not much more than speculation and one conversation overheard. FitzRolf blustered in that evening with the storm, the leather of his cloak crusted with snow. He was drunk, and hard with some emotion I couldn't fathom, his speech confused and slurred, and he and his friends—"

"Friends?"

"No, my lord," she shook her head, "I cannot name them. If ever I had seen them before, I do not now remember it. They were strangers to me. FitzRolf knew many I did not, many he never brought into our hall. One of the two bore, I think, a scar high on his left cheek, but that is common enough. They were intent on getting themselves drunker. I knew the signs. I sent food and wine and withdrew to my solar. I knew they would carouse until they slept in their own vomit.

"Later, I know not how much later, there was a great crash. I worried that my lord had hurt someone in a drunken rage. It has happened. I pulled back the hangings of my bed. My maid sleeps at its foot, and she roused with my waking. The other servants, all but the old chamberlain, had been sent away, well aware of the type of mayhem that might ensue with his carousing. FitzRolf often pulled a shroud of secrecy around his drunken revels. Mistrust and suspicion stalked his mind at the best of times, and when drunk? Suffice it to say that a drunken rage could be expected. Often it was over no more than the forfeiture of a stray cow. How was I to know that this was different? I started down the stairs. There is a bend in the stair, and many feet have worn it away since the keep was raised.

"The first words I heard were ''Twas well done.' Not a voice I knew. Then another said, 'Oh, aye,' followed by… I think I have the words, or something like 'Stephen. Stephen sits safe in Blois. Such guile.' Before I could parse the meaning, a third voice said, 'He will have the crown, like as not, when the old lion dies, despite the claim of the empress.' Had these men—my husband among them, and led—I shrink to think it—led in their perfidy by Stephen of Blois—plotted to rid the country of William, Henry's heir? Had they fed the oarsmen and the ship's master enough wine so that the boat ran aground, drowning all but a fortunate few? The idea was astounding, but not beyond thinking, as I myself had seen the casks trundled up the gangway.

"The first voice then continued, light and nasal, 'When think ye it first came to him to try for it?' I assumed that meant when Stephen of Blois and the others had plotted to kill the crown prince. 'Bremule. Chasing the king.' FitzRolf sounded glad."

Isabel's eyes fixed on the memory and she shook her head. "My mind reeled. Regicide. I knew the king would find out, sooner or later. He had placed me and my sons in horrible danger. Were it known that FitzRolf had caused the death of the crown prince, all members of my family would be suspect and certainly killed. I turned, petrified. These were words I shouldn't have heard. It was dark, and I missed the stair and fell. It was a horrid moment. They heard my fall, of course. How could they not?" Isabel leaned her head back against the wall.

"Best tell us the rest, my lady," said the sheriff.

Isabel brushed a tear from her cheek. "They overturned benches to get at me, but they were drunk, and I was not. They tangled their feet in their clothes or slipped on grease or were hindered by the dogs. I know not. They swore. I struggled upright and ran as fast as I could back up the stairs. One of them bellowed, grabbed my leg, and pulled me down. In the hall, FitzRolf dragged me by my hair," she rubbed her head, "what there is of it.

"By then FitzRolf was, of a sudden, quite sober. He glared at me and fingered his dagger. Said something. The others paced close around me. Wolves waiting. FitzRolf had his knife and a whip." She shook her head. "It would have been easy to kill me, but he did not."

"Why not?"

"Too obvious, I imagine. They bound me with my girdle, stuffed my coif in my mouth, and left me. I must have slept, must have fainted. When next I knew, FitzRolf was saying to Peter— Peter my sworn man—'Kill her.' Just those words. 'And leave her where she won't be found. I'll put it abroad that she ran away,'"

"So," the sheriff said.

"So, the wreck of the White Ship wasn't an accident?" questioned one of the sheriff's knights, a man dressed beyond the station of a mere knight. "By the rood, it must have been well planned."

"'Twas," agreed Isabel. "I never could understand why FitzRolf ordered more wine in Barfleur for the White Ship and then jumped off instead of staying to carouse with the prince. That must have been their wicked plan."

"'Tis said Prince William was like his uncle William, the red king." This came from another of the sheriff's men. "Wild carousing. Unspeakable debauchery. A sodomite. Cruel and ruthless."

The first knight nodded. "Many heard the crown prince vow—several heard him say it—that he would grind the English into the dirt from which they had risen."

"Mayhap that spurred them on to treason, but—my God—there were with the prince a boatful of innocent lives."

"Say you that Stephen of Blois jumped off the White Ship just at the last moment?"

"Aye, indeed, just like FitzRolf. I myself saw him scuttle down the gangplank to join the king's ship."

The sheriff shook his head, firmed his lips, and turned to examine FitzRolf's remaining men, bound and forced onto the ground.

After a moment, the sheriff said, "These remaining shall be punished?" It was a question.

Isabel looked around at the sorry remnants.

"Let them go, all but Weldon. The others were merely following orders. Treacherous, vicious orders, but… I know these men, have seen some of them grow to manhood. What use to strike back? The canker has been removed. They can take FitzRolf's body… home."

The sheriff considered. "If I remember aright, the honor was in your family name? You were the heiress and twice wed?"

"That too is true, my lord. And I have two sons from my first marriage, both in their majority. They will soon arrive, I hope. A missive was sent, I believe." She looked to Cecily for confirmation. The abbess nodded.

"Until one or both of them come to convey me home, I will remain here."

The sheriff frowned. "I think, my lady, that they may still be at court. I will tell them to go and bury FitzRolf before they come to you."

"But you," Isabel's eyes softened as she noticed Will standing awkwardly alone, "I owe you my life. I sense mayhap your anger at FitzRolf may have had a deeper root than the succor of a defenseless woman?"

He nodded, pointed to his own scarred mouth and then toward the end of the lane where the body of FitzRolf was being lugged.

"'Twas he carved out your tongue?"

Will nodded.

Isabel said, "When?"

Will looked at his fingers as if for a way to sign his answer, but the numbers were far beyond him. Averilla found her voice. "From the scarring on his tongue, the first part of Advent, I would guess. Mayhap a little later."

Will nodded.

Bleakness seared Isabel's eyes, "Then I imagine Will must have lost his tongue for the same reason I was trussed and left to die—the pursuit of power."

No one spoke.

ON THE WAY TO VESPERS, Averilla limped over to the abbey parapet, removed veil and wimple, and let the wind cleanse her. She felt bruised and dirty, but more violated spiritually than a loss in her belief in humanity could account for. Though her rib was probably broken, and she was forced to take shallow breaths, and though she would see through only one eye for a time, she was alive. Snow landed on her head. Flakes ruffled across her lashes and mingled with the crust of her earlier tears.

The bell for Vespers rang and she turned.

My Lord, I was so frightened. You saved me. How can I repay you?

The beloved voice bloomed in her mind. Repay me?

Aye, I would.

> All you need do is desire my presence. My love is
> a freewill gift. Return it to me.

Averilla felt tears well behind her eyes, and awe and peace
steal through her limbs. She reiterated as if into a dense mist, *But
I dearly want to give You something. It is in me to show You my
love and gratitude, but to You I cannot give anything that was
not already Yours. Nothing have I.*

> Tend the sick.
> Feel my peace.
> Show my love.
> Empty yourself of yourself.
> Tend them not in haste but in serenity.

Averilla felt her heart ease. *So, my rushing about—*

> Pours salt on their misery.

CHAPTER THIRTY-SIX

DECEMBER 18–24

THE ABBEY

There was little time for the community to reflect upon or discuss the chaos of the previous few days. The urgency of Christmas was upon them. In the church there were new settings for the Mass to be practiced, the sung tropes to be perfected, and the finest liturgical plate to be lugged up from the treasury and polished. All the extraordinary tasks that had been deferred during the pandemonium of the last days fully occupied them.

As if in a trance, Averilla moved through the aisles of the infirmary. She found herself folding bandages, toying with the mortar and pestle, or gliding to the window to stare out through the horn glazing. Often, unaccountably, she stood in the officina, obsessed with keeping the herbs from mildewing. She would fixate on little things that she could control and make right. She toyed with the placement of the surgical implements in their leather case, and rearranged the baskets of bandages. When her hands stopped, she would stand idle for long moments. When thought reengaged, she was unable to remember what she'd been doing, and would lift a lid or unroll the case again and peer inside. Every nook and cranny reminded her of Ethelind. She would see the back of a tall nun and start forward, joy foaming, only to dissolve when the nun turned out to be Agnes or Emma. Averilla felt small and vulnerable, lessened somehow. The slightest misplaced word could engender a raft of tears. The dreaded shaking had not returned to her hands, but even of that she was unaware. Everything in her felt troubled. She would start at shadows, and though she could now see through her eye, she would often finger the bruise near it. Above all, she wanted the reassurance of Maud's expertise and the comfort of her presence among them. So aware of her failure and guilt had Averilla become that she, who was never frightened, feared to do anything.

ON THE TWENTY-SECOND OF December, it began to snow in earnest. Not the earlier stinging sleet or little gritty flakes, but great puffs drifting down. It muffled the sounds of the town and insulated the abbey from everything outside its walls. The novices slogged back and forth through the drifts to the orchard to retrieve the yew, mistletoe, and holly that they had stored there. They massed the greens into great bundles, and staggered to the calefactorium where the ropes to make garlands had been placed. In their movements, Averilla saw Ethelind going off to find mistletoe and pleading for reassurance. *Which I gave her not. Just one word could I have spoken!*

Some of the novices were sent up ladders to interweave a great garland of the holly, ivy, and mistletoe through the apertures in the rood screen. Others teetered on ladders to decorate the fire baskets on the church pillars with sprigs of holly. The great round circle of iron that held the candles above the choir was winched down and hoisted back up, pine and yew intertwined between its candles. Ivy festooned the lamp stands in the chapter house, and holly was placed in bowls in the refectory and dortor. Fir broadcast its fragrance into the closeness of the calefactorium.

LADY ISABEL WAS AGAIN CONFINED to the infirmary. The strain of walking on her injured leg had so inflamed it that Averilla had been forced to cut off the leather, and Isabel was kept in bed, leg raised on a pile of pillows. She was impatient for the arrival of her sons. "They have been told, surely," she complained, as Averilla came to plump the pillows.

Averilla nodded reassuringly, and, trying not to sound irritated, said, "It is as well that they delay, for you are not yet fit to travel." She added, with what she hoped was a conspiratorial grin but was more of moue of sadness, "Lady, you are still healing. Were you well, their tardiness would not vex you so."

Isabel gave a small "pah" in disagreement, but the sides of her lips quirked.

"In any case," Averilla continued, "seeing to the burial and now the depth of the new snow will have slowed them. They will be here, my lady, and you will have the energy to greet them properly."

Isabel sighed. "Verily, you are probably right, but I worry the king will somehow hear what FitzRolf did on the White Ship, ascribe the guilt to my sons, and lock them up in retribution."

"My lady, be at ease. Remember you what the sheriff said. Your sons are merely delayed."

Isabel nodded uncertainly, turned, and said, "Might Will be summoned to take me to the kitchen? Cooking would distract me from this dogged worry."

Will was summoned. Averilla accompanied them to the kitchen. Cook's uncertain temper and fierce protection of her territory were well known. Will deposited Isabel in the heat and chaos of a kitchen in full preparation for a great feast.

Breads and pastries lined a shelf, ready for the oven. On a long table, onions, leeks, and turnips were sliced by lay sisters who then placed them in pottery jars and bowls. Cook turned from the bubbling cauldrons and heat of the fire to glare at the intruders. Isabel was meek. "I would help you. My wifely skills are not inconsiderable."

Cook huffed.

"I could at least stone raisins and currants," Isabel continued. "Surely you can use another hand."

Cook had been preparing for the Christmas feast since the beginning of Advent. This close to the actual day, she was indeed, as Isabel had known she would be, overwhelmed. Yes, the geese were hanging, had been since the third week in advent. Yes, on Advent Sunday the pudding cake had been prepared with oats, suet, mincemeat, dried plums, and cider. Yes, she had seen to the storing of casks of ale and bushels of apples during the fall. Yes, the cellarer had purchased from the markets enough cloves and allspice for a grand wassail bowl. And yes, this year there would be the crowning glory of a marchpane cake, but still there were the breads that had to be fresh, and the meat, and the trussing of birds to be seen to. Relenting, cook nodded, "Aye, that I cain, and welcome, my lady. Ye might even move the spit now and again."

Thus it was in the kitchen that Isabel's sons, Michael and Gaston, found her. "Just like Mother," said Michael, leaning against the doorjamb. "Always cooking."

Lady Isabel, seated at a table, craned around at the familiar voice, gave a yelp of joy, and opened her arms to be engulfed by the tall, strapping young men bundled in layers of leather and fur.

"My dear boys. My dear, dear boys." She hugged them for as long as two men would permit, and then both knelt before her, heads bowed. "Your blessing, mother. And forgiveness."

"For what?"

"Our lateness." Gaston grimaced. "We would have come sooner, but the sheriff bade us bury FitzRolf. We were told little of what happened, just that you were here with a broken leg and needed us."

"But the note? Surely you received my missive." She looked from one face to the other. "Dame Joan was to have sent you a note when I was rescued from the tree."

"We received it not. We were with the king in his mourning. But even so," he shook his head, "we received no such missive." Then, as her words registered, "What tree?"

She laid her hands on the two wet heads and, emotion brimming, blessed them, then motioned to the door. "We mustn't disrupt the kitchen. We can use the Lady Parlour. I have much to tell you."

They carried her through the drifts and into the parlour. When they had made her comfortable and finished fussing over her, Isabel related all that had taken place.

"FitzRolf ordered you killed?" Michael asked.

"Because I heard him talk of plotting with Stephen of Blois to have Prince William drown on the White Ship. Our lives would have been forfeit had the king found out."

"But why did they plot to kill the prince?"

"He was debauched." This from Gaston, who made a face of disgust. "Like his uncle. With William as king, England would have descended into butchery and disorder. King Henry's peace is fragile.

"So, Stephen of Blois, in company with FitzRolf, plied the seamen with wine and ale, hoping for the ship's destruction."

"And if the crown prince drowns, Stephen is next in line for the throne and beloved of the king." Gaston's voice was grim.

"There is the empress, the king's only other child."

"She is a woman, and wife to the Holy Roman Emperor."

"So you were to be silenced."

Michael changed the subject. "Your leg, it is healed?"

"Not healed. I reinjured it trying to…" Then another thought surfaced: "It was the sheriff who told you to come?"

"Aye. And bade us attend the burial. To save you from… we thought that mayhap you…" He looked at her to see if she wanted to hear more about it, but her face remained impassive. "Then it started to snow in earnest, and we have had the devil of a time getting here."

"And now you have reached me, despite the snow. Thank God."

CHRISTMAS EVE DAWNED WITH NO lessening of the ceaseless snow, leaving the courts and garth blanketed in white. The round of prayer and praise went on as usual, but there was a certain lack of focus among the younger nuns.

It was full dark as Vespers approached. Even before the bell had rung, the elder members of the community, arrayed in the serenity of age, placed themselves beside the door to the chapter house, a coffer of tapers at their feet. Aethwulfa spoke into the darkness:

> In the beginning God created the heaven and
> the earth
> Darkness was upon the void
> And upon the face of the deep.
> And God said, "Let there be light."

Aethwulfa lighted her own candle and then sang, "Oh, gracious light, Lord Jesus Christ…," her contralto deep and warm and unwavering. Those around her took up the hymn, and each young nun, as she passed through the door, stooped for a taper, lighted it from Aethwulfa's candle, and entered into the dark and cold of the chapter house. Even that first candle pierced the darkness. As the others entered, the room became brighter and brighter.

The abbess entered last and alone. The now brilliant light glinted on the diamonds of her pectoral cross. She began a long, intricate plainchant that incorporated the Creation, the Flood, Abraham's sacrifice, Israel's deliverance, and all of the Old Testament leading to and presaging the birth of the babe.

Her voice rose.

> Oh come, oh come Emanuel.
> Who ransomed captive Israel.

The full strength of the gathered women joined in, voices undergirding the one lone voice, harmonious and yearning, hovering and blending,

> O, Adonai.
> O, Root of Jesse.
> O, Radiant Dawn.
> O, King of Nations.

So it went, until

> Oh come oh Wisdom from on high.

As Aethwulfa had begun Vespers, so it was she who spoke the closing words:

Oh, God, grant us we beseech thee, that as we
have known the mystery of Your light upon the
earth, so may we also perfectly enjoy Him in
heaven where with thee and the Holy Spirit He
liveth and reigneth, in glory everlasting."

Averilla watched and sang, but her voice lacked life and joy.

Chapter Thirty-seven

December 25, 1120

Christmas morning dawned clear and sparkling. The Christmas Mass, after more food, seemed to go on forever, and Averilla's exhausted soul could do no more than observe. She tried to sing, tried to feel the exaltation of the Savior's birth, but the loss of Ethelind lurked in her weariness and muted her soul. It was all she could do to wade through the familiar antiphons, psalms, and readings. *Elizabeth?* The thought came suddenly into her mind. *I haven't been thinking of Elizabeth. The mass. She needs… and so do the lepers. Oh, my Lord, so wrapped up in my own feelings that...*

With renewed purpose, she settled back into a gentle peace until the nun next to her jostled her arm, alerting her to move into procession. The Mass had ended. She shuffled unsteadily, the somnolence of peace still wrapped around her. Her limbs felt loose and somewhat disjointed. At the great doors, instead of exiting, she waited. Two novices, under the cellarer's supervision, were hauling down the great iron circle above the choir in order to extinguish the candles. It was quiet as Averilla made her way back up the nave. At the nave altar, a lone figure knelt in prayer. Averilla tasting the lingering smell of burnt beeswax and soot, lowered herself onto the floor beside Father Merowald, and let herself drift into the tranquility of the moment, feeling his prayer beside her.

After what could have been forever or no time at all, he spoke. "Averilla?"

"Father."

"What troubles you, child?"

"Elizabeth. And the lepers."

Merowald sat back on his heels. After a moment, he said, "Yes, yes, I see. Elizabeth has the quiet and the peace, but not the sacrament."

"Could we take it to her?"

He thought about it. "There is indeed a little time before I celebrate mass in St. James. We can take the reserve sacrament. I will remove it from the monstrance. If you could go into the aumbry and retrieve a pyx?"

Before he could change his mind, Averilla mounted the three steps and ducked into the little sacristy tucked under the rood screen. The round silver box, little bigger than the wafer it was designed to hold, was in a small cupboard with others like it. Father Merowald took the pyx, tucked the sacramental wafer inside, and stowed it in the small leather scrip that dangled from a cord around his neck.

Averilla's eyes rounded. *He was intending to do this even before I thought of it!*

Unspeaking, they exited into the snow-bright light of Christmas morning. The courts were mostly empty. The last of the parishioners were just entering the hall of the gatehouse, lively with light and laughter. Various lay sisters hurried across the court, laden with platters and steaming bowls from the kitch-en. Merowald paused, inhaling the rich mingling of scents, and turned to Averilla, eyes dancing.

"The bread of life feeds the soul, my child, but what of the body? Could we?"

"Oh, Father, yes!" A barrow stood beside the stables. As Averilla went to fetch it, Merowald intercepted the closest lay sister, lifted the concealing napkin from the bowl she carried, and peered inside. Averilla couldn't hear what was said. The girl looked dubious, then smiled and gave it to him, raising her hands in a gesture of surrender. When Averilla reached him, he said, "Pheasant," and carefully placed the bowl in the barrow.

The next girl, having watched the earlier transaction, eyed him warily. "What have you there, Sister?" The girl raised her eyebrows and untucked the napkin.

"Buns." Merowald sniffed appreciatively. "We need to take them to the poor."

"But Father, the poor are inside today."

"Not all of them."

Confused, but a smile lurking, she allowed him to take the buns, saying, "Father, you know I can deny you nothing."

"A good meal, this," he said, and together Merowald and Averilla pointed the barrow toward the pilgrim's gate. They were near the kitchen when he said, "Just see if there is a pie?"

Averilla entered the kitchen with her usual trepidation. Cook was removing her apron and turned. "Averilla?" But she didn't seem surprised.

"I was hoping there might be something for the lepers."

"There on the table. Venison pie. With carrots and leeks. It should be enough."

Beside it stood a full wineskin and a Christmas pudding.

"Oh, Cook, bless you." Cook raised an eyebrow and smiled. "Nothing more than what we agreed to.

"Oh, but Cook, you remembered. And I, God forgive me, forgot."

Cook smiled and gave her a friendly pat. "My child, I think you may also be forgetting that you are human."

THE ABBREVIATED MASS HELD OUTSIDE the lazar house had none of the pomp of the earlier one in the church, but the effect was glorious. Merowald said the words, his mouth rounding on each syllable, and Elizabeth and Averilla responded. The lepers, seated inside, watched it all with peaceful eyes. Ellen was even able to take the host from Elizabeth's hands and put it in her mouth. They oohed and aahed at the bounty in the barrow. On the way back, Merowald looked at Averilla. "You didn't seem to mind being near them."

"No."

"Everything else palls before His peace."

"I don't need to prove myself to Him. I thought I did. Now I see that I will never be good enough to deserve His love. It is His own gift, and I need only accept and give back to others what He so freely gives to me."

The old priest smiled.

SHE LEFT HIM AT THE pilgrim's gate and walked slowly through the court where the opening of the slot door in the gate caught her eye. A donkey bearing a hooded and cloaked figure entered, followed by the horses of three men-at-arms. *A woman?* Whoever it was drew back her hood. *A veil—a nun?* Averilla's heart gave a lurch and she felt a glimmer of hope as the woman, stiff and aching, dismounted and said something to one of the ostlers. Averilla's eyes narrowed. *Who?* The ostler and nun both looked around, and when the former pointed at Averilla, the nun smiled broadly. Bowing briefly to the men, the nun— *Maud, oh, Maud!*—started toward Averilla, her gait unsteady from the hours on a donkey. Averilla, tears streaming, rushed to her mentor. Maud's arms opened, and Averilla fell into them, resting her head on the other's chest as great sobs wracked her body. "You've, you've come back."

All the grief and self-doubt of the last weeks were heaved from the depths of her soul onto Maud's shoulder. When the storm had somewhat ebbed, Maud said, "Oh, my child, my child. The abbess summoned me, told me Ethelind had been killed. I came as soon as I could. The storm delayed my departure. What a heavy burden for you. Ethelind was… such a joy to all of us. We must remember that, even as our hearts break. We will speak of her and remember her sweet soul."

Maud held Averilla away from her, then jerked back in consternation, really seeing the half-closed eye and the great blooming bruise. "What happened? How did you—?"

Averilla shook her head. "'Tis a long story."

"Then you shall tell it to me. I am cold and tired and eager to taste all the good things that I smell. Come."

They entered the large hall of the gatehouse and swam into the light and laughter. "Oh, blessed, blessed warmth." Maud looked around. The trestle tables, crammed with people, were bright with candles down the centers. Bits of greenery decorated the walls, and the fresh, clean scent of the woodlands mingled with the smells of cinnamon and cloves and roasted fowl and pig.

Maud maneuvered Averilla, who was still wiping, unsuccessfully, at her eyes and her nose, toward a bench in a deep corner. "We will have a bit of privacy here. Help me off with this cloak." Maud continued her stream of prattle, hoping the everyday matters would stem Averilla's brimming hysteria. "Oh, Wat!" Maud saw him at the nearest table. He looked over, a smile hovering. When he recognized Maud and took in Averilla's state, he rose. "If you would be so kind. Some wassail would not go amiss." He nodded and hurried off.

Averilla told it all as she ate and drank everything that was put before her.

"So, I did everything—absolutely everything—wrong," she finished, voice so soft that Maud had to lean in to hear her. "With Will and Ethelind. And I felt so alone."

Maud's chin jutted. "Mayhap, but mayhap not. Yon huge man? I don't recognize him. He must be the Will you speak of. He seems hale enough now to eat and drink and make merry even if he is still convalescing. Him you did only good. And Ethelind. Well, that could have been handled better, but don't forget you were tired and scared and times like that are the times Satan uses to bring out the worst traits of our flesh and uses them to our—or most likely someone else's—hurt. We always must wrestle with our flesh, and we are weak. Remember too that Ethelind chose to wander off, her thoughts on herself. Remember as well that her disobedience led to the rescue of Lady Isabel.

"Now, however, you need and must have rest, my child. Sabbath. We must be rested to engage in this continual strife with Satan and with those parts of our flesh that rebel. Had you been rested you would not have said those words to Ethelind that so torment you."

"But you see, that is the very point of my trespass—I went on the Sabbath."

Maud frowned. "Why were you in the forest on that day?"

A flush of shame flooded Averilla's cheeks. "We were to look for mistletoe for the service of penance."

"That is ironic. But whose idea was it? The abbess's?"

"No. It was mine." Averilla sank further down. "I- I wanted to find a spring Madge knew of, that could cure the shaking in my hands. "Ethelind wouldn't even have been there if not for my trespass."

"Have you confessed?" When Averilla shook her head, Maud said, "Confession is good for what ails you, but then you must rest, and more than one day. Perhaps even the whole Christmastide will not be enough. I will take over now. And as for being alone, certainly I was not there, but you are never alone. You know that. Christ is always with you, but you must, and most fervently during these times of trial, plead for His help. And rely on it."

AT THE END OF THE FEAST, when the candles, saved and savored for such occasions, had started to gutter, most of the villagers made their way reluctantly back to their own hearths, replete and slightly drowsy. Isabel and her sons rose from their places beside the abbess and made their way down the length of the hall to the sheltered bench on which Dame Averilla, eyes bright with medicinal wine, still held fast to Maud.

"My sons would be known to you, Dame Averilla. Without your care, I…"

OVER THE NEXT FEW DAYS, the sounds of festivity continued around the abbey, though muted by the solemn feast day of Stephen, the first martyr, and that of the Holy Innocents.

Averilla found herself drawn not to Dame Maud, though she was warmed by her presence, or to Father Merowald, as that encounter would require more work than she knew how to give in her neonate state.

No, it was to Scholastica that she increasingly turned, drawn by Scholastica's smile, so different from those offered by others, which were weak pallid things that turned up at the edges, eyes sorrowful and questioning.

The first time Averilla went to see her, Scholastica's smile, her usual wry twinkle, was followed by a raised eyebrow. "I understand your prayer time in the Brode Hall was not all you had hoped."

Averilla couldn't help herself. A great guffaw burst forth, startling the other nuns and waking some of the patients. The laugh was followed by a lone tear that trickled from her left eye.

"I think I need to learn how to pray. I did try." Averilla continued haltingly. "I allowed calm to steal into my mind, but..."

"But then you had a visitor."

Averilla shuddered. "And found myself clinging to the hem of God's mantle."

"And you have felt God's presence since?"

"I have, warm and comforting, but," she made a fluttering motion with her right hand, "I am not giving back."

Scholastica squirmed against the mountain of pillows. Dutifully, Averilla plumped and straightened.

After a moment, Scholastica said, "My novice mistress, Dame Marigold, was… unusual." Scholastic tilted her head back. "A simple soul. English. She started her teaching on prayer with the comment that she was not learned, that was for priests and abbesses and such, but over the years she had learned to depend on God. To see him as a refuge. But understanding the nature of the refuge differed with her needs. Key to this was the Trinity."

At Averilla's frown, Scholastica again raised the sketchy eyebrow. "I know. The Trinity. The most knotty of theological problems, one that priests either avoid or speak of in lofty riddles. But Marigold was different. She insisted the concept was simple. "Saint Patrick showed us the shamrock with its three leaves," she said. "One leaf with three separate parts, three in one. As is the Trinity. When you sit in quiet to pray,' she continued, 'and a thought rises, examine it in light of one of the three aspects of God. Do unexamined sins fester in your heart? Take them to God Almighty, the ruler and judge, for you must repent. From confession springs the water of forgiveness.'

Scholastica paused. There was the comforting drip of thawing ice from the eaves. " 'Or,' Marigold continued, 'is your dis-ease a sorrow that is too great for words? Does it need the empathy of the Son, bone as we are bone, betrayed as we are betrayed? Let Him sit beside you."

"'Or, do you need,' Marigold finished, 'the life-giving energy of the Holy Spirit? See him giving new life to Mary or leading

Christ into the wilderness. The wind that comes we know not whence and goes we know not where. To lift us and shake us until His will is done.

Scholastica's eyes drooped. "So, as you rest in Sabbath, Averilla, take the gnarly knots of the last tumultuous days and allow these aspects of God to minister to you. As you thus pray, you will find yourself drawn down, and you will have no words, and then you can enjoy His companionship, that ineffable sweet peace.

Her last words were almost inaudible: "Above all remember, dear one, it is the loving that matters."

THE END

Come unto me, all ye that labour and are
heavy laden and I will give you rest.
Take my yoke upon you and learn of me, for I
am meek and lowly of heart, and ye shall find
rest for your souls.
For my yoke is easy and my burden is light.

Matthew 11:28–30

ACKNOWLEDGMENTS

Because this book has taken such a long time to write, I fear I may have omitted someone from the following list. If so, I am so sorry. My heartfelt thanks to all those who labored hard and long over the various iterations of this manuscript:

William Geisler, Melissa Geisler Trafton, Robin Miller, Carolyn Cavalier, Marilyn Isherwood, Betty Miller, Adele Ghio-Sale, MS CCC/SLP Supervisor Hearing and Speech Department, Marin General Hospital, Amy Saunders Simpson, Jayne Davis, and Jennifer Cook, and the wonderful folks at Cypress House: Cynthia Frank, Roberta Morrow, and Richard Hays.

Notes

The Abbey

Shaftesbury Abbey was built by Alfred the Great after the Battle of Eddington, around 888. The abbey was later rebuilt. I postulate that it was rebuilt under Cecily FitzHamon. There is physical evidence to bolster the supposition of the existence of an abbey of that size at the time. Such buildings were constructed with surprising swiftness—Winchester was completed in thirty years.

Shaftesbury Abbey is now a ruin. It is unfortunate that, when the great monasteries are now spoken or written of, Shaftesbury is rarely mentioned, though it was one of the largest and richest in the country, its nave rivaling that of Winchester. Is this silence due to the destruction accomplished under Henry VIII, or is it perchance because Shaftesbury was a convent for women?

Lichen

The supernatural effects produced by old Madge's lichen to provide an eerie glow through the forest could have been *Omphalitis olearius* or *Armillaria mellea* or perhaps something else. More than seventy-five species of bioluminescent fungi have been scientifically identified; thus Madge made educated use of a naturally occurring substance.

Magic

Madge followed the accepted practice of ancient wise women in requiring Averilla to go three times around the well to cement the efficacy of the spell. For their effectiveness, wortcunnings and leechdoms required physical as well as mental exercises such as going out during a full moon.

THE HOLY WELL

RESEARCH OVER THE LAST DECADES, including but not limited to that of Peter J. Preston, M.D.; Rick Maizels at the University of Edinburgh; Joel Weinstock at the University of Iowa, and Jorge Correale and Mauricio Farez at the Institute of Neurological research in Buenos Aires, has demonstrated the link between intestinal worms in humans and protection against various auto-immune diseases, including multiple sclerosis. I posit that walking barefoot in an area where such worms might flourish by virtue of other people and animals having been there might have reduced or eliminated Averilla's condition.

THE ENGLISH OAK

THESE MAGNIFICENT TREES, MANY UP to 1,000 years old, were once abundant in the English landscape, but were cut down ruthlessly during the late middle ages and after to produce timbers for the ships needed by the Royal Navy. In earlier times some were coppiced—a process of woodland management wherein the tree is cut down near ground level, and the shoots that emerge are allowed to grow, producing a stool, or stump. Such a woodland is called a copse. If a tree is undisturbed, the interior is hollowed out by beetles, which produce a reddish mast. These interiors provided spacious rooms that people used for shelter. One, in fact, was a well-known inn. For more information I recommend the book by Aljos Farjon, *Ancient Oaks in the English Landscape*, Kew Publishing, 2017.

HERBARIUM AND OFFICINA

THE HERBARIUM WAS A PLOT around the infirmary, planted with medicinal and other useful herbs. The officina was a separate hut, kept warm for the drying and preservation of those herbs.

Stephen of Blois, King of England

Stephen was born sometime between 1092 and 1096. When his father, the count of Blois, died, his mother, Adele, a daughter of William the Conqueror, brought him to England where he was raised in the court of his uncle, King Henry I. Stephen was on the White Ship in 1120, but ran ashore before it sank. Apparently a winsome youth, he was later knighted and granted lands by King Henry. As Henry lay dying in 1135, he reiterated to those at his bedside, including Stephen, that his daughter, Matilda, was his heir. Stephen ignored this command, boarded the first ship he could find back to England, and took the throne despite previous oaths to his uncle that he would not try to wrest it from his cousin Matilda (Maud), Henry's legitimate heir.

The White Ship (Blanche Nef)

An original account of this disaster is in the work of Ordericus Vitalis, the chronicler of the abbey of St. Evroulet in Normandy, but it was not added to the chronicle until later. Several notable things in the account have caused confusion over the centuries. First is the date of the tragedy, which Ordericus gives as late November 1119, whereas other contemporary historians refer to December 1120. The index of the original four-volume translation from the French by Thomas Forrester, in 1856, entirely omits a reference to the White Ship, though the account occurs in a footnote in the body of the narrative. Ordericus recounts: "Stephen, count of Mortain gave the mariners three casks to drink... and [with] several others came onshore."

I find his account suspicious. Stephen gave the already drunk mariners more wine, thus ensuring a drunken crew, and then promptly left the ship on which the only legitimate male heir to the English throne was a passenger.

Maslin Bread

Maslin was the common bread of the medieval period. It consists of wheat mixed with rye, barley, or whatever grain grew best in a farmer's field. As an aid to rising, some of the bran was removed, and the bread was risen with sourdough. While wheat-only bread was much preferred, many regions in England weren't good for growing wheat, so farmers planted mixtures of grains to ensure that at least one would produce well in any given year. A recipe for maslin bread can be found at http://timetravelkitchen.blogspot.com/2017/02/maslin-bread.html.